Flight to Coorah Creek

Janet Gover

Published 2014 by Choc Lit Limited
Penrose House, Crawley Drive, Camberley, Surrey GU15 2AB, UK
www.choc-lit.com

A CIP catalogue record for this book is available
from the British Library

ISBN 978-1-78189-097-4

MIX
Paper from
responsible sources
FSC® C020471

FSC
www.fsc.org

Printed and bound by CPI Group (UK) Ltd, Croydon, CR0 4YY

For John.
I could probably do this without you
– but I never want to.

Acknowledgements

When people ask where I get my ideas from, it's sometimes hard to answer. Ideas can come from nowhere or from everywhere. Some years ago, in the central Australian desert, I found myself in the care of the Royal Flying Doctor Service. In places where the nearest doctor is hundreds of kilometres away, the RFDS saves lives. In part, this book is my way of saying thank you.

Even more years ago, I met a Catholic nun who worked as a nurse in a children's hospital. In the face of the most tragic suffering, she remained serene and never lost her faith in people. I always wanted to write a story worthy of such a character.

These are the people who inspired this book.

As a result of a chance meeting on a plane, I offered the name of one of my characters to be auctioned to raise funds to help the people of Haiti, still recovering from the shocking earthquake. Thank you Andrea Geroldi for your generosity – I hope you like 'your' character.

It takes more than inspiration to write a book – an author needs a lot of help ... Thank you Jamie White for advice on flying – or not – a light aircraft. Any technical mistakes in this book are entirely my fault.

Thank you to my friends and fellow writers in the
Romantic Novelists' Association – in particular
Jean and Rachel and the girls (and occasional guys)
who meet up in London, Reading and Oxford.
You help more than you will ever know.

Thank you to the Choc Lit authors who welcomed
me with open arms. I love you all. Thank you to
the team at Choc Lit who turned my manuscript,
with all its flaws, into this beautiful book.

And thank you to John – for the many cups of tea,
the proof reading and for sharing the pain and the
joy. Marrying you was not an entirely bad idea!

Chapter One

'It's no big deal.'

The loud voice and angry tone suggested it was in fact a very big deal.

'Honestly! She's only a bridesmaid for goodness sake. It's not her decision to make,' the woman almost shouted into her mobile phone.

Jessica Pearson shifted uncomfortably in her seat, moving an inch or two further away from the woman sitting next to her. From all parts of the airport lounge, eyes began to turn in their direction. Jess felt the first small twinge of fear. What if someone recognised her? A man seated opposite sighed very loudly. He glared at the woman on the phone, who either didn't see him or chose to ignore him. He caught Jessica's eye and shook his head, his mouth fixed in a disapproving line. Jess avoided his gaze and ducked her head to stare at the page of the book she wasn't reading.

'I know she's his sister, but this is my wedding ... And before you ask, I will *not* talk to her.'

The woman was becoming even more strident. Was she totally unaware of the looks she was getting from her fellow passengers? Jess was tempted to move, but that would only draw some of those eyes her way – and the last thing she wanted to do was to attract any attention. Right now she was just an anonymous face in the crowd, another nameless passenger in Sydney's busy airport. And that's just what she needed to be.

'Excuse me, miss?'

The voice caused Jessica's heart to leap. Had she been

recognised? Slowly she looked up into the face of a uniformed airline agent.

'Is this yours?' the agent asked, indicating a black bag on the carpet near Jessica's feet.

'No.' She shook her head.

'It's mine,' the woman next to her said, without removing the phone from her ear. 'Is there a problem?'

Jess ducked her head, glad to be out of the spotlight – but she wasn't that lucky. More eyes turned her way as the passenger snapped her phone closed and began to argue with the airline agent over whether her bag was carry-on size.

Oh, no! Jess thought. Please!

She risked another quick glance around the lounge. Two men sitting on the other side of the room were looking directly at her. One said something in a low tone to his companion.

Jess felt her heart clench. She couldn't hear their voices and she wasn't even sure they were discussing her, but her mind filled in the words she'd heard so many times over the past few days.

Gave up her lover to escape jail. Turned him in to save her own skin. Just as guilty as the others. A drug runner who should be in prison.

She wasn't a drug runner, but neither was she entirely innocent.

The speakers overhead crackled into life announcing that it was time to board the flight. Jess leaped to her feet. She was in no great hurry to board the plane, but she was eager to be out of the curious gaze of her fellow passengers.

The flight attendant smiled mechanically as he checked her boarding pass.

'Welcome on board, Miss Pearson.'

He didn't recognise her name. Jessica nodded briefly and quickly moved towards her seat at the back of the plane, hoping that her fellow passengers would be too busy settling into their seats to notice her. She reached up to touch the ends of the hair that feathered around her face. She still wasn't used to this new super short haircut. She wasn't hiding her identity as such, but all the press photos and the TV footage taken outside the courthouse during the trial showed her with long dark hair. Her new hair was simply a symbol of her new life. That life was starting today.

It felt so strange to be a passenger and not in the pilot's seat. Not in control. But she hadn't had much control over her life during the past few months. This flight was the first step in getting it back.

As she settled herself in the last row, Jessica sent a brief plea to whatever deities were responsible for travellers and people starting over: if she had to have a travelling companion in the seat next to her, could it please be someone willing to sit in silence. Above all, could it please not be the annoying bride-to-be from the lounge! The gods were kind and the seat beside her remained empty as the aircraft doors were finally closed, and the plane taxied for take-off.

Jessica's every sense was tuned to the moment the wheels left the runway and the plane soared free of the earth. Ever since she had been a child watching the birds in the clear blue skies, she had wanted to fly. There was a lot of hard work involved in becoming a pilot, but that hadn't deterred her and the day she got her wings was one of the happiest of her life. More than anything else in the world, she loved to fly. Every time she left the ground behind, her heart sang.

But not anymore. That had been taken from her along with so much else.

Unlike most of the other passengers, Jessica didn't look down at Sydney's famous harbour bridge or the glorious beaches. They were a part of the life she was leaving behind. Her eyes were closed. As much as she tried to believe she was starting a new life, deep in her heart she couldn't shake the feeling that she was running away. Looking for a safe place to hide.

'Ladies and gentlemen, the seat belt sign has now been turned off and you are free to move around the cabin ...'

She was tired. So very, very tired. It seemed like years since she'd had a good night's sleep. Every time she closed her eyes she saw the courtroom and the faces of the judge and jury. She heard the crisp clear voice of the prosecutor. And she saw Brian. Brian Hayes – her boss. Her lover. The wealthy jet-setting businessman with the brilliant blue eyes and the killer smile. The man the press had labelled 'Heroin Hayes'.

They'd had a name for her too. Jezebel, they called her. The woman who betrayed her lover to save herself from prosecution. But that wasn't how it was. She was the one betrayed; when the man she loved hid those packets of white powder on her aeroplane. All she had done – all she could do when she discovered them – was try to atone by contacting the authorities.

But that hadn't stopped the accusations. In the media. Outside the courtroom ... where she came face to face with a mother's grief.

My son is dead. The woman screamed over and over again, her brown eyes filling with tears. *Because of you. It's your fault. You brought that poison into the country. You killed my son ...*

Jessica's eyes shot open as she suddenly jerked awake. Her hands were clenched around the arms of the seat, her breath coming in short sharp gasps. She wiped a hand over her face.

'Are you all right?' The flight attendant leaned over her.

'I must have fallen asleep,' she stammered, as she fought to regain her composure.

'Yes, you did.' The attendant smiled in understanding. 'And for quite some time. You missed the refreshments. We're going to be landing at Mount Isa in just a few minutes.'

'Thank you.'

As the attendant carried on his inspection, Jessica gathered her scattered wits. She glanced out of the window. The countryside below her was red-brown and looked very dry. They were circling the town. She could see the streets and houses and on the outskirts of the town, the great scar on the landscape that was the mine. She remembered reading about the outback mining towns at school. They had seemed a world away from her safe home in the Sydney suburbs. But today Mount Isa was just the first stop on her journey. She still had further to go.

When Jessica ran away – she went all the way.

Jessica emerged from the terminal building, if such a grand name could be applied to it, and glanced about her. The airport was little more than a runway with a motley collection of small buildings, most of them built of corrugated iron. The arrival of the Sydney flight must have been rush hour. There were three taxis parked outside, the drivers looking her way in the hope of a fare. They were going to be disappointed. To her right she could see a collection of smaller buildings, and a few light aircraft parked on the apron. That was her destination.

She shrugged her rucksack higher on her back and started walking, rolling her small suitcase behind her.

It was hot. Within a few moments she could feel the sweat starting to prickle in the small of her back and on her forehead. In Sydney, winter was only starting to fade, but this far north it would always be hot. She had better get used to it.

There was no fence around the apron where the light planes were parked. No security. No guards. The irony of that struck home with some force. All those other airports she'd seen. All the guns and uniforms and checks ... yet here she was, free to walk past the parked aircraft and into the dim interior of the hangar.

She let the rucksack fall to the ground, as her eyes adjusted after the brilliant glare outside.

'Hello?' she called, her voice echoing a little.

'Hang on!' The muffled shout came from inside the aircraft parked a few metres away.

Jessica took a closer look at the plane and the green logo emblazoned on its side. 'Goongalla Mine Air Ambulance' was stencilled in red under the cockpit window. This, she guessed, must be her new plane. She gently ran one hand along the wing's leading edge. The Beechcraft was a nice aircraft. Maybe it would give her back some of the things she had lost ...

'G'day!'

A man emerged from the plane. He wore blue jeans and a stained white T-shirt – but the tools he carried identified him immediately. No doubt he was the one responsible for the aircraft's good condition.

'Hi.' Jessica stepped forward and held out her hand. 'You must be Jack North.'

'That's right. You are ...?'

'Jessica … Jess Pearson.' She watched his face, waiting for that moment of recognition. Waiting to feel him draw away. Waiting for the silent accusation. It never came. The man's brow creased.

'Sorry?'

'I'm your new pilot.'

Realisation spread slowly over the man's face. 'We were expecting a bloke.'

'I'm not a bloke.'

Jack North looked her up and down. 'Yes, I can see that.' He wiped his hand carefully on his T-shirt, adding considerably to the stains, and took her offered hand. 'Sorry. Pleased to meet you. Welcome on board.'

Jess guessed Jack was a few years older than her. Probably in his mid-thirties. He was quite tall, several inches taller than her, and he was a big man. Solid with muscle. The hand she shook was strong and calloused with hard work. His face was open and friendly. It was very obvious that her name and face meant nothing to him. Perhaps she had run far enough.

'And I'm pleased to meet you, too,' she said. 'This is a nice aircraft. I'm looking forward to flying her.'

'Yeah.' The engineer turned with obvious pride. 'She's a beaut all right. Got the blended winglets. They really help the performance.'

'And they look pretty cool too,' Jess offered as she stroked the upturned wingtip.

'Yeah. What have you been flying?'

The question so casually asked struck close to her heart. 'Small jets,' she said briefly.

The engineer raised an impressed eyebrow. 'Lear?'

'Gulfstream,' she admitted, and was rewarded with a soft whistle.

'Very nice indeed.'

'Yes, it was,' Jess answered. The jet had been beautiful and a joy to fly, but when she last saw it, it was no longer beautiful. The lush interior had been ripped away by the drug agents. All the joy was taken from it. And from her. Maybe this new aircraft would give some of it back.

'Is she ready to go?' she asked.

'You bet. Let's get your things and put them on board.'

Jess indicated the rucksack and the small suitcase. 'That's it.'

It seemed she had surprised him again. Jess bit back a grin as she let him get her bag. She climbed the aircraft stairs and it was her turn to be impressed.

She had stepped into something that was a cross between a doctor's surgery and an operating theatre. There were two stretchers lining the bulkheads, and three seats. Custom built wooden cabinets filled most of the luggage space. She guessed they would hold medical kit. This was no rich man's toy. This was a plane with a purpose.

'We can take two on stretchers – and three in seats,' Jack said, as he stepped into the plane behind her. 'There's a defib machine stored there. Heart monitor. Blood pressure. All with its own battery power. It's ready to go. All we need is the patient.'

'And the doctor,' Jess added.

'Oh, him we have,' Jack said. 'You'll meet him when we get to Coorah Creek.' He carried her bags to the back of the plane, placed them in a recess, and tightened the cargo net around it. As he did, Jess couldn't help but notice …

'I don't mean to pry,' she said, 'but is that a tattoo of Donald Duck?'

'No. Of course not.' Jack grinned broadly as he slid his T-shirt sleeve higher to give her a clear view. 'Why would a grown man have a tattoo of Donald Duck? It's his Uncle – Scrooge McDuck.'

Jess stifled a smile. She had a feeling there was more to her engineer than met the eye.

Jack took the co-pilot's place. Jess buckled into the pilot's seat for the first time since the trial. It felt good to be back there. She felt a moment's nervousness under the engineer's close scrutiny, but it didn't last long. She settled into the routine of pre-flight checks. Tower clearance came as soon as she asked for it, and she taxied to the runway. She held the plane in check as she pushed the throttle forward, feeling the power build. The Beechcraft quivered with eagerness to be away. Jess released the brake. The aircraft raced down the runway and climbed into the brilliant blue sky.

Although the joy was still missing, Jess did feel her heart lighten just a little as the landing gear clunked into place, and she pointed the plane's long sleek nose towards the south.

It was an easy journey. The aircraft almost flew itself, allowing Jess to spend some time gazing out of the window at the vast expanse of sun-baked earth beneath her. She had known she was coming to the outback. Coorah Creek was one of the last towns before the great desert that covered half the continent, but she still hadn't expected such emptiness. Within just a few minutes of leaving Mount Isa, it was as if she had stepped back in time several millennia. There were no roads. No buildings. Nothing to show where man had made his mark on the landscape. In the distance, she could see the dark red rocks of a long low mountain range. Here and there she saw the winding track of a creek, but seldom was there a glint of water. This was a dry place. And harsh.

'It's beautiful,' she said, almost to herself.

'It sure is,' Jack agreed with her.

Most of the flight passed in a companionable silence. Just as her instruments told her they were nearing the end of the journey, Jack touched her arm.

'There it is.'

She followed his pointing finger, but saw nothing to indicate a town. She started her descent. A few moments later she saw it. A long ridge ended in a sheer red cliff. At its base, a line of trees mapped out a narrow watercourse. That would be Coorah Creek. She'd looked the Aboriginal word up on the internet. It meant woman. At the time she'd thought that might be a good omen. Of the town that bore the same name, she could see little. The Goongalla Mine, however, was another matter. The open pit was far larger than she had expected. As the plane dropped lower she could see machines moving slowly on the sides and base of the cut, carrying their load of uranium ore to the surface. It took a few seconds for her to realise how huge the machines must be to be visible from such a height.

She banked the plane and dropped even lower. Now she had a better view of the town which had grown up on the banks of the creek, in the shadow of the escarpment. It sat where two roads met in a giant Y shape to form a single track heading south-west towards the desert. A railway line ran parallel to the east-bound road and turned south to its terminus in the mine compound. A short spur led into the town itself. The houses were set in large blocks of land. In a place where rain was more common, there would be gardens around those homes. Instead, Coorah Creek had just a very few small green patches of carefully tended lawn. The rough red of the outback soil predominated. Near the middle of the town, Jess blinked at the incongruous sight of a square of brilliant blue.

'You've got a swimming pool?'

'The school does. Courtesy of the mine.'

'Like this aircraft.'

'You got it,' Jack replied. 'Without the mine ...'

'There'd be no town.' Jess finished for him.

'Pretty much. Before the mine came, this place was just a pit stop on the Birdsville Road. A petrol station and pub and half a dozen houses. Now look at it.'

A population of almost three thousand, Jess recalled from her reading. With a police station, shops and a town council. There was a church and a hospital too, small but very well equipped. The mine looked after its own. Jessica circled the town as she reduced her height, trying to get a feel for this place which was going to be her new home. The mine was south of the town and the airstrip was right next to it, which made sense if the mining company was paying the bills. They'd no doubt use it for flying company executives in and out. The strip itself had an all-weather surface, not that rain would be much of a problem out here. There was a single large building made of corrugated iron, with a flat roof and a large round metal water tank at the side. Jess guessed that was the hangar for the plane she was now flying.

Jess brought the Beechcraft in for a gentle touchdown. Following Jack's directions, she taxied the plane towards the large corrugated iron shed that served as the air ambulance hangar. She was still some yards from her destination when a car shot at high speed around the corner of the building and began sliding towards them as the driver stood too heavily on his brakes.

'What the ...' Jess jammed her brakes on and brought

the plane to a halt, its spinning propellers just a few yards from the car.

She was about to shut down the engines, when a man leaped out of the car, waving his hands.

'Get back,' she yelled, knowing as she did that he couldn't hear her. The lunatic was running forward, in very real danger from the spinning propellers.

Jack said something as he ducked between the seats into the back of the plane, but Jess didn't hear him. She watched horrified as the madman on the tarmac dived under her wingtip. A few seconds later, she saw a woman in some sort of strange headscarf follow the madman. That's when Jack flung open the aircraft door.

Jess's heart started to pound as she heard booted feet race up the aircraft stairs. It was as if she had stepped back into her nightmare ... Flashing lights and sirens ... Angry men with guns, shouting and threatening. Knives tearing into the seats of her beloved jet, to reveal the packets of white power hidden there ...

Jess shook her head and turned towards the interior of the plane. The tall man who looked into her startled face wasn't wearing a uniform. His hands were holding a small rucksack.

'What the hell?' Jess shouted at him. 'You idiot. You could have been killed.'

The madman waved her words away with an impatient hand. 'We've got to get in the air. Right now.'

'What?'

'There's an injured man. About two hundred kilometres west. You've got to get me to him.'

'What's going on?' She looked to Jack North for help. He grinned at her and nodded to the madman.

'Jess Pearson – pilot, meet Adam Gilmore – doctor.'

'Oh.' Jess did a classic double take. This lunatic with a death wish was the doctor? He didn't look much like any doctor she'd ever met. He was wearing jeans and an open-necked shirt with long sleeves rolled up to his elbows. He appeared about thirty, and he needed a shave. His dark hair and brown eyes were quite unremarkable – for a madman.

'We don't have time.' The doctor was obviously not one for pleasantries, or even manners.

Jess felt her hackles rise. She was the pilot. She was responsible. This plane was going nowhere unless she wanted it to. She wasn't going to let another man use her and her aircraft.

'He'll die if I don't get there fast.' Adam's eyes blazed with an almost fanatical intensity.

A tense silence settled in the crowded confines of the small aircraft – for about three seconds.

'Where?' Jess reached for her map case and spread a map out on the nearest stretcher.

'Here.' He pointed to a place on the map. 'Warrina Downs. They've got an airstrip.'

'How long is it?' Jess asked, as she looked down at the map.

'How the hell should I know?' Adam snapped.

'Well, I need to know if I'm going to land this plane on it,' Jess retorted.

'It's long enough,' Jack offered calmly, as he passed a couple of medical bags into the cabin. 'We've been there before. And you'll be fine for fuel. They've got plenty out there.'

As Jack was the only person she'd known for more than ninety seconds, Jess guessed she would have to trust him.

She glanced out of the window. 'There's not a lot of daylight left. If we run out of light …'

'You won't if you get this damn plane in the air right now.' Adam was too tall to stand up straight in the cabin, but Jess could feel him looking down at her in anger. 'That man is dying.'

A woman's face, streaked with tears. My son is dead. It's your fault.

Jess closed her eyes and fought down the emotions surging through her. 'All right,' she said through gritted teeth. 'Stow those bags. Get yourself strapped in and I'll get this damn plane in the air.'

She opened her eyes and looked straight into the lined face of a small elderly nun standing at the top of the aircraft stairs.

'Oh,' she gasped. 'Sorry. Sister … I …'

'That's quite all right, my dear,' the nun's gentle voice sparkled with humour. 'I'll just strap myself in too so you can get this damn plane in the air.'

Chapter Two

Adam looked at his watch again. Somewhere below them a badly injured man needed his help. They were taking too long to get to him. Shaking his head, he turned to look out of the window. The sun was sinking very close to the horizon. From this height it was still light enough to see, but closer to the ground, the vast open plain was being eaten up by shadow. He felt a twinge of concern. If they weren't on the ground soon …

He looked towards the cockpit. From his seat he could only see the back of the pilot's head, but he could feel the intensity of her concentration. Occasionally, she would reach up to tug at her short dark hair, as if trying to lengthen it. She seemed to know what she was doing at the controls for someone who was quite young – no more than her mid-twenties. She was attractive too, he suddenly realised. She looked more like a model than a pilot. He wondered for a few seconds what on earth would bring a woman like her to a place like Coorah Creek. Then his eyes dropped back to his watch.

'I'm starting the descent now.' The pilot – Jess – turned to look back at him. 'We're about ten minutes out. I've got them on the radio. They want to talk to you.'

Adam unbuckled his seat belt and moved forward into the cockpit. He slipped carefully into the co-pilot's seat and reached for the radio handset.

'This is Adam Gilmore.'

'I'm glad you're almost here, Doc. He's in a bad way.' The voice from the radio was distorted, but the concern was still obvious. 'His side's ripped open. We padded it like you said on the phone, but there's still a lot of blood.'

'Where is he?'

'At the homestead. Are you going to fly him out tonight? We can bring him to the strip.'

'We're not going anywhere else tonight,' Jess said sharply. 'No light.'

'I know,' Adam said impatiently, very aware that the swiftly falling darkness might cost the injured man his life. He thumbed the microphone open. 'Don't move him. Keep him as still as you can and keep pressure on the wound. Have a car meet us.'

'Okay, Doc.'

Jess took the handset from him and thumbed it on. 'This is the pilot again,' she said. 'We're running out of light up here. I'm going to need your help to get down. I need landing lights.'

Landing lights? Adam frowned. Didn't she realise she was talking about a graded strip of red dirt in the back of nowhere?

'Send out cars.' Jess gave instructions in a crisp clear voice. 'At least two – more if you have them. I need one on the south-east corner, pointing up the eastern side of the strip. The other one at the north-west corner, pointing down the western side. Tell them to have their lights on high beam.'

'Okay.' The voice at the other end of the radio sounded hesitant.

'I'm starting my descent now and I can barely see the strip. I need those lights and I need them right now.'

Adam heard some muffled words shouted at the other end of the radio.

'They're on the way.'

He looked out of the window. He could distinguish a cluster of buildings, illuminated by a series of small lights. Huge white letters across the roof of the shearing shed identified Warrina Downs. They were barely readable in the low light. The landing was going to be more than just difficult. It was going to be dangerous. He caught a glimpse of a pale line in the earth. The landing strip. Even as he watched, it faded from sight as the light failed. He could see the headlights of two vehicles moving at speed away from the homestead.

'There they are,' he said.

'I've got them. Strap in. This isn't going to be the best landing you've ever experienced.'

Adam did as instructed. Glancing sideways at Jess's profile, he saw her brow furrow. He wasn't afraid of flying. In his job he'd chalked up more than a few difficult landings in his urgency to get to someone who needed him. But this ... He looked out of the window again. The cars had stopped moving. He saw the bright beams of their headlights – but he couldn't see a landing strip. He felt a twinge of something that might be fear.

He turned to look back at Sister Luke. The nun was securely strapped into her seat. Her face was calm, but he rarely saw her any other way. Her hands were closed around the wooden cross that hung down the front of her habit. Adam wasn't a religious man, but he always felt slightly comforted when Sister Luke was praying.

A small sound beside him drew his attention back to Jess. She was saying something, but not to him. She was speaking too softly for him to hear, almost as if she were talking to the plane. Adam could almost feel the intensity of her concentration as she lowered the nose of the aircraft. Unconsciously his hands clenched into fists.

The plane settled lower. To Adam it seemed they almost clipped the roof of the first car as they passed over it. He could see the ground now. The aircraft's wheels brushed the dirt, and the plane bounced a few feet into the air. Again the wheels touched, and this time they gripped. The headlights at the end of the runway seemed to be racing towards them, even though Adam knew the car was stationary. Jess's hands moved quickly and assuredly over the controls and the plane rapidly slowed. In the faint light of the cars' headlights, Adam could see the tin shed that served as hangar for the airstrip. Jess turned the plane and brought it to a complete stop with its nose pointing at the shed. The two cars converged on them, their lights providing an eerie illumination to the scene.

In the back of the plane, Sister Luke was out of her seat before the propellers had stopped turning. She released the catch and lowered the aircraft stairs. She was gone by the time Adam had their medical bags out of the lockers. He passed them out to willing hands.

As he stepped through the doorway, he turned to look back. Jess was out of her seat, watching him. She looked tired and relieved as she ran her fingers once more through her hair. He wondered for a moment if her hands were shaking.

'Thank you.' Adam felt he should say something more, but he didn't have time. He turned and descended the aircraft stairs in two great bounds.

Sister Luke was already in the front cab of the utility. Adam leaped onto the flat tray where his bags were waiting. He banged his fist on the metal side of the ute to signal the driver and the vehicle surged forward. Adam stared back at the plane, as Jess slowly descended the steps, where the driver of the second car was waiting for her.

In the harsh glare of the headlights she looked a little lost and very alone.

It was amazing what the human body could stand. Adam sat by the bed, looking down at the face of the sleeping stockman. He was just a kid. Twenty. Maybe twenty-one. Despite the deep hollows that pain had carved under his eyes, the kid still looked soft. City soft. According to the property manager, he'd only been in the outback for a few weeks. He'd come seeking adventure and excitement as a jackaroo – a trainee stockman. This was much more than he'd bargained for.

It was hot in the room. His sleeping patient was covered only with a light sheet that had been folded back so Adam could see the dressing he'd placed over the wound. The kid had disturbed a feral pig. He should have known better than to go near the huge boar as it was gorging on the carcass of a young calf. He carried a rifle, but his aim wasn't good enough. The wounded beast had turned on him. One of the other stockmen heard the screams and killed the boar, but by then the kid had been badly mauled by the creature's razor sharp tusks. He'd probably walk with a limp for the rest of his life due to the damaged muscles in his leg. But the wound in his side could have killed him. If they'd been a bit longer getting here …

The outback was a tough place. Mother Nature could be very cruel. Almost as cruel as people.

Adam stretched to relieve the tension in his back, rubbing the left side of his neck and shoulder. He leaned forward to place a hand on his patient's forehead. No sign of a fever – yet. He'd stitched the wound and administered a huge dose of antibiotics, but the fight wasn't over. A saline drip hanging above the bed would help with the loss of blood, but this kid needed watching tonight. Hopefully he'd stabilise and in the morning they'd fly him to Mount Isa. He needed better care than Adam could give at his tiny facility in Coorah Creek.

'Why don't you go and get something to eat?' a gentle voice behind him said.

'He should sleep for a few hours,' Adam said, as he gave up his chair for Sister Luke. 'He's had some painkillers, but if he wakes—'

'I'll call you,' Sister Luke said. 'I've done this before.'

'Yes, you have.' Adam smiled, suddenly feeling very tired. No one knew better than him just how good Sister Luke was. He rubbed his shoulder again, stretching his neck against the stiffness there. His patients had always been in safe hands with Sister Luke. This boy would be too. With a final look at the unconscious figure on the bed, Adam left them and stepped out into the darkness.

Like most outback homesteads, this one had a deep veranda running along all four sides of the house, to offer sanctuary from the blistering sun. Almost every room had at least one door opening onto the veranda. Adam had no idea of the time, but he imagined it must be quite late. The last vestiges of the sunset had long since vanished from the western sky. He walked to the edge of the veranda, rested his hands on the wooden railing and stared out into the night.

When people from the city came to the outback, one of their first reactions at night was to notice the silence. Adam knew better. The outback is never silent. To those who listen, the night is filled with sound. He could hear the gentle ticking of the corrugated iron on the homestead roof, contracting as it cooled after the heat of the day. To his left, behind a high post and rail fence, he could hear some animals moving around. Probably the horses the stockmen had been riding that day. A faint breeze was blowing, carrying the metallic clank of the windmill as it continued its never-ending circles – pumping life-giving water from deep below the earth. Occasionally, the breeze brought faint sounds of human voices from the stockmen's quarters. His nostrils flared as he caught a whiff of smoke. In the distance the restless light of an open fire captured his attention, mesmerising in its slow dance.

Adam took a long slow breath trying to relieve the tension of the past few hours. The injured boy was safe. He'd made it here in time. Thanks to the new pilot. She'd done a great job. Now he had time to think, he was rather impressed by that difficult landing. And on her first day. He probably should find her and tell her. The other thing he should find was food. He suddenly felt very hungry. He set out in search of the kitchen. Turning the corner of the veranda, he saw a figure standing in the dim light, staring out into the night. Just as he had. Adam knew why he often stood alone staring into the darkness. He wondered why Jess did. Her tall slender body was tense, as if ready to dart away at the slightest threat. She was taking no comfort from the stillness of the night.

She turned as she heard him approach. 'How is he?'

'He'll be fine,' Adam said. 'He's lucky. That was a great landing, by the way.'

'Thanks. Just don't tell the authorities. I'd like to keep my licence.'

'I guess they'd frown on a landing like that.'

'It's not the worst thing I've ever done.' She seemed almost to be speaking to herself, and her voice was full of regret.

What other things, Adam wondered, could Jess possibly have done that were more illegal than a late landing on an unlit airstrip? He watched her face as she turned back to the night. She was tall for a woman, but still shorter than him. Her hair shone softly in the light that streamed out of a window. He had always liked long hair on a woman – but he realised he rather liked this short gamine cut. It framed a face that was quite beautiful. He was struck by a desire to see her smile. Their acquaintance so far had been short – and not exactly designed for smiling. He found himself wanting to change that.

'You did well today.'

'Is this where you tell me I saved his life,' Jess said, her voice a little brittle and defensive.

'No. I saved his life. But you got me here so I could do it.'

She was silent. He sensed her surprise. Perhaps she found him a bit brusque. Well, he believed words existed to help people communicate – not to hinder them. He didn't mince his words.

'You've had a rough first day,' he said.

She nodded. He could feel the tension in her. That was easy to understand. The more he thought about the past few hours, the more he realised just what a tough welcome Jess had received in her new home. Perhaps there was something he could do about that. He certainly wasn't about to leave her staring out into the night, brooding. He knew from long experience that no good would come from that.

'Have you eaten anything?'

'I … the family offered me dinner. But … well, I guess I didn't feel much like eating.'

'I know what you mean. The smells coming from the kitchen weren't very appealing, were they?'

Jess turned quickly towards him. The corners of her mouth twitched as she almost smiled. That was better.

'But you should eat. We both should. Come with me. I happen to know the best restaurant in town.'

She looked at him then, her eyebrows raised in question.

Adam led the way down the wooden steps into the baked red earth and together they strolled towards the distant campfire. As they got closer, the smell of smoke got stronger. Adam ignored the smoke and focused on the cooking smells. His stomach rumbled.

'G'day,' Adam called, as he approached the fire. 'Any chance of some tucker for a couple of hungry fliers?'

'Sure, Doc,' said a voice in the darkness.

The men sprawled around the campfire were almost uniformly dressed in blue jeans and well-worn cotton shirts. The sun had long since vanished, but each still wore a battered Akubra hat, as if he had been born wearing it. To a man, their brown skin and dark curly hair declared their Aboriginal heritage. Some sat on the dry earth. Others on logs that had been set around the fire.

'This is Jessica. She's our new pilot. She hasn't had any dinner.' Adam guessed Jessica hadn't managed much in the way of lunch either.

'Sure thing. Pull up a log, Missus.' Another stockman waved Jess to an empty place. Adam sat down next to her. The man nearest the fire, obviously the cook, reached for metal plates, and ladled some steaming stew out of a big black pot that sat amid the coals.

'Thank you,' Jessica said, as she took the offered plate.

'It's the best food for a hundred kilometres,' Adam said, as he accepted his meal. 'Better that anything you'll get at the homestead – which is the only other food for a hundred kilometres.'

'Too right,' the cook said.

'Is everyone okay at the camp?' Adam asked.

'Grandpa had a fall today hunting kangaroo.'

Adam saw Jessica start and glance down into her bowl. Her mouth stilled and he saw a touch of panic in her eyes.

'It's all right,' he said softly, leaning towards her. 'Dave's grandpa hasn't actually caught a roo for ten years or more. You're eating good outback beef.'

A chuckle around the campfire suggested he wasn't the only one who had noticed her sudden lack of enthusiasm for the food.

'It's gotta be more like twenty years,' Dave offered cheerfully. 'But Grandpa don't give up easy.'

'Do you want me to take a look at him?' Adam asked.

'It's all right, Doc,' Dave said. 'Sister Luke came down and sorted him out. She says he'll be hunting again in a few days.'

'Sister Luke?' Jess asked.

'Her order works with the Aboriginal people,' Adam explained. 'That's why she's here.'

'Oh, I thought she worked for you.'

'No. I'm just her charity case.'

She almost smiled at that. Adam wondered if she would smile if she knew just how close that was to the truth.

'By the way,' he turned his attention back to the stockmen. 'Where's Blue?'

'Gone walkabout,' was the reply.

'Walkabout?' Jess said.

'It's something they do,' Adam started to explain. 'The Aborigines have always been nomadic. Sometimes they just walk into the wilderness – particularly the young men. It's like a rite of passage for them.'

'I know what it is,' Jess said. 'I just didn't think in this day and age ...'

'We still do it, Missus,' the cook said. 'To talk to the spirits of the Dreamtime.'

'Oh.' Jess looked very serious.

'It's better than a sickie to get off work,' Dave explained, his teeth flashing white in the dim light as he grinned. 'I like to go fishing. Pete over there is too lazy to go into the desert proper. He just likes to get away from his wife and kids.'

The men around the camp laughed loudly.

For a brief moment, Jess looked uncertain. Then it came. A slow smile that spread across her face like the light of the sun peeping over the edge of the desert at daybreak. Adam watched her in the gentle glow of the fire. Again he wondered what had brought Jess Pearson to this remote place on the edge of nowhere. Whatever it was, at this moment, he was glad she was there.

The flickering of the fire dragged his eyes away from Jess. Flames curled around the dead tree branches. Sinuous. Seductive. Dangerous. Adam rubbed his shoulder, feeling remembered pain. Beside him, one of the stockmen leaned forward to drop more wood on the fire. Glowing red and orange sparks flew high into the night sky to mingle with the brilliant stars. The harsh crackling of the flames drowned out the ongoing conversation around him. Adam could feel himself being drawn into the flames. Losing himself as the flames reached for him. Then a sound pulled him back. A soft gentle sound. The sound of Jess laughing.

Chapter Three

Jess was trying to fight her way through a wall of noise and flashing light. Leering, lusting faces in front of her.

'Jessica, how does it feel to send your lover to jail?'

'Jessica, shouldn't you be charged, too?'

She raised her hands to fend off the microphones waving just inches from her face. She ducked her head so her long dark hair fell forward, covering her face as the cameras flashed. Hunching her shoulders, she started to push her way through the crowd, but she made no headway. Then a man appeared in front of her, using his body to shield her.

'Thanks, Dad,' she gasped.

But his brow furrowed. 'You ignored the signs? Why Jess? Why?'

There was a boy. So young. His face so pale. His body painfully thin. Then Jessica heard a scream.

'It's your fault. You killed my son!'

A grey-haired woman. Her lined face streaked with tears.

'This was my son!' The woman held a photograph in her hand. She thrust it at Jessica. 'You killed him with that poison you brought here. It's your fault my son is dead.'

'No,' Jessica's voice came out as a croak. 'I didn't know what was happening. I didn't know the drugs were on the plane.'

'Didn't you?' the woman said, in a cold harsh voice. 'You were the pilot. How could you not know?'

Jess woke suddenly, her breath coming in shallow gasps as she tried to shake herself free of the nightmare. Her pulse raced and she felt the tears pricking the back of her eyes. The boy had been just sixteen years old. Dead of a drug overdose. There was no way of knowing if the drugs that killed him had ever been on her plane. But for a grieving mother, that was irrelevant. She sat in the courtroom every day, her haunted eyes following every moment of the high profile trial. And when it was over, facing a life without her child, the woman had struck out at the only target within reach. Jess. The prosecutor told her not to take it personally. But how else was she to take it? What was more personal than a dead boy?

She pounded her fist into the bedclothes in a mixture of anger and pain. Would the ghosts of the past never leave her?

As her heartbeat slowed, Jess became aware of her surroundings. She lay in an unfamiliar bed, staring up at a fan circling slowly to stir the warm air against her sweat soaked body. Still struggling to regain her grip on the daylight world, she heard a baby cry. It took a second cry for her to realise it wasn't a child at all. Somewhere not far away, a crow was crying ... a long mournful sound that in her mind was somehow associated with loss ... and death.

Not the young drug addict. Another boy. The injured jackaroo.

Suddenly fully awake, Jess slipped out of bed. She pulled on her jeans and T-shirt as the events of the day before came flooding back with a little too much clarity. She had to find out how the injured boy fared. She had to know that the mad dash from Coorah Creek to this remote outpost hadn't been in vain. She had to know that this time, she had helped. That this boy would live.

She walked to the bedroom door and opened it. Almost opposite her, the door to another room stood half open. Through it she could see the foot of a bed and a figure draped in a white sheet. Silently on her bare feet, she entered the other room. The jackaroo was stretched on the bed, a drip attached to one arm. His eyes were closed, but she could hear his slow deep breathing. In a chair beside the bed, his back to her, sat Adam. His head was bowed forward and he was rubbing his neck. She couldn't see his face, but his weariness surrounded him like a cloak.

'How is he doing?' Jess whispered, as she approached the bed.

Adam looked up at her. His brown eyes were shadowed with exhaustion. Jess realised he must have been sitting with his patient all night.

'He's stabilised,' Adam spoke in a whisper, too. 'We'll take him back to Mount Isa today. They can do more for him there.'

Jess looked down at the boy on the bed. 'But he will …?' Jess couldn't put the thought into words.

'Yes. He will.'

Jess felt a profound sense of relief. 'Thank God.'

'I'm sure Sister Luke already has.' The slow smile on his tired face softened the words.

Silence fell between them as they watched the sleeping boy, and brought with it a strange sense of intimacy. Together they had saved a life. In this moment, Jess felt closer to Adam than she had to any human being for such a very long time.

'Adam …' It was the first time she had called him by name. Without really thinking, she reached out to lay a hand gently on his shoulder. Afterwards she wasn't sure why she had done it. The need to touch him, to make human contact was just so strong.

Her fingers were like burning embers on his skin. Adam flinched away from her. He felt her snatch her hand

28

back, and that was even more painful than her touch. He wanted to tell her it wasn't her fault. That the problem was his. But he couldn't look at her. He didn't want to see her face. Instead, he reached for the drip line attached to the boy's arm. As if it needed checking.

'I want to get him to the Isa as quickly as possible,' he said, his voice rough. 'I imagine there are things you need to do to the plane.'

'Yes. There are.' Her voice was little more than a whisper. 'If you're looking for breakfast ...'

'I can find the kitchen. I'll send word when we are ready to leave.'

Adam didn't so much hear her go as feel her absence. He dropped the drip line, and tentatively rubbed his shoulder, feeling the roughness of the skin beneath his shirt. There was no new wound there. No burn. Why then did it hurt?

Because it always did. When people got too close they hurt. They laughed, or they left or they just hurt. The only way to avoid the hurt was to keep people away. He was very good at that. Oh, people liked him. He was friendly. He cared about his patients. There were times he knew he touched their lives. But that was different. No one touched his life. No one touched him.

Adam took a deep breath and regained his equilibrium as the only person who had never deliberately hurt him walked into the room.

'I'll look after him if you want to get some breakfast,' Sister Luke said.

'Thanks. I'll go in a minute. I just want to check the wound.' Adam busied himself with his patient for a few minutes. Sister Luke was, as always, the perfect nurse – assisting him without being told what he needed.

'It's probably safe to go into the kitchen now,' Sister Luke said, as they finished.

'I don't know what you mean?' Adam fiddled with the drip in his patient's arm again rather than look into the nun's too-knowing grey eyes.

'I heard Jess asking for someone to drive her to the airstrip. My guess is she's finished her breakfast and gone.'

'That's good. We need to get this kid to hospital,' Adam said, firmly ignoring Sister Luke's tone. 'Can you stay with him while I get something to eat? I don't want to disturb him any more than we have to, so I won't shift him until Jess sends word that the plane is ready.'

'Of course.'

Sister Luke was smiling in that annoyingly satisfied way she had. Adam almost snorted as he left the room.

Sure enough, there was no sign of Jess in the homestead's big kitchen. The station owner and his wife were effusive in their thanks as they served him a huge breakfast of steak and eggs, with more coffee on the side than he would drink in a week.

Just as he was finishing, the loud clump of boots on the wooden veranda heralded the return of one of the stockmen. Removing his hat, the man put his head inside the door.

'Doc, the plane is ready to go,' he said.

'Great.' Adam got to his feet.

'Jess said you'd probably need the stretcher from the plane,' the stockman continued. 'It's in the ute.'

The stretcher. How had he not thought of that? That was unlike him. He put it down to tiredness.

With the assistance of another stockman, they carefully carried the jackaroo out of the house, and laid him in the back of the ute. Adam rode with his patient, wincing every time the slow-moving vehicle hit a pothole in the red dirt track. There were far more than Adam would have liked, but thanks to the drugs, the injured boy was oblivious to the harsh bumps.

At the airstrip, the plane was waiting, the steps lowered. As the driver pulled the ute up close to the aircraft doors, Adam could see Jess in the pilot's seat making her pre-flight checks.

'Gently now,' Adam cautioned, as together the driver and the stockman lifted the stretcher from the back of the vehicle. They carried it to the plane and manoeuvred it through the door. Adam followed them on board to make sure his patient was safely strapped in for the flight. The straps secured across his chest and legs would keep him safe through any turbulence they encountered. Making sure the saline drip was still in place; Adam knew they were ready to go.

Sister Luke was already on board. He stepped to the doorway.

'Thanks a lot,' he called to the stockman below, as he pulled the stairs up and latched the door.

He leaned into the cockpit, where Jess was strapped in to the pilot's seat.

'Are you ready to go?' she asked, without turning to look at him.

Adam hated that she didn't meet his eyes. He hated the distance in her voice. Hated the knowledge that he had put it there. And most of all, he regretted that was the way it had to be, but at this moment, he needed that distance. So did Jess. And so did the injured boy in the back of the plane. He was their first priority.

'Yes. We're ready,' he said, and made his way back to a seat close to his patient.

Chapter Four

Jack parked his dusty ute in front of the railway station. The doc had called earlier this morning to say they were flying the injured jackaroo to Mount Isa hospital. They wouldn't be back in Coorah Creek until late this afternoon. Jack shook his head. What a way to start a new job! He hoped Jess wasn't already regretting her decision. It was hard enough to get pilots willing to work in the outback, without this sort of an introduction to their new life. He wondered just what had brought Jess to the Creek. She appeared fragile, but Jack had the impression she was a lot tougher than she looked. He hoped she was strong enough to stay. They needed her.

Jack got out of his vehicle just as the train pulled into the station. It should be carrying some parts for the emergency power generator at the hospital. Trains came in and out of the mine compound on a regular basis, carting the ore back to the coast. On some days, the mine train broke into two parts, the smaller engine and just a few carriages heading along the short spur to the town itself. Those trains carried freight. Supplies for the stores. Equipment ordered from back east by local businesses and outlying cattle stations. And, very occasionally, a passenger.

Today there were three of them.

The first passenger to alight was clutching a large and battered teddy bear. She had fine blonde hair and a big brother attached to one hand. The boy was trying to look tough, but his wide eyes gave him away. Jack didn't know much about kids. He guessed the little girl was maybe five, her brother a year or two older. Where was their mother? A few seconds later, he saw movement in the train's doorway. Someone was struggling to get a large blue suitcase out of the carriage. The suitcase suddenly slid forward, then toppled sideways. The little girl darted out of the way, tripping over her brother as she did, and went sprawling to the rough wooden platform. The resulting cries were staggeringly loud for such a small girl.

A woman darted out of the train and bundled the little girl up in her arms. Jack couldn't see much of the woman, but the protective arch of her body as she cradled her child said everything he needed to know.

'Do you need some help with your bags?' Jack touched one finger to the brim of his Akubra hat.

The woman looked up at him. She had the bluest eyes Jack had ever seen, but right now they were glistening with unshed tears. The woman was obviously fighting to hold herself together for the kids.

'Thank you,' she said. 'There's two more, just inside the door. If you could ...'

Before she'd finished speaking, he had the bags in a pile on the platform. The woman stood up, smoothing her cotton skirt. Jack smiled down at the little girl, who retreated behind her brother and peeked up at him with eyes almost as blue as her mother's.

'Do you need a ride?'

The woman looked around. The railway station was at the eastern edge of town. From the platform there was little to see. A few shabby wooden huts. The railway line leading to the mine and some scrubby bush beyond. Jack realised that to a stranger, it must seem the edge of nowhere.

'No. Thank you. I'll take a taxi.' She offered him a polite, but distant smile.

'There aren't any taxis,' Jack said with a rueful grin. 'If you're heading to town, I'm very happy to give you a lift. My ute is just outside. It's a long walk for a couple of tired kids.'

The woman reached out a hand to rest on her son's shoulder. Jack could see her hesitate. She knew she needed a lift, but he could read the wariness in her eyes. Something wasn't going to allow her to accept.

'I'm Jack North,' he said, removing his hat and holding out a hand. 'I work for the local air ambulance.'

'You're a doctor?' she asked.

'No. The engineer.' That was strange. Usually he referred to himself as the maintenance man. Engineer always seemed too grand a title for a man who just fixed things.

'Nice to meet you.' The woman finally held out her hand. 'I'm Ellen Parkes.'

She looked to be in her early thirties. She was quite small, barely reaching his shoulder. There were lines around her mouth and eyes. They should have been laughter lines, but Jack had the impression they had been etched into her face by a difficult life. Her hand when he took it was a little rough. The nails were blunt and unpainted. This was a woman who understood hard work. But when Jack looked at her eyes, all he saw was how beautiful she was.

'So, now that we've been introduced, will you let me give you a lift?' he asked again.

Still she hesitated.

'I have to pick up some packages. Why don't you think about it while I load them?'

He located his packages in the freight car. He could sense Ellen watching him as he carried the heavy boxes out to his ute. They were clearly addressed to him, at the Coorah Creek Hospital. Maybe that would make her feel more secure in accepting his help. After loading them into the tray of his vehicle, Jack turned back to find Ellen and her children standing at the station entrance, looking down the road towards town. The look on her face said enough.

'Let me get your bags.' Jack retrieved the suitcases and placed them in the back of the ute. 'It's going to be a tight fit, the cab only seats three.'

'Bethany's so small, she doesn't count,' a boyish voice piped up.

Jack crouched down to bring his own eyes level with the boy's.

'What's your name?' he asked.

'Harry.'

'How old are you, Harry?'

'I'm seven.'

'And Bethany is your little sister, right?'

'Right. She's five and a half. She's only in prep school.'

'Well, Harry, can I tell you a secret?' Jack said in a serious voice. The little boy nodded. 'Girls always count. Especially little ones like Bethany. It's our job, as men, to look after them.'

Harry was silent. He looked up at his mother. Jack glanced at Ellen too. Her lips were pressed tightly together, as if to stop herself from crying. She nodded to her son.

'See, your mum knows the secret too,' Jack said. 'It's supposed to be just for men to know, but I think it's okay if your mum knows. What do you say?'

'I think so too,' Harry said importantly.

'All right then.' Jack stood up and turned to open the car door. 'How about you squeeze in the middle, young

35

Harry? Then Bethany can sit on your mum's lap. Does that sound all right?'

Harry nodded and scrambled up into the ute.

Ellen seemed to hesitate one last time, then climbed into the cab after her son.

What was she thinking? Ellen's emotions were running on adrenaline – and not going in a good direction. What on earth had possessed her to bring the kids to this town on the edge of nowhere? She had to get away, but surely she could have picked somewhere better than this? She had two children who needed a home and a father. She hadn't done very well so far in providing them with either. Although she'd long since given up any hope of a fairy tale ending for herself, her kids deserved to be safe. They deserved a future. But was this the right future?

Here she was riding into some town at the back of beyond, in a beat-up old ute, with a strange man at her side. She cast a quick sideways glance at Jack. His face was tanned and he needed a shave. She had also glimpsed a tattoo on his upper arm. Ellen guessed he might be a year or two younger than she was. The hands gripping the steering wheel were possibly not the cleanest she'd ever seen, but they were the hands of a man who was not afraid of a bit of hard work. He was a big man, but not frightening. He'd been so gentle with the kids. And it was good of him to give her a lift. Town was a longer walk than the kids could have managed, tired as they were from the journey. She was tired too, but not tired enough to let down her guard. Jack North seemed nice enough, but she'd met a 'nice' man once before and still carried the scars.

Jack turned and smiled in her direction. Embarrassed at being caught watching him, Ellen turned to look out of the window. They drove past a line of wooden houses. The paint was faded and peeling and the yards messy and overgrown with weeds. Here and there the wrecks of cars sat rusting under the outback sun. The homes looked deserted and reeked of failure. Not only that, it was far hotter than she expected. Already she could feel the sweat staining her armpits. And the dust! A cloud of it seemed to follow the car as it moved. This was no place for her kids.

'Don't be put off.' As if he'd been reading her mind, the man at her side indicated the row of shabby buildings. 'Those were originally part of an old Aboriginal reserve. They've been empty for years. They should have been pulled down long ago, when the mine built better houses.'

That wasn't very comforting.

'Where do you want me to drop you off?'

It was an obvious question – and she had no answer.

'The motel?' she said hesitantly.

'Sorry. There isn't one.'

Ellen's heart sank another notch. No motel? Then where would she and the kids stay? She'd been in such a hurry to get away, she hadn't given any thought to finding somewhere to stay. After all, every small town had a motel. Except, it seemed, this one.

'Caravan park?' She hated the thought, but if there was no motel …

'Not really,' Jack said. 'There's a campsite near the river, but no vans for hire.'

This was just getting worse! Ellen tightened her arms around Bethany. The little girl was exhausted after the long journey. So was Ellen. All she wanted right now was a bath and a bed. Somewhere she could close her eyes and know her children were safe.

They were approaching a T-intersection. To her left was a petrol station. On the right she saw a large two-storey pub with beautiful wrought iron railings around the upper veranda. As they turned right, Ellen could see a long straight road, with shops either side. It wasn't exactly a city centre shopping mall, but things were looking a bit better. Almost immediately Jack swung the car off the road, to park in front of the pub.

'I hope you don't mind, but I need to stop here for a moment. While I do, you can have a think about where you want to go.'

He was gone before she could answer, and Ellen felt the fear start to rise. It was barely lunchtime and here they were at a pub. This Jack was just the same as the loser she had married. From bed to bar and back again. That was it. Why had she thought things would be any different here?

'Mum, I'm hungry.'

Harry's plaintive voice dragged Ellen back from the gulf of self-pity at her feet.

'I know, honey,' she said, dropping an arm around his thin shoulders. 'It won't be long now. I just need to find us somewhere to stay.'

She kept her voice cheerful, for Harry's sake, but inside she felt nothing but despair. No motel. No caravan park. Was there a church somewhere? Maybe a priest would know of somewhere safe for her to go. Or perhaps if she went to the hospital, they might suggest something. There was no one here who knew her. No one who would help her. She would have to rely on charity, but not for long. Just for a few days. Until she got her feet back under her. Then she'd find a job, a place to live and start again. This time she'd do it all herself and not rely on anyone else. Especially not a man.

'Mrs Parkes?'

The woman standing beside the car had to be in her sixties. She had short, silver-white hair that framed a lined face and a pair of sympathetic brown eyes. She wiped her hands on an apron that looked to have seen a lot of service.

'Yes.'

'I'm Trish Warren. My husband Syd and I own the pub.'

'Oh. Nice to meet you ...' Ellen said hesitantly.

'Jack is helping Syd with some barrels. Despite what Syd thinks, he's getting a bit old for the heavy lifting. It's really good of Jack to help him out like he does, but that's Jack all over. Anyway, he said you needed somewhere to stay the night. You and your kids.'

'Well, yes. But ...'

'I know, it's a pub. Not your first choice for a place to stay. Particularly for the kids. But please believe me when I say that it's okay. Out here, the pub is the centre of the town. Families come here. It'll be fine for your kids. Honestly. Besides, it's the only place in town,' Trish added with a smile.

'Well.' Ellen didn't like it, but what other option did she have? 'All right. Is there a room I can have for the night? Somewhere away from the bar,' she added quickly. 'The kids are going to need to sleep.'

'There's a big room on the top floor at the back which is just what you need,' Trish said with a smile. 'Two beds. I guess it will be okay for the little ones to share? It's nothing fancy, mind you. But it's clean and comfortable. You have to share a bathroom, but there are no other guests at the moment.'

'That'll be fine. How much?' Ellen held her breath. She didn't have a lot of money.

Trish named a price so low Ellen could hardly believe she heard it right. 'Thank you,' she said.

'It's no problem at all. Now, kids, I'm Mrs Warren. Why don't you come with me to the kitchen? You must be tired and hungry after your long trip. I think I've got some chocolate biscuits. And milk. I hope you like milk. It's really good for you.'

That seemed to do the trick. Harry and Bethany scrambled out of the cab. Ellen and the kids followed Trish inside the pub. It was cool and dark after the heat outside. A long polished wooden bar ran almost the entire length of the room. Behind it, from the open door of a giant cool room, Ellen could hear men's voices.

They made their way through the bar into a lounge area, liberally dotted with tables and chairs. Although it was empty, it had an aura of homeliness that Ellen found very welcoming. A door on one side led to a large and airy kitchen, which was spotlessly clean. Trish headed for the fridge and removed a bottle of milk. From an adjoining cupboard she produced a container of what were obviously home-baked biscuits. In a few seconds, Harry and Bethany were seated at a well-scrubbed wooden table, happily working their way through a generous serving of both.

'I bet you'd love a cup of tea,' Trish said, as she filled an electric kettle. 'I always think tea helps. Whenever I'm tired or stressed, I just take the time to sit and have a cuppa. I always feel better too.'

'Please, don't go to any trouble,' Ellen said. Her voice quivered a little. She didn't know how much longer she was going to be able to hold things together.

'It's no trouble at all,' Trish replied, without pausing in her task of putting tea bags into two big mugs. 'There are people who say you can't get a good cup of tea out of a bag. I think they're wrong. You just have to go about it in the right way. Trouble is, most people just don't let the bag sit for long enough.'

'Ah ...'

'Like anything that's worth doing, you just have to take your time.' Trish didn't seem to need any response from Ellen. 'Help yourself to milk, and the sugar is in that blue bowl.'

Ellen took the offered steaming cup. She reached for the sugar bowl then turned to see Trish's eyes narrow.

No! Ellen pulled down the sleeve that had ridden up as she reached across the table. Please! Don't let her see the bruises. I need to start a fresh life. I don't want anyone to know.

She busied herself adding milk and sugar to her tea, then refilled Harry's glass of milk. When at last she looked up at Trish, she saw compassion in the woman's face.

'When you're done with the tea, I'll show you the room,' Trish said. 'And I think I've got some books and things stashed somewhere for the kids, if they'd like them. Keep them occupied while you sort yourself out.'

'Thank you,' Ellen said. 'I guess I should pay you in advance for the room. And for—'

'No need,' Trish interrupted her. 'The room rate I mentioned was for a single night. If you stay longer, you'll get a discount. Long-term residents' rate. So why don't you and the kids just relax and we can worry about it later.'

The kindness in her eyes was the final straw. Ellen blinked back the tears. 'Thank you.'

Trish nodded. Her eyes were also suspiciously bright. 'I'll leave you with the kids for a bit. I'll get Jack to carry your bags up to your room.' With an understanding nod, she left, closing the door behind her.

'Are you all right, Mummy?' Harry asked, from the other side of the table.

'I'm fine, darling. Just a bit tired. How are the biscuits?'

'Really good,' her son said.

Ellen's heart nearly broke. Those home-baked biscuits were the first good thing Harry had experienced in far too long.

Chapter Five

Jess looked down at the cluster of buildings as she circled for landing. Was it just twenty-four hours ago she'd been doing exactly the same thing – preparing to land at Coorah Creek? She recognised the green slash that the creek created against the red soil. There were the houses and the railway line. The mine and the incongruous blue of the school swimming pool. It was familiar – but she had not yet set foot there. That first landing had been ... interesting. At the time, she had thought she was tired, but that was nothing to how she felt now. She was beyond tired. Now all she wanted to do was go home, curl up somewhere quiet and sleep for a week. Home? That was a bit of a joke. It certainly wasn't her home. Yet. Would this cluster of buildings on the edge of the desert ever become her home? Or was it just a hiding place? She could only hope that today she would get a chance to actually leave the aircraft.

She began her gentle descent towards the airstrip. At least this time she wouldn't have to worry about a madman decapitating himself as he ducked past her propellers. The madman was safely ensconced inside the plane with her. She glanced back over her shoulder. Adam Gilmore was sound asleep, strapped in to one of the forward seats. He was a tall man, and his legs stretched forward into the narrow aisle. He didn't look much like a madman any more. He had incredibly long eyelashes that lay softly against his skin. His longish dark hair had a gentle wave to it. Lying across his cheek, it made him seem younger, although she guessed he would be a few years older than her – early thirties, perhaps. Asleep and in need of a shower and a shave, he looked positively harmless. Vulnerable, even. And perhaps just a little bit handsome.

No. No. Jessica stopped her thoughts right there. Adam was her boss. She wasn't about to let herself feel attracted to him. Especially not as he was a madman. Getting involved with the boss was a bad idea. She'd made that mistake with Brian, and it had almost destroyed her. She would not do it again. This job was all about getting her life back in order. Taking control again. The last thing she needed was to feel anything for Adam. She was already regretting that moment of weakness this morning, when she had reached out to touch him. She could blame exhaustion. Or the nightmare that always left her emotions fragile. Whatever the reason, she should not have let it affect her like that. What had she been thinking? She was a stranger here. If she was going to make a success of this new life, she was going to have to put those sorts of errant emotions behind her and just focus on her work. This first rescue flight had gone well. The boy was going to live. She had to focus on that. She had helped save one life. It wasn't enough … but it was a start.

'Adam's a very good doctor, you know.' Sister Luke had chosen to ride up front with Jess during the trip back to the Creek.

'I thought he might be,' Jess said.

'He cares – sometimes too much,' Sister Luke said, her voice softening as she spoke. 'He'll sit up all night with a patient. Just holding their hand. I swear he talks them better.'

Jess raised an eyebrow. 'That seems a strange thing—'

'For a nun to say,' Sister Luke finished for her, her gentle voice sparkling with humour.

'Well, yes. I guess so.'

'He talks. God listens. The patients recover. Do we really have to define who does the healing?'

'I don't suppose we do.' Jess felt a twinge of envy. Sister Luke spoke with such surety. There was little enough that Jess was still sure about in this world, let alone the next.

A few minutes later, Jess guided the plane to a smooth touchdown on the airstrip and brought it to a halt well short of the end of the runway. The rituals of take-off and landing were a comfort to her. The rituals assured her safety and gave her control of her surroundings, something her life had lacked in the roller coaster of the past few months. There had been a time when she thought she might never fly again and at this moment, the act of landing the small air ambulance on the long, thin grey strip of tarmac in the middle of the bush seemed something of a miracle. The fact that her efforts had helped save a young man's life ... perhaps there was something miraculous about that as well.

She taxied the Beechcraft towards her hangar. The hangar she had yet to set a foot inside. She parked the plane and looked back into the passenger seat. Adam was still asleep.

'How can he sleep through a landing?' she wondered out loud.

'He didn't sleep last night,' Sister Luke said, as she unbuckled her safety harness. 'He relieved me about midnight and stayed with the patient.'

'Talking him better,' Jess suggested.

Sister Luke nodded. 'Adam has a one track mind when his patient needs him. He doesn't give much thought to himself – or anyone else other than his patient.'

Jess could believe that. Finding Adam with his patient this morning hadn't really been a surprise. She'd already guessed that his devotion to his patients ran deep. She wished they hadn't had that awkward moment when she reached out to him. But they'd get past that. Compared to the other problems she'd had to overcome, a moment's tension was nothing.

Sister Luke moved back into the plane's cabin. Jess expected her to shake Adam awake, but the nun's hand stopped a couple of inches from Adam's shoulder. Jess wondered if maybe it wasn't just her. Maybe the doctor didn't like to be touched by anyone.

'Adam,' Sister Luke said quite loudly. 'We're home.'

He started awake. His eyes flew open and for a few seconds they looked around wildly. Then they settled on Sister Luke's face, and he visibly relaxed. Even from the front of the plane, Jess could see that there was some sort of special bond between the two. She wondered what it was.

'We're home, Adam,' Sister Luke said again.

Adam nodded and looked past the sister to where Jess was watching from the pilot's seat.

'Nice landing,' he said, his lips curling into the suggestion of a smile.

'How would you know?' she countered. 'You slept through it.'

'That's how I know.' He slowly unfolded himself from the seat and lowered the aircraft steps.

Jess was the last to exit. Adam was waiting for her on the tarmac. 'Welcome to Coorah Creek,' he said formally. 'I'm sorry I had to drag you away so quickly yesterday. You didn't even get to leave the plane.'

Looking at his tired face, Jess thought she could see

sincerity there. Jess wanted this new job to work – for so many reasons. She took a deep breath and decided to start all over again with both the town and its doctor.

'I'm just glad the patient was all right,' Jess said, as she stretched her neck and shoulders to relieve the tension of too many hours in the air.

'It gets a bit like that out here. Sometimes there just aren't enough hours in the day. Other times you'll be dying of boredom.'

'Boredom sounds pretty good to me right now,' Jess said. 'As does a shower and some clean clothes. I am supposed to get somewhere to live as part of the job. You wouldn't happen to know where that might be and how I can get there?'

'Ah, yes. Your accommodation,' said Sister Luke. 'Adam can tell you all about that. Can't you, Adam?'

Surprisingly, the question caused Adam to drop his eyes to his shoes with the air of a child who knows he is in trouble.

'I'll take Jess to the pub,' he said shortly.

'The pub?' Jessica's heart sank. 'I'm not staying at a pub.' The words came out louder and more strident than she had planned. But that was exactly how she felt. According to her contract she was to have accommodation provided as part of the job. She hadn't expected anything fancy, but she had imagined a small house. Certainly not a room at some outback pub. Then there was the ever-present fear that someone would recognise her. They had newspapers and television even out here.

'Just for a couple of nights.'

'Adam,' Sister Luke said in a chiding tone. 'Please don't tell me you forgot.'

'Not so much forgot as didn't think about it,' Adam

replied. 'Well, I got the call about the injured jackaroo. And I had a couple of patients I had to ring. To cancel appointments. I never got around to it.'

Jess was starting to get a bad feeling. 'Never got around to what, exactly?'

'We were expecting a male pilot,' Adam explained. 'The last pilot just stayed with the mine workers at the single men's accommodation.'

Jess's eyes widened in horror.

'So,' Adam hurried on before she could say a word, 'when Jack met you yesterday, he rang and asked me to sort something out for you.'

'And?' Jess looked at the doctor.

Adam had the grace to look ashamed. 'If you could just stay at the pub for a couple of nights – a week at the most – I can get something organised for you. There are a couple of houses attached to the hospital. I'm sure one would suit you.' He rubbed the side of his neck as he spoke, as if to relieve the tension.

'No Adam. Not those houses,' Sister Luke interrupted. 'They've been empty for eons. She needs a nice place to live.'

Jess wasn't sure whether she wanted to laugh or cry. She'd wanted to get away from her old life. Being taken to an outback pub by this absent-minded madman of a doctor was as far away from her old life in luxury hotels with Brian as it was possible to get. She took a long slow breath and decided that right now a room at the pub was definitely better than nothing. In a town this small, how busy could the pub be on a Wednesday night? She had wanted privacy and anonymity, but right now a shower and some sleep sounded much more appealing. And besides, no one she'd met since leaving Sydney had recognised her. Maybe they didn't have newspapers way out here after all.

'Does the pub have a hot shower?'

'Of course.'

'And a bed?'

'Yes.'

'Then the pub will be fine – just for a couple of days,' she warned. 'At least it's not a jail cell.' As soon as the words were out of her mouth, Jess wished she could call them back. That was a part of her past that she wasn't going to share. Not with these people. Not with anyone. Ever.

'Oh, we've got one of those,' Adam said with a rueful smile. 'But the pub is a far better idea.'

Jess forced a laugh, at once grateful and ashamed. Grateful to be among people who would assume she was joking … and ashamed that she was, in fact, not joking at all. Those terrible nights spent behind bars after her plane was seized still haunted her. As did the thought that she could well have spent years in such a place, had she not chosen honesty over love … or what she thought was love.

'I'll take you there now,' Adam said. 'Jack will see to the plane and help Sister Luke.'

Jess hadn't noticed Jack's arrival. He backed his ute up close to the Beechcraft, ready to unload the medical supplies they'd picked up in Mount Isa. He also retrieved Jessica's luggage which he'd loaded twenty-four hours and many, many kilometres ago. Ordinarily, Jess would never have left her plane in someone else's care. She always checked her own aircraft. Made sure it was secure for the night and ready for a quick take-off in the morning if needed. Just this once, she was going to let Jack do it.

The way she felt right now, she was more likely to make a mistake than he was. And she'd made more than enough of those recently.

Adam's car, the one she'd almost collided with the day before, was parked next to the hangar. On the way into town, Adam was all business. He gave her a running commentary on everything they passed.

'The town's really changed in the past few years,' he said, as they drove along a gravel road next to a high cyclone wire fence. As they passed a gate and a small guardhouse, a man in uniform waved. 'That's the mine. Uranium. It opened a bit over five years ago. The vein is really rich. The mine turned a two-horse truck stop into a thriving town. Brought in the railroad. Jobs. Me. And now you.'

He turned and smiled at her in a friendly, if distant, way. That was just fine by Jess. If she was going to have to work with Adam that was exactly the way their relationship had to be.

'The highway runs south from here towards Birdsville. We go there every year to provide medical cover during the race meeting. You'll get to come too this year. It's only a few weeks away and it's a lot of fun.'

In the closed confines of the ute, Jess was very aware of Adam, his shoulder almost touching hers as he steered the car around a sharp corner. Almost touching. Not quite. She wondered which one of them was more determined to avoid that touch.

They had turned off the gravel road and onto a long straight stretch of grey bitumen. On either side, scrubby bush lined the road. Red dust, blown by the wind, left bright lines across the dull surface of the road. Jess felt as if she could drive for days, and see nothing but the red soil, the bright blue sky and the bush.

A kilometre further down the road, the first of the town buildings appeared.

'That's my hospital,' Adam said proudly, as he pointed to a long low building, built on wooden stumps with the ever-present wide veranda. 'The mine pays for it, of course. They built it originally to treat anyone injured at the mine. There are always a few of them, but luckily the injuries are usually slight. I had trouble convincing them they needed to expand it – but when the first baby was delivered there, they finally got the message. It's pretty well equipped now, but anyone requiring surgery has to go to Mount Isa or Longreach. We also treat the people from the Aboriginal community. That's why Sister Luke is here.'

Jess liked the pride in his voice as he spoke. How wonderful to have something to be proud of. She'd had that once. Pride in her skill as a pilot. Maybe this job would help her find that again.

More buildings started to appear. They were remarkably similar timber structures, all raised clear of the ground on wooden stumps. The paint on every building was faded by the blistering heat of the sun. There was nothing resembling the green lawns and colourful gardens of Jessica's suburban upbringing. Out here there was barely enough water for people, let alone for plants. The vehicle started to slow down as they approached the intersection that Jess had seen from the air. The signpost on the corner pointed east towards Longreach and north towards Mount Isa. They had reached the centre of town. Jess took a deep breath and looked along the town's main street. There wasn't a single person to be seen. Not a car moved, apart from the one she was in. Coorah Creek was a long way from anywhere ... slow moving and quiet. Some people would no doubt find it boring.

It was exactly what Jess was looking for.

In no time at all, Adam pulled up in front of the only two-storey building in the town. 'Come on in and let me introduce you to the Warrens. Syd and Trish run the place. I should warn you, Trish does talk rather a lot. They're good people. Most of the people here are. They'll welcome you with open arms.'

Adam grabbed her bags and ushered her through the doors into the pub's one big room. It was cool inside, and dark after the sun's glare outside. Adam left her in the lounge and vanished through an archway into the main bar in search of the publican. Jess turned slowly around. She hadn't ever spent a lot of time in pubs. Brian had been more a restaurant and wine bar sort of person. This place would not have suited him at all. The big high-ceilinged room held a mismatched collection of tables and chairs and a pool table dominated one corner. The walls were painted wood panels, decorated by framed posters of outback scenes. It wasn't exactly something out of *Vogue Living*, but Jess decided there was something to be said for the pub's gentle homeliness. The wooden floors gleamed softly with much polishing. In a nearby kitchen someone was baking a cake, or biscuits. It smelled good. There was no television, which made Jess feel just a little more secure.

She was starting to wonder what had happened to Adam, when she heard a scurry of feet behind her. She turned and by instinct caught a small blonde girl as she darted past. Just as Jess dropped to her knees in front of the girl, a slightly older boy appeared at a run. His hair and similar blue eyes proclaimed their relationship.

'Bethany.' The boy called and the little girl giggled happily.

'Well, hello,' Jess said, as the boy came up to her.

'Bethany ran away,' the boy said, taking the little girl's hand.

'And you were looking for her?' Jess fought back a smile at the boy's serious face.

'We have to look out for girls. Jack says so.'

Could the boy be talking about her mechanic? Maybe. He hadn't mentioned a family, but then, she hadn't asked either. Asking someone else about their life usually meant similar questions being asked of her, and Jess tried to avoid too many questions. At least from adults.

'Well, he's right,' Jess said. 'What's your name?'

'Harry. What's yours?'

'I'm Jessica. Where's your mum, Harry?'

Before the boy could speak, the answer came in the form of running footsteps. A woman appeared, her face a mask of concern.

'Harry! Bethany! I told you not to leave the room.'

'I'm sorry Mummy, but Bethany ran away. I had to come and find her.'

The woman swept both children into a hug. 'You must never go off alone. I was so worried.'

Jess stepped back to give the woman a moment with her children. She could feel the concern and love emanating for the woman. Her desire to protect her children from harm was evident in everything about her.

My son is dead. It's your fault. You killed my son!

Jess took another step back. Her foot caught a chair and it crashed noisily to the floor. The woman looked up.

'I'm sorry,' she said, slowly getting to her feet. 'I fell asleep upstairs, and when I woke they were gone. We're new to town and I guess I panicked ...'

'It's fine,' said Jess, replacing the chair under the table. 'I think they might have been heading for the kitchen.'

'Mrs Warren cooks really great biscuits,' Harry offered by way of explanation.

'I'm Ellen Parkes,' the woman said, 'and you've already met Harry and Bethany. We just arrived in town today. We're staying here for a day or two.'

'Jess Pearson. I arrived yesterday – sort of, and I think I'm staying here, too.'

'Yes, you are. And you are very welcome.' A smiling, elderly woman approached. She had short grey hair and her lined face seemed to almost glow with good humour. 'We've had a few of the Flying Doctor pilots here from time to time. And once a pilot who was flying a plane for a politician. But we've never had a female pilot before.' The woman wiped her hands with a dishcloth and Jess guessed she was the one responsible for the great cooking smells. 'The pub hasn't had this many guests since last year's election,' the woman continued before Jess could greet her. 'We had two politicians and two election officials here then, plus the pilot, of course. This is going to be much more fun. I see you've met Ellen and the kids. I'm Trish Warren.' The woman didn't seem to need to pause for breath. 'Let me show you to your room, Jess. It's going to be such fun. All us girls here together. And with the kids, too. I'm sure we'll all get on famously.'

Chapter Six

Ellen opened her eyes and stared up into the darkness. The silence surrounding her was as unfamiliar as the room in which she lay. For a split second she had to think to remember where she was. Of course, her room at the pub. She remembered the train journey, and the man ... Jack ... who had come to her rescue. Then she raised herself on one arm to look at the next bed. Beth and Harry were sound asleep, curled up under the covers against a surprisingly chilly night. They'd been exhausted when she put them to bed. She hadn't heard a peep from either of them since. Then what had woken her? A glance at the window told her the sun was only starting to peek above the horizon. She'd been just as exhausted as the kids last night and had fallen into a deep sleep not long after they had. Something must have pulled her from that blissful rest.

A cry. From a nearby room.

Ellen listened intently. There was silence for a few seconds then she heard it again. A low cry. A woman's voice. She slipped out of bed and even though it was dark and she was alone, she pulled down the sleeve of her nightshirt to cover the bruises. Then she padded softly to open the door just a crack. The hallway outside was deserted.

As far as Ellen knew, there was only one other guest in the pub. Jess.

Last night, Trish had insisted both women and the kids eat their dinner at the big kitchen table. She claimed she wanted someone to talk to, but it had seemed to Ellen that Trish actually didn't need any other person. She seemed quite capable of doing all the talking herself. Still, Trish was a kind woman, and Ellen was more grateful for that kindness than anyone would ever know.

Muffled sounds from the bedroom across the hall suggested Jess had woken. Ellen ducked back into her room. In their short time together, she had formed the impression that Jess was a very private person, who wouldn't be at all pleased to know that someone had heard her crying in the night.

Jess was out of bed very early. She always was when the nightmares came. She probably wouldn't be able to get back to sleep, and if she did the bad dreams would be waiting. It was easier just to get out of bed. She dressed and headed downstairs into the silent pub. There was no sign yet of the publican or his wife, so Jess unlocked the side door. She hesitated for a few moments before pushing the door open, enjoying the knowledge that she could just walk through it. Without being accosted. Without facing a barrage of questions. For such a long time, even that simple act had been denied her. And not just her ...

'Get off my lawn. Do you hear me.' Her mother's voice was shaking with anger. 'And just leave my daughter alone. She was the one who turned them in. She was the one who stopped them.'

The front door slammed and her mother slumped against the wall, tears coursing down her face. Outside, the media scrum remained on the lawn, trampling her mother's flowerbeds and tossing cigarette butts onto her father's carefully tended lawn. Jess stood in the living room and cursed herself for bringing this into her parents' lives. Cursed Brian for using her.

And wondered ... was there something she should have seen? Some hint of what Brian was doing? Could she have stopped him earlier?

Stepping through the doorway, Jess took a long deep breath. The air had a crisp freshness that only comes at dawn. It helped clear her head, if not her heart. The sun was just beginning to peer over the horizon, bathing the town in a gentle golden glow. It was still chilly, but that wouldn't last much longer. The streets were empty of movement, apart from a black and white cat sitting on a nearby fencepost, carefully washing his paws. He stopped for a few seconds, one paw still raised as he watched Jess walk past in the direction of the town's main street. In the far distance, a kookaburra laughed. A crow cried as if in answer. This early in the day, the sounds of nature far outweighed the sounds of the town, and she liked that. It felt safe.

Coorah Creek wasn't exactly a bustling metropolis. Apart from the pub, there were no more than a handful of shops. Diagonally opposite the pub was a grocery store. It was quite large, and Jess guessed it was the only one in town. The clothing shop next to it was also probably the only one of its kind too. Underneath the wide awning that was a feature of all the shops in the street, Jess could see the displays in the window. One window was full of men's clothes. The other was for the women. She didn't have to cross the road to guess that there would be no designer labels in that window. That was fine by her. She was done with designer labels. Blue jeans and a T-shirt were all she needed or wanted for this new life.

Jess walked a little further along the road, past an electrical goods shop that also seemed to offer repairs and an electrician who made house calls. There was a hardware shop with a window packed with rolls of fencing wire and wicked looking tools – the use of which was a mystery to her. She seemed to be on the rural side of the street. The next building sold stock feed. She crossed to the other side, drawn by a sign that offered hairstyling and beauty treatments. It was a small salon – if indeed it really deserved that name. According to the sign above the door, it was run by a woman named Olga. Jess didn't think she'd be patronising Olga's Outback Salon any time soon. A café, a small furniture shop and an even smaller newsagent-cum-bookstore-cum-souvenir shop seemed to complete the commercial district. Jess wondered briefly what souvenirs a town like this might boast and just who would buy them.

Jess was almost back opposite the pub already. Her last stop was an area with possibly the greenest grass she had seen since leaving Sydney. The square of carefully tended lawn was weed free. A small statue in the centre seemed to suggest that this was the official part of Coorah Creek. The square was bounded by a police station and post office, and at the rear was what looked to be the only building in town made of bricks rather than wood. The bricks were the same deep red as the earth and the building's roof was made of tiles, not corrugated iron. According to the sign, this grand, two-storey edifice was the Town Hall and office of the mayor. Jess felt some of the tension ease from her shoulders as she stood on that tiny patch of carefully tended grass. She'd wanted a quiet place to hide – and this small community seemed to fit the bill perfectly.

All she needed now was a house to live in – and a cup of coffee!

Feeling more cheerful than she had in a long time, she headed back to the pub, not really expecting to find anyone awake, but the smell of coffee reached out to tickle her nostrils the moment she opened the door. Trish Warren greeted her cheerfully as she entered the kitchen, produced the coffee and set about making breakfast.

'Just some toast will do fine for me,' Jess insisted. 'I don't want to put you to any trouble.'

'It's no trouble,' Trish assured her. 'Nothing beats a good cooked breakfast. I have to make breakfast for those two kids when they wake. I'll guess their mum could use a good breakfast too. She looked quite pale last night. Of course, she could just have been tired after the journey. Poor girl, she must be so pleased to get away from ...' Trish bit off the next words, and she was silent as she furiously beat eggs in a mixing bowl.

Jess gratefully accepted the steaming plate of eggs and bacon, and found to her surprise that she was ravenous. It must be something about this outback air!

'The ABC radio was predicting rain this morning,' Trish continued, as she threw another round of bacon onto the grill, 'but I don't think so. The wet season's gone now. It's going to start to get warm pretty soon.'

Start to get warm? Jess wondered about that, but was happy to let Trish's chatter just wash over her while she ate. But eventually, she had to interrupt. 'Trish,' she said tentatively. 'Is there somewhere I can hire a car for a day or two?'

'Hire a car? No. The town doesn't even have a taxi. Never needed one, I guess. Everyone has their own car.'

'I was supposed to get a car with the job ... but then I was supposed to get a house as well. I'm beginning to think I got it wrong.'

'Adam will know. Or more likely, Jack. He's the practical one.'

'Okay. I'll get in touch with him.'

'In the meantime,' Trish came over to refill her coffee mug, 'there's a ute out the back. Take that.' She dropped a set of car keys onto the table.

'No. No. I couldn't!' Jess was startled by the offer.

'Oh, go on. I am not going to be using it today. There's no other way for you to get out to the airstrip. Or to the hospital.'

'But it's your car …'

'Out here we help each other. That's just the way it works. You need the car more than I do. Take it. You can bring it back once Jack has got you sorted out with your own transport.'

Jess hid her face in her coffee cup for a few seconds while she took a deep breath. Her recent experiences had taught her that no one ever did something for nothing. Stop it, she told herself. There's no catch. Trish is just trying to help. Accept the offer in good grace.

'Thank you,' she said.

'Just watch the brakes. They're not too good,' Trish added. 'I told Syd to get them fixed, but he hasn't yet. Of course, most men would fix the car themselves, but not my Syd. He's a good man, mind you, but totally hopeless when it comes to cars. Or anything else mechanical, for that matter. Thank goodness for Jack, that's all I can say. If it wasn't for him—'

'Thanks so much for the car,' Jess interrupted, before Trish could really get up a head of steam. 'If you need it, just call me. I'll bring it right back.'

'All right, but don't you worry. Syd's got a car too; although why we have two I don't know. We certainly don't need them.'

'Maybe it's so you can lend one to people like me?'

Trish laughed. 'Maybe.'

A clatter of eager feet outside the door heralded the arrival of Bethany and Harry, their mother in close pursuit.

'I'm hungry,' Bethany announced.

'Bethany,' her mother chided, 'that's not very polite. You should say good morning to Mrs Warren before you demand food.'

'Good morning,' both children chorused at the same time.

Trish ruffled the blonde heads as the children climbed onto two more chairs around the big kitchen table. 'And I bet you'd like some juice.'

'Yes!' The children chorused.

'Yes what?' their mother demanded in mock severity.

'Yes, please!'

'Well, let me see what I can do.' Trish turned back to her huge refrigerator.

'How are you this morning?' Ellen enquired, as she took a seat next to Jess. 'Did you sleep all right?'

Something about her tone caused Jess to hesitate. Ellen was only a few years older than her, but her voice held the same sort of concern she had heard in her own mother's voice on those nights when she'd sought comfort in the family home. Nights when the nightmares caused her to cry out in her sleep.

'It's always hard to sleep somewhere new,' Ellen offered. 'I'm sure you'll sleep better when you get settled into your own place.'

Jess felt a twinge of gratitude for Ellen's empathy. They were two very different women, but Jess had a feeling they had at least two things in common – a good reason to come to Coorah Creek and a strong desire to keep that reason secret.

'Speaking of my own place,' Jess said, 'I'd better find Adam. Thanks for breakfast, Trish. I'll take good care of the car.' She escaped before the conversation could get any more personal.

'You know, Doc, for a smart man, sometimes you really get it wrong.'

'You can fix it. Can't you?' Adam asked.

'There's a lot to fix,' Jack pointed out.

Adam turned his head slowly, looking around the room. Jack was merely stating the blindingly obvious. Maybe this was a mistake. This house adjoining the hospital grounds was the official doctor's residence. Adam had moved in here when he first arrived in the Creek, but quickly abandoned it to move into the hospital. He told people he liked to be closer to his patients, but the truth of the matter was that he didn't like living alone in a house. Alone in a hospital was different. It was a place of work. A place of healing. A house was just empty and quiet ... and lonely.

He vaguely remembered the house as being quite an acceptable place to live. But that was then and this was now. In the past five years, he'd stripped it of a lot of its contents. Some had been put to use in the hospital. Some he'd given away to people in need. He hadn't realised just how little remained.

'I guess I still pictured it like it was when I arrived.'

Jack opened the door to the kitchen, raising a small dust storm as he did.

'She's not going to be impressed.'

Jack was right. Jess wouldn't be at all pleased to hear him say this was her new home. Well, not if she saw it like this.

'How long is it going to take to fix it up?'

'That depends,' Jack's voice floated out from the kitchen. 'Does she cook?'

Frowning Adam followed him. 'How should I know if she cooks ...? Oh.'

The kitchen was even worse than the living room. Under a thick cloud of dust, marks on the lino floor showed where the refrigerator had once rested.

'The cupboards would come up all right with some paint,' Adam said doubtfully.

It didn't take long for them to inspect the rest of the house. Then Jack delivered his verdict.

'Doc, I can fix this but it's going to take some money. And some time. There aren't a lot of home decorating shops in the Creek.'

'Money we have.' Or rather, the mining company did. 'Time, however, is a bit of an issue. I don't think our new pilot is all that keen on staying at the pub.'

'Then I had better get started. I think I have an idea that might help.'

Adam left him to it. If anyone could make that house liveable, it was Jack. The man had a knack for finding things in unexpected places. Adam would put money on his having a refrigerator and some furniture lined up by the end of the day.

Back in the hospital, Adam headed for the bathroom to wash off the accumulation of dust he had acquired during his visit to the house. He had an appointment this afternoon with a young couple expecting a baby. A clean shirt was in order too. He walked through the door into his quarters and felt the familiar sense of sanctuary. In this place he didn't need to hide any part of himself. He had no fear of someone getting too close. This was his place. A room of books and music. A room for a man who didn't need – or want – people.

Adam took a clean shirt from the wardrobe. Like all his shirts, it was light, soft cotton and long-sleeved. As he always did, he rolled the sleeves up to his elbows. Then he set off for his office. He didn't make it. Through the open front doors of the hospital, he saw Jess. She was standing outside, studying the building with some interest.

Adam realised she couldn't see him, standing as he was inside the dim hallway. Without the needs of his patient to occupy his thoughts, it was as if he were seeing her for the first time. She certainly made her T-shirt and blue jeans look good and he liked the way the short hair framed her face. Adam had been impressed by her skills as a pilot on their dangerous night landing. Outside the cockpit, she really was a lovely looking woman.

What on earth could have brought her here? Coorah Creek was not the sort of place beautiful women came. He'd love to ask her. But he wouldn't. If he asked her about her past, then she would probably ask about his, and that was something he wanted to avoid.

Jess finished her inspection of the hospital's exterior and walked through the front door. Once out of the bright daylight, she spotted him instantly.

'Hello,' she said.

She looked relaxed and refreshed. The stress of the past couple of days seemed to have dropped from her body, and from her voice.

'Hi,' he said.

'I was supposed to report to the hospital administrator,' Jess hurried on. 'Do you know where I might find him?'

'You have. I guess I should have told you. I am the

hospital administrator, chief resident, head of surgery, obstetrics and anything else you can think of.'

'You're the only doctor?'

'That's right. I can't claim to be the receptionist and bookkeeper. Sister Luke does that.'

'There's just the two of you?' Jess seemed shocked.

'Most of the time. There are no other doctors in town. One of the RFDS guys drops by if we need help.'

'RFDS?'

'Royal Flying Doctor Service. They're great guys. You'll meet them soon.'

Jess nodded, then smiled tentatively. 'Well, I guess that I've reported for duty.'

'I guess you have.'

'I was hoping we could sort out this business of my accommodation. And there's also the matter of a car.'

Adam felt a twinge of guilt. 'I can give you some good news about the car,' he said. 'The pilot's car has been at the garage since the last pilot left. It's had some work done and is ready for you whenever you want to pick it up.'

'That's good news.' Jess almost smiled. 'And the house?'

'Come with me.' Adam led the way towards the rear of the hospital.

'There is a doctor's residence as part of the complex,' Adam said, pointing across the baked earth to the nearest building. 'That should suit you.'

Jess halted in her tracks. 'But, I can't live with you ... I mean. I can't impose on your house.'

'No. No. I didn't mean that.' Adam was equally shocked. It was so long since he'd shared a home with anyone, he honestly had not even considered she might misunderstand. 'I don't live there. I use the resident's quarters here at the hospital. I like to be close to the patients.'

'Oh.'

'So I thought you could have the doctor's residence. It's been empty for a while, but Jack is over there now fixing a few things.'

'Can I go and take a look?' Jess asked.

Adam wanted to say no. If she saw it now, she might turn tail and leave, and he needed a pilot!

'Well. I really want to let Jack do his thing first,' he said quickly. 'Get it cleaned up for you. It's been empty a while and needs some new furniture and stuff.'

'Still, I would like to see it.'

Something about the way she said it reminded him of Sister Luke. The nun could be a stubborn woman when the mood took her. Adam gave in as graciously as he could and they set out across the hospital yard. There was no garden worth speaking of, and the lawn, if that's what it was supposed to be, was just a few clumps of burnt brown grass on a pan of cracked dry earth. The house, like most of the others in the town, was wooden and raised on stumps.

'It's probably a stupid question ...' Jess began, 'but why are all the houses on stumps?'

'It allows cool air to flow underneath in the summer,' Adam replied, 'and it keeps the snakes out, of course.'

'Of course, the snakes.' Jess didn't look happy at the thought.

She looked even less happy when he opened the door and ushered her into the house. Jack had left; no doubt in search of supplies for the job in front of him. The scuffed marks the two of them had left on the dusty floor merely added to the decayed look of the house.

'You are not honestly suggesting I should live here?'

'Well, yes. I know it needs a bit of work.' Adam ran his hand over the bench top, disturbing a cloud of dust.

'And a good clean,' Jess added.

'Yes, but—'

'And some furniture,' she continued.

'All right.' Adam held up his hands. 'There's a lot to be done. But you can stay at the pub in the meantime, and if we all pitch in, it won't take too long.'

'You won't be pitching in today,' a quiet voice behind them said. Sister Luke walked into the room. 'We've had a call. Adam, you need to get to the mine. Someone's been hurt.'

'Will he need transporting?' Jessica asked.

'Probably,' Sister Luke replied.

Adam had already turned towards the door. 'Jess, go straight to the airstrip. I'll bring him there.'

'Of course.'

'I had an appointment this afternoon—' His mind was racing.

'I've got it,' Sister Luke said. 'Now get going.'

Relieved of the things that didn't matter, Adam started to run.

Chapter Seven

The sign over the door said Le Chat Noir. The Black Cat. A newspaper cutting taped inside the window had a headline suggesting this was the best French restaurant in Mount Isa. Jess guessed it might well be the only French restaurant in Mount Isa. The clipping was yellow with age.

Le Chat Noir. That was a pretty fancy name for such a small and unassuming restaurant. In fact, Jess wasn't at all sure she should even call it a restaurant. It was really a café with delusions of grandeur. The paint on the wooden building was faded. The tables inside were wooden, and boasted neither tablecloths nor candles. Jess tried to focus on the menu taped on the inside of the window, under the aging clipping. She tried not to think about another restaurant called Le Chat Noir. In a place a long way from here. And a man who was as different from Doctor Adam Gilmore as night from day.

That night had been hotter than this, and far more humid. They told her that was typical for Vietnam. The restaurant was on the ground floor of their hotel in the old quarter of Ho Chi Minh City. The hotel was a lovely restored colonial building, with all the elegance of France transported to a tropical paradise. Despite a turbulent history, the hotel had proudly preserved its French past, and was now one of the best in the city. The tablecloths were fine linen. The long-stemmed glasses were crystal. A breathtakingly beautiful and delicate orchid adorned each table. And the man sitting opposite her was handsome and rich and charming.

Life as private pilot for international businessman Brian Hayes was beyond her wildest expectations. She loved the Gulfstream jet that she flew. She loved the exotic places they visited while Brian attended to his business. And she loved Brian. What woman wouldn't? He was handsome and smart. A self-made millionaire with business dealings throughout South-East Asia and Australia. And when he began courting her she had fallen. Hard. He could be funny at times, at others, deeply serious and caring. His generosity extended not just to the gifts he gave her, but also to the help he offered others. He was strong and protective, but at the same time allowed her to be the woman she wanted to be. When he made love to her, he made her feel as if she was the centre of his world.

That night, at that other restaurant called Le Chat Noir, she had been as happy as it was possible for her to be. Brian was in a good mood. His business dealings had gone well. They'd dined extravagantly, and then retired to their suite, where they made love and watched the sun rise over the sleeping city. Her life was everything she had ever dreamed it would be. And more.

The most perfect night.

The last perfect night.

The next day, while Brian was attending to business, she'd planned to carry out a few maintenance checks on the jet. That's when she'd found it. The package hidden inside the lining of one of the seats. A package of white powder. At first she couldn't believe it. Someone was trying to smuggle drugs on board the plane. On her plane. Her first instinct was to call Brian. But something stopped her. She didn't believe Brian was involved. He couldn't be! He wasn't a drug smuggler.

That's when she began to remember. Small things that she had chosen to ignore. When she asked Brian about his business, his answers had always been vague. There were meetings late at night. And phone calls hastily ended when she entered the room. And their destinations. Brian's business all seemed to be centred in the infamous Golden Triangle – Vietnam, Thailand and Laos. The world's largest heroin producers. Had she been that naïve or was it true what people said? Love really is blind. In one heart-stopping moment, the niggling questions had turned into a blinding certainty.

Instead of calling Brian, she had gone to the authorities. She had played her part well. For the next day and a half, she had smiled and pretended nothing was wrong. She pleaded a headache and slept alone in the spare room of their suite. The journey back to Australia the next day had been routine up until the moment the police had surrounded the aircraft at Sydney airport. Even as the drug squad had torn apart her beautiful jet, she had still hoped Brian was innocent. But one look at his face told her everything she needed to know.

She had never felt such pain, and anger and guilt. Not until that day after the trial. The woman outside the court. The agony in her voice. *You killed my son! It's your fault!*

Jess blinked back the tears. Like Brian, she had been led away in handcuffs from that last flight, but her stay in jail had been brief. The prosecutor had believed her innocence, and enlisted her help as a witness at Brian's trial – her evidence just one more plank in the case that sent her lover to jail. The prosecutor may have believed she was innocent, but the mother of a dead son hadn't. To that mother, Jess was part of the drug ring responsible for importing the heroin that killed her son. In that mother's eyes Jess was guilty.

That mother would never forgive her.

She would never forgive herself. She was the pilot. Her plane – her responsibility.

Jess dashed the tears from her eyes. This new job was supposed to put all that behind her. Surely today she had taken another small step towards atonement.

They had brought the injured miner to the Mount Isa hospital. Sister Luke had not accompanied them this time. While Jess flew, Adam had stayed in the back of the plane, keeping an eye on his patient. The injured mineworker had been awake for most of the flight, and Jess had heard Adam talking to him. Reassuring him. Talking him better. Adam hoped that they could take the miner back home tomorrow, after his injuries were treated. That meant staying the night at a nearby hotel. Jess had organised rooms – but Adam had vanished to the hospital. She'd heard nothing from him since. She'd set out in search of dinner and her steps had brought her here, to a small restaurant that brought back so much that she desperately wanted to forget.

Jess brushed some imaginary dust from her T-shirt. She must remember to keep a bag packed with a few essentials stowed in the back of the plane for occasions just like this one. Maybe tomorrow before they left she'd have time to do a bit of shopping. There were some things she needed that she was pretty certain wouldn't be available in Coorah Creek. She wasn't a big shopper. Not anymore. She no longer needed the designer dresses that she'd once worn just to watch the light in Brian's eyes when he looked at her.

Damn it!

She shook her head, determined not to cry. Would those memories never leave her?

Jess was hurting. Adam could see her pain as clearly as he'd seen the pain on the face of that miner in the back of the plane today. She hadn't seen him yet. Some quirk of fate had sent them both to the same place in search of dinner. He had expected to dine alone and he still could. He could just slip away and give her the privacy she seemed to want. That was the sensible thing to do. The safe thing to do. The pain on Jess's face was not the sort of pain he could deal with. It wasn't a bleeding wound or a broken bone. Her pain was deep inside her. And that was dangerous. That was the sort of pain that could only be healed by caring and understanding. He had sworn never to get that close to anyone. Ever. But he could no more walk away from her than he could have walked away from that miner. Jess was hurting and Adam's whole being longed to help her. Whatever the danger.

'Hello, Jess.'

She gave a small cry as she realised he was there. 'Adam. You startled me.'

Adam could see the effort she was making to bring her errant emotions back under control. Carefully he ignored the suspicious shine to her eyes, and turned his attention to the menu taped inside the window.

'I was just walking back from the hospital and I saw you here.'

Jess's voice seemed a little calmer as she asked, 'How is Ed doing?'

'He'll be fine.' Adam raised an eyebrow. 'I didn't think you knew his name.'

'I heard you talking to him. In the back of the plane. You called him Ed.'

'Oh.'

A long moment of silence followed. Adam's eyes searched her face and then he smiled, a long, slow, sweet smile that made Jess feel they had shared a moment of intimacy.

'We won't be taking him back tomorrow. He'll have to stay here for a few days.'

'All right.'

'Were you planning on having something to eat here?' Adam asked casually. 'Because the nurse at the hospital suggested this place as I left. She says the food is pretty good.'

'I hadn't really thought about it,' Jess offered.

'Why don't we see if they have a table?' Adam said. It wasn't a date, he told himself. They just happened to be at the same place at the same time.

Fewer than half the tables in the restaurant were taken. A waiter seated them and offered menus. The menu was a single page and the only thing French about the offerings were the fries. For a few minutes they were involved in ordering food and a bottle of wine. Like the food, the wine had never been in the same hemisphere as anything remotely French.

Then the waiter walked away, and they were alone.

'So, it's been a bit of a busy start for you in the new job,' he said.

'Yes, it has,' Jess replied. 'But nothing I can't handle.'

'I can see that,' Adam said. 'I think you're going to be just great at this. Tell me, what made you take a job out here in the back of nowhere?' It was the question he had promised himself he would not ask.

'Well, it's a part of the world I have never seen before, and I liked the idea of doing something worthwhile.'

It was like she was reading the lines from a script. Adam didn't doubt that she was new to the outback or that she wanted to do something worthwhile. He equally didn't doubt that there was more to her story than she was telling.

'But still,' Adam studied her face intently, trying to read what lay behind the words. 'It's a strange place to find someone like you.'

'No stranger than finding someone like you here,' Jess countered. 'What brought you here?'

He opened his mouth to give the same glib answer he'd used a hundred times before. To talk about the adventure and the attraction of being one of the legendary flying medics. Looking across the table into Jess's clear blue eyes, he was suddenly compelled into honesty.

'I worked in a hospital for a while, but I have no patience with the staff politics and the intrigue that goes with it. I wanted to heal people, not waste energy on politics. Or on paperwork. That meant private practice was off the table. Sister Luke was coming here to work with the Aboriginal people. I came too.'

'How long have you been here?' Jess asked.

'I originally came for six months. I learned more about how to heal a human being in those months than three years interning at a city hospital.'

'And you stayed.'

'Five years so far. Out here, people have to work hard to survive. No one comes to the doctor if they have a cold or hit their thumb with a hammer. In the city, half my patients weren't sick. They were wasting their time and mine. Here, people seek help when they need it. I have seen some terrible injuries. And seen people recover from them, at times by sheer force of will. It's given me a great respect for the human body – and the human spirit.'

'You know Sister Luke says you talk patients better.'

Adam smiled. 'Sister Luke is amazing,' he said, with genuine affection. 'She won't tell me her age, but I suspect she's nearly eighty.'

'Eighty?' Jess was stunned. 'I wouldn't have thought her much over sixty.'

'I know. I've seen Sister Luke do things that would test a woman half her age. I have the easy job. I heal bodies. Sister Luke helps me do that, and then her real work starts. She heals souls.' His voice trailed off as painful memories threatened to surface.

'How did you meet her?' Jess asked softly.

'In a hospital. There was a boy. Ten years old. There was an incident ...' Adam paused, but the memories would not be denied. 'It was a terrible thing. A custody battle. It was very nasty. A lot of bad feeling. And the boy's father – he sprayed petrol on the family home and set it on fire. His son – he got caught in the fire.'

'No!' Jess's face paled at the horror of it.

'The boy was badly burned. He survived, but his recovery was slow and painful. And not just his recovery from the burns. Sister Luke sat with him, day after day. The doctors may have healed his body, but she brought his soul back from the darkness.' Adam fell silent. He raised his hand to gently rub his left shoulder.

'She must be quite a remarkable woman,' Jess said softly.

'She says her strength comes from her faith. How she could hold onto that faith in the face of something like that ...' Adam stopped speaking. He had told her only part of the story, but he feared if he said one more word, the floodgates would open and the secret he'd hidden for so long would come rushing out.

Before Jess could speak, the waiter arrived with their food.

Jess waited until the waiter was out of earshot, then she leaned forward to look closely at the plate in front of her. She smiled, a mischievous smile that seemed to light the whole room.

'I've eaten French food before,' she said, her eyes sparkling. 'But I have to tell you it didn't look like this.'

Adam felt his mood lift. He looked at his own plate and nodded his agreement.

They talked as they ate. About books and movies. Politics was raised and dismissed very briefly. Adam told her some stories about his adventures at Coorah Creek. In return, she told him about the trials of being a female in what was still essentially a man's realm.

As he laughed at one of her stories, Adam suddenly realised that it was a very long time since he had laughed so easily.

By the time Adam paid the bill, they were the only diners left in the restaurant.

The walk back to the motel took only a few minutes. A long, low line of rooms was spread through carefully tended tropical gardens. Adam escorted Jess to her door.

'There's no hurry flying out tomorrow,' he said. 'I want to drop by the hospital to see how Ed is doing.'

'And I would like to do some shopping,' she countered.

They arranged a time to meet at the airport for the journey back to Coorah Creek. Adam bid her goodnight and left.

'Adam,' Jess stopped him before he'd gone too many steps. 'I have to ask. What happened to the boy?'

Adam turned slowly around. He was standing in the shadows, but he could see her clearly in the light above her door, her face softened by a look of gentle concern. He was struck again by her simple and unadorned beauty. Once more he spoke the truth. 'He decided to become a doctor when he grew up. He wanted to make Sister Luke proud of him.'

'I imagine she is very proud of him.'

'I like to think so.' His voice was very soft in the darkness. 'Goodnight Jess.'

As he walked back to his room, Adam was tempted for a few seconds by the lights in the motel bar. His steps slowed. No. He'd been down that route once, and wasn't about to do it again. He didn't drink alone any more. When he reached his room, he stripped off his shirt and tossed it casually over the back of a chair. The rest of his clothes followed and he headed for the shower. He turned the water on full blast and stepped under it. This was his way of easing the tension of his day. The cool water running over his skin took more than dust with it. He knew he felt his patients' pain too keenly. But that was the sort of man he was. This ritual washing away of the day's tensions was as necessary to him as sleep.

Except tonight there was a different kind of tension to wash away.

He stood with the water streaming over his body and thought about Jess.

She was so beautiful. A man could lose himself in her eyes and if she knew the effect those tight jeans had on any red-blooded male, she might blush. She was intelligent and funny and gentle. The sort of woman any man would be pleased to have sitting across from him at a restaurant. Or around a campfire. Or in his bed ... But there was something else. She did a good job of hiding her pain, but it wasn't buried deep enough to hide it from someone who knew pain as he did.

The physician in him wanted to heal her.

The man wanted something more – something he knew he could never have.

Adam turned off the taps and stepped out of the shower. He wrapped a towel around his hips, and walked back into the bedroom. There was a large mirror on the opposite wall, above the dressing table. For the first time in an age, he approached the mirror and half-turned his body. They had faded with time, but burn scars never go away. His back was a total ruin, the skin puckered and pale. The scars continued over his left shoulder and down his arm, stopping just above the place where his shirt sleeve habitually sat. His upper thighs were also heavily scarred; some caused by the flames and others by the doctors taking skin grafts. He closed his eyes but he could still see the scars. He could still see the flames and feel the pain. He could still see his father's face.

He hadn't spoken about that day for years. Only Sister Luke knew about his past. What was it about Jess that had made him want to tell her? There was so much he hadn't said. He hadn't told her that he was that burned boy. And he never would. She would never see the scars on his body. She would never learn the true horror in his past. Not even Sister Luke knew the whole story. He would spare both women that knowledge.

Chapter Eight

Ellen was tired. She felt as if she had walked for kilometres – which she hadn't. If she walked that far, she would have been well outside the town. Right now, getting out of Coorah Creek seemed a good idea – if only there was somewhere to go. She wished she'd never laid eyes on this no-horse town somewhere west of everything.

What had she been thinking? Coming all this way – and dragging the children with her. Sure, she'd been desperate, but in the cold harsh light of day, were she and the kids any better off? What were a few bruises compared to knowing Harry and Bethany had a roof over their heads and would have food on the table every day? Had she put herself ahead of her kid's welfare? No! She might be able to manage if the bruises were hers alone, but next time it might be one of them at risk. She would not have her children grow up in a violent home! Even if she had to starve, or scrub floors for a living, she would make a safe home for them.

Ellen took a deep breath, fixed a smile on her face and walked through the door of the petrol station.

'G'day,' the man behind the grimy counter said as she approached. He looked to be about fifty years old. His skin was wrinkled and dried by years in the harsh outback. Ellen suspected the lines on his face were put there by bad temper, not by laughter. He was reading a car magazine, and his hands were dirty.

'Hello,' she said, keeping her voice cheerful even though she was dying a bit inside. 'Are you the owner?'

'Yeah.'

She'd done this so many times already today. In every shop in the main street. She had a feeling this was going to be the worst yet. 'I'm looking for work,' she said. 'I don't suppose you need anyone? Even part-time?'

'What? Here? Don't make me laugh. There's barely enough customers to support one person, let alone two. Sorry, lady, you're outta luck.'

'I understand,' Ellen said. 'I don't suppose you know of anyone who might have some work available?'

'You could try the pub.'

Ellen glanced across the road. She had hoped she might be spared asking Trish Warren for work.

'No. Not that pub. The other one.'

'There's another pub?' Ellen was surprised. The town seemed to have only one of anything.

'Yeah. Down near the railway station.' The man looked her up and down, taking careful note of her well-ironed white cotton blouse and dark skirt. 'Of course, it's mineside. And a bit rough. Might not be to your taste.'

'Thank you for your help.' Ellen made a hasty exit and turned her steps towards the railway station.

It was hard to keep her spirits high as she walked past the row of dilapidated and empty houses she had seen on the day she arrived. This part of the town obviously hadn't benefitted from the prosperity brought by the mine. The sagging roofs and peeling paint of the abandoned homes felt like an added burden of despair as she walked past, trying not to wonder about the people who had once lived there. She reached a corner. A gravel road led off to her right. Looking down the road, she could see more buildings. They looked less dilapidated than the ones she had just passed, but were still not very appealing. This, she guessed, was the accommodation for the single mine workers. On the other side of the road, fronting both the highway and the gravel road, was a pub.

Ellen's courage nearly failed her as she looked at it. It was a long, narrow, single storey building. The yellow paint had been faded by the sun. The corrugated iron roof was rusty in patches. The obligatory wide veranda along the front of the building had no railing, and the floorboards were weathered and rough. The windows were dark and even from this distance she could see the layer of dust on the glass. There was no attempt at a garden, or any sort of decoration around the building. Just a wide bare patch of hard packed dirt where the customers could park. Down the side of the pub she could see a pile of metal kegs, and a forty-four gallon drum overflowing with empty bottles.

It took every ounce of her courage – and her desperation – to cross the road and walk into the bar.

Her eyes needed a few seconds to adjust to the dim light after the brightness outside. Slowly she became aware of her surroundings. A long wooden bar ran the length of the room. The top of the bar was pitted and stained. Despite the laws against smoking inside buildings, the whole place reeked of cigarettes and stale beer. The floor was bare timber ... not polished, but rather blackened by many years of grime. Rows of upturned beer glasses covered a bar towel. There were beer taps on the bar, and on a shelf behind it, bottles of cheap whisky and Bundaberg rum. Despite the fact that it was barely lunchtime, there were several men on bar stools, looking like they'd been there for some time. They were all staring at her.

'Hey, Pete. Get out here,' one of them yelled in the direction of the open door of the big cold room behind the bar.

'Just hold your horses. The beer ain't going nowhere,' a disembodied voice answered.

'There's someone here I think wants to see you,' said the speaker. 'I don't think she's looking for me, more's the pity.'

'What are you on about …?' The man who emerged from the cold room was surprisingly young. Early thirties, Ellen guessed. He was very thin, his skin pale among the tanned faces of the men around him. He had pale grey eyes and a voice as reed thin as his body.

'Can I help you?' he asked Ellen.

'Are you the owner?'

'The manager. Name's Pete. The owner would never set foot in here. All he does is take the money each month.'

'I'm looking for work,' Ellen said, thinking that this time she would welcome the refusal.

'Work? Not much work around this town, unless you're a miner,' one of the men at the bar suggested.

Ellen wanted to just curl up and die. She started to turn towards the door, knowing that at least she could say she'd tried every possibility.

'Can you cook?'

She turned back to face Pete. 'Well, yes. I'm not a chef, but I can cook.'

'We don't need a chef,' he said. 'We need someone on Friday and Saturday nights who can burn a steak and mash potatoes. Can you do that?'

'Yes. Yes. I can.' Ellen tried not to sound too eager.

'And you might need to pour a beer or two. It gets pretty busy in here on Friday and Saturday nights.'

'I can do that too.'

'And you'll have to clean the kitchen. At least well enough to keep the health inspector off my back.'

'That's no problem.'

'All right.' Pete glanced about at the interested faces of the men at the bar. 'You should look at the kitchen before you agree to anything.'

It wasn't the nightmare Ellen had feared. But it wasn't good either. The kitchen boasted a huge hotplate, an equally large oven on one wall and a big sink under the window on another. There was a large refrigerator and an even larger freezer, and a big wooden table sat in the centre of the room. It would all benefit from a good clean, but Ellen knew how to clean. It wasn't ideal, but it was the best – the only – offer she'd had all day.

'All right,' she said. 'Let's talk about money.'

Jack saw Ellen the minute he pulled up in front of the pub. She was walking up the street from the direction of the railway station. For a minute he wondered if she had just booked her journey home. That thought was strangely disappointing.

'Hello,' he said, as she approached.

'Hi Jack,' she replied, with a slow smile.

'How are you and the kids doing at the pub? All right?'

'We're fine,' Ellen said. 'Thank you for bringing us here. Trish Warren has been just wonderful. She even offered to look after the kids today while I went looking for a job.'

'How did that go?' Jack knew there wasn't a lot of work to be had outside the mine.

'I have a part-time job cooking at the pub. It's only Friday and Saturday nights, but it's something.'

'Really? That's great. Trish and Syd are good people.'

'No. Not this pub. The other one.'

Jack's heart sank. She obviously had no idea what she was letting herself in for. 'Ellen, that pub's not … well. It's mineside.' He couldn't think of any other way to describe it.

'Mineside? You're the second person who's said that. What does it mean?'

'Well, the town really has two parts. Townside is where the families live. With kids. Shops. The school and so forth. And the Warrens' pub is a sort of family gathering place. The other side, the mineside, is where the single men live. The mine workers. It's not ... nice.'

The word was totally inadequate. Jack knew he sounded like a snob, which he most certainly wasn't. But he didn't know how to explain to Ellen what life was like for a miner in a place like the Creek. There was hard work at the mine and there was hard drinking at the pub. That was all they had. Jack didn't judge the miners. He'd been one for a time. He'd come to Coorah Creek to work in the mine. It was good money for a youngish man with no real training or skills, and no family to worry about. He worked the mine for a year before people started to notice how good he was at fixing things. His life had changed since then. He no longer came home exhausted after eight back-breaking hours, covered in dust and with a thirst that might kill a man. He no longer drank at The Mineside. But he had few illusions about what happened there on Friday and Saturday nights.

'I don't have much choice,' Ellen insisted. 'I need a job and it was the only one going.'

Jack saw the way she held her head, clinging on to her pride. He thought about trying to find her something else, but there probably wasn't anything and the look in her eye told him she wasn't about to accept charity. It wasn't his place to tell her where she could or could not work. But the thought of Ellen in that pub on a Friday night ... Well, he didn't like it.

'I was wondering,' he said tentatively, 'if you are still looking for more work. I have an idea.'

'Yes?'

'There's some stuff needs doing on the hospital house. We're getting it set up for Jess – the pilot.'

'I know. Jess and I met at the pub.'

'I'm doing all the repairs and stuff, but there's some cleaning and so forth. It's just a couple of days work. It won't pay much.'

'I'll do it.' The eagerness in her voice told him more than she probably would have liked. 'I'll be happy to do it. Will it be all right if I bring the kids? I don't want to impose too much on Trish. I haven't enrolled them in school yet. I wanted to be sure ...'

Her voice trailed off, but Jack knew what she didn't put into words. She wanted to be sure she was staying before she went through the paperwork at the school.

'Of course you can bring the kids,' Jack said. 'But what about when you're working at the pub in the evenings? Trish won't be able to look after them because she'll be busy.'

'I am sure there'll be some teenager willing to babysit,' Ellen said firmly. 'Jack, I appreciate your concern, but I need to work. And that job at the pub is the only option I have.'

He heard the desperation in her voice. He was surprised by how deeply that touched him. He heard the determination, too, and that he admired.

'Do you want to come and have a look at this house?' he said, changing the subject. 'We need to get it done fairly fast. The doc was supposed to organise accommodation for Jess, but ...' Jack paused. 'It's complicated. Why don't you get the kids? I can explain as we drive over there. Then, if you're willing to take it on, we can get started.'

'All right.'

Ellen seemed to find Jack's explanation about the house rather amusing. 'I'm looking forward to meeting this doctor,' she said with a smile, when Jack finished the story.

When they walked into the silent house, Harry and Bethany took one look around at the big empty rooms and raced off to explore.

'How long was this left to decay?' Ellen asked.

'The doc has been here for five years. He moved into the hospital a couple of months after he arrived. I guess that means it's been empty since then.'

'And he expected it still to be liveable?'

'That's the doc,' Jack said. 'He doesn't think much beyond his work.'

'And the furniture has gone where?'

'I guess Adam took some of it to use at the hospital. A chair or two. He gave some bits and pieces to Sister Luke for one of the Aboriginal families that needed help. I remember helping him shift the fridge to the hospital. And I think the bed in the maternity ward came from here.'

'This is a lovely house,' Ellen said, as she stood in the centre of the living room, slowly turning in a circle. 'Or it will be by the time we've finished with it. It needs a good clean, of course. And furniture – a sofa over there. That room through there could be the main bedroom – but there are those other two rooms around the back. Then here – for a dining room table.'

Jack listened to her. In her head this dusty shell was already a home.

'It's such a shame to see such a lovely big house empty,' Ellen continued, almost as if talking to herself. 'It would be the perfect home for a family, with that other big room out the back. Perfect for kids. You could do so much with it.'

Jack almost heard the ping of the light bulb springing into life above his head. Now there was an idea! He'd have to be careful how he went about it – but if he played his cards right ... two birds with one stone.

Chapter Nine

The pub kitchen was buzzing when Jess went down for breakfast, attracted by the smell of fresh coffee.

The kids were seated at the big table, busy devouring cereal covered in chopped fruit. Ellen was making toast and Trish was muttering to herself as she surveyed the big pantry, notebook in hand.

'Good morning. I hope you slept well,' Ellen said, as she poured some coffee into a mug.

'Yes. Thanks.' As she spoke, Jess realised that she really had slept well. Since the trip to Mount Isa two days ago, her nights had been undisturbed by nightmares. She slid into a chair at the table, smiling at Ellen's kids as she did.

'Jessica, dear. Would you like some eggs?' Trish emerged from the pantry. 'I could cook some you know. I always think a big breakfast is important. Gives you energy for the day. And in your job ... Well you never know, do you?'

'No thanks,' Jess said. 'Coffee and a slice of toast will do me just fine.'

'You girls these days, always watching your figures. It's not healthy ...' Trish was still speaking as she left the kitchen.

Ellen caught Jess's eye and they shared a smile. 'I wonder if she stops talking when she's asleep,' Jess said with a grin.

Ellen nodded. 'She does talk rather a lot, but she has been very good to the kids. And to me.'

Ellen placed the fresh toast on the table in front of Bethany and Harry and slipped two more slices of bread into the toaster.

'I can do that.' Jess started to get to her feet.

'No worries. I'm here now. By the way,' Ellen paused for a second before continuing, 'Jack has asked me to help him get the house ready for you to move in to. I hope that's okay?'

'Of course. If you're willing. There's a lot of work to do.'

'I don't mind the work. And he's going to pay …' Ellen's voice trailed off, and Jess sensed the older woman was just a little embarrassed. Of course, with two kids she'd need the money. Jess could understand that.

'Have you had any luck finding a job?' she asked.

Ellen's face lit up. 'Yes. I have a job cooking at the other pub. The Mineside.'

'That's great.' Jess meant it.

Their conversation was interrupted by the door swinging open.

'Is there any more coffee?' Sister Luke asked, as she walked in.

'Of course.' Ellen reached for another cup.

'Jessica, I came to ask a favour of you,' Sister Luke said, as she slid into a chair. 'I am heading back east on the train today and I was hoping you'd drop by this afternoon and just make sure Adam doesn't need anything.'

'Of course,' Jess replied. 'But he's a big boy, Sister Luke. He can look after himself.'

'He can be an idiot sometimes,' Sister Luke responded, a fond smile spreading over her face. 'But he means well. I told him I'd be away for a couple of days, but he's quite likely to forget. I would feel better about being gone if I knew you were around.'

As any emergency involving Adam was also likely to involve Jess anyway, in her job as pilot, it didn't seem a big thing to ask.

'Sister Luke, are you ready?' Trish popped her head around the door. 'Syd's just about to drive down to the station. He can give you a lift.'

'Thank you.' Sister Luke quickly finished her coffee, smiled at Jess and Ellen and left.

'I'd best be going, too,' Jess said. 'I need to get down to the strip. Thanks for the breakfast.'

'You're welcome.' Ellen's response was drowned out by Harry and Bethany's exuberant goodbyes. Jess walked out of the pub feeling almost as if she were leaving a family home.

It was late morning by the time she made it to the hospital. She walked through the empty corridor towards Adam's office. He was engrossed in some paperwork on his desk, and didn't hear her approach. She watched him rub the side of his neck with his left hand. In such an unguarded moment, he seemed tired. Or lonely. Or both.

She stepped back into the corridor and away from the office door. This time as she approached, she made a bit more noise. When she stepped into his office, he was ready for her.

'I'm glad you're here. We need to talk about our trip to the Birdsville races.'

The day got considerably brighter for Adam as Jess slid into the chair opposite his desk. He did need to talk to her about their job providing medical cover during the races. But he was also beginning to discover that a day with Jessica Pearson in it was far better than a day without her.

'What do you know about the races?' he asked.

'What everyone else knows,' she said. 'A bunch of people and horses. A weekend race meeting. Lots of partying.'

Adam nodded. 'That's about it. Our role is to provide medical cover. For about six thousand people.'

'Six thousand? All the way out here?' The shock was evident on Jessica's face.

'Birdsville is even further out than we are,' Adam said. 'It sits right on the edge of the desert and it's tiny. There's the pub, a few houses and a general store. The airstrip, of course, and that's about it. There's a clinic, too, but it makes this one look like the Royal Brisbane Hospital.'

'And six thousand people turn up for a horse race?'

'It's a weekend of racing – but yes, they certainly do!' Adam leaned back in the chair. The Birdsville Race meeting was one of his favourite events and this year he was looking forward to it more than usual. If he were to be honest with himself, he would probably admit that was because he was eager to share the experience with Jess. He wanted to watch her face as she experienced the wonderful madness of the event. He wanted to hear her cheer on the racers. Laugh at a joke. He wanted to walk into the desert with her and share the beauty of the place. And he knew that would never happen.

He pulled his mind back to the present. Some dreams were better left unrealised – because the reality would never match the dream.

'We're not the only medical cover are we?' Jess asked.

'No,' Adam said. 'The Royal Flying Doctor Service goes too. You'll like them. They're good guys.'

'But where do they put all those people?'

'Most of them camp at the airstrip,' he answered. 'There's no accommodation, apart from the pub.'

'And we have to camp too?'

Adam looked at the expression on her face and

laughed. 'It's all right – the medical team get first shot at real beds at the pub.'

Her relief was obvious. Adam had a feeling Jess wasn't a camping sort of a girl. She would probably be happier in an upmarket hotel. She looked pretty fine in the jeans and T-shirts she wore, but he guessed that in a designer dress, she wouldn't look out of place in the best hotels in the world. Which made it even more curious that she was sitting in his office way out here at Coorah Creek, talking about the Birdsville Races.

'We're busy, but serious injuries are pretty rare. It's a fun weekend. Surely you've seen it on TV. It's one of the few times the media acknowledges that we exist way out here.'

'It's on television?' Her voice sounded wary.

'Yes. Reporters come from everywhere. Newspapers. Radio. TV, too. Last year I treated one of the TV reporters for severe sunburn and dehydration. He got drunk and passed out on the side of the airstrip in the middle of the day.' Adam chuckled. 'He was fine, but I imagine he didn't spend a lot of time in front of the camera during the next few days. His face was lobster red.'

Jessica's face was frozen. Something flashed in her eyes and she looked like a frightened animal poised for escape. He didn't think she was hearing his words. It was as if her mind was seeing something other than the inside of his very ordinary little office.

'They're not a bad bunch really,' Adam said quickly. 'But they do like to drink.'

His attempt to lighten the moment fell flat. Whatever had put that look on Jess's face must have been pretty serious. Serious enough to drive her to the ends of the earth?

'Jess? Is something wrong?' he spoke gently.

For a moment he thought she was going to tell him. Her clear blue eyes held his. There was a world of pain in their depths. Pain that was so much more than the mere hurt of a physical wound. Pain that was all too familiar to him. The room was so still, he could almost hear their hearts beating. Somewhere deep inside him, Adam felt the beginnings of a need he thought long since quenched. He wanted to reach out and take her hand. Human contact would comfort her. Would comfort him. There was danger in that thought. In Jess. Because if he got too close …

The telephone on his desk rang – a harsh note that cut through the room like the shattering of ice. Jessica jumped as if someone had slapped her.

Adam wasn't sure whether to be grateful for the interruption – or to curse it. But, in either case, he was a doctor. He couldn't ignore it. He reached for the phone.

'Doc. It's happening. Right now!' The male voice at the other end of the line sounded very young and very frightened.

Adam knew instantly who it was. 'It's all right, Steve. Calm down. It's going to be all right.'

'I gotta get her to the hospital. Right?'

'Yes you do. But you've got plenty of time. Don't break both your necks driving like a madman. Okay?'

Movement across the desk dragged his attention back from the call. Jess was getting to her feet, obviously leaving. He shook his head and motioned for her to stay.

'Everything is going to be fine,' Adam said into the phone. 'I'll see you soon.'

Jess was standing by the door as Adam hung up. 'Jess, I need you.'

'I'll head for the airstrip. Where are we going?'

'Oh, we're not going anywhere.' Adam grinned. He couldn't help himself. 'We're about to deliver a baby.'

Her face paled. 'What do you mean ... deliver a baby?'

Adam moved out from behind the desk. 'Have you ever seen a baby born? It's the most wonderful moment. A miracle.'

'Let's get back to the "we" part,' Jess said.

'I need a nurse. And that's going to be you.'

'No. No.' Jess started backing thorough the doorway. Her face was a mask of fear.

'Sister Luke is away,' Adam said. 'She took the train east this morning. Some business with her order, I think. It's you and me, Jess. You are in for such a treat.'

'No. Absolutely not. I know nothing about babies ... especially about giving birth to them.'

'But I do,' Adam reassured her. 'I know everything we need to know. What I do need is an extra pair of hands. That's where you come in.'

'No. No.' Jess backed even further away. 'That couple don't want me there. Intruding.'

'Trust me, they won't care,' Adam said. 'They'll have other things on their mind.' He stepped closer to her. 'Jess, you'll do great. I need you.'

Jess shook her head again. But the conviction was gone from her face.

'Please,' he asked one more time, knowing that he had already won.

'All right. I just hope you don't regret this.'

'I won't, and neither will you.'

Jess wasn't so sure about that, but it looked like she had no option. Adam had simply overwhelmed her with his passion and his optimism and his need. He was walking down the hospital corridor now, issuing instructions to her as he went. For a few moments, she was tempted just to turn and run. What could he do to stop her?

But she didn't. If she ran away from this, where could she possibly go?

At that moment she knew that she was going to accept the assignment in Birdsville as well. Yes, she was worried about the media, but they would probably not even see her – far less realise who she was. And if they did? Somehow she'd deal with that. It would be easier than telling Adam why she couldn't go. It would be easier than admitting to herself that she was still running away.

Just a few minutes ago, she had come so close to telling Adam about her past. She wanted to be truthful with him, but was terribly afraid of how he would react. His entire life was devoted to saving lives. To healing. If he knew that she had carried that poison on her plane, he would never forgive her. He would look at her with disgust. She couldn't bear that.

'Jess. Come on. I need you to focus,' Adam called from a doorway just down the corridor.

'All right.' Jess took a deep breath and pushed aside all thoughts about the past or the future. The next few hours were going to be tough enough without letting things she couldn't change get in the way.

Adam wheeled a metal instrument trolley into what was to be the delivery room ... a bright clean room with a traditional hospital bed.

'Doesn't this happen in an operating theatre or something?' Jess asked, as she helped cover the bed first with plastic sheets – then with crisp white cotton.

'Not unless something goes wrong,' Adam said. 'I try to stay out of the operating room. It tends to frighten the parents.'

'They're not the only ones,' Jess muttered, as she tucked and folded.

Adam turned to check his instrument tray. Not for the first time, Jess noticed how his long dark eyelashes curved against the tanned skin of his face. Most women would kill for eyelashes like that. They were wasted on a man. Then he lifted his eyes. Velvet brown eyes, with a hint of gold. Jess felt a tiny frisson somewhere deep inside her as his eyes captured hers. No. Those eyelashes were not wasted at all.

'You enjoy this, don't you?' she asked, to distract herself from the disturbing thought starting to form in her mind.

'This is the very best part of my job,' he said. 'You'll enjoy it too.'

Jess wasn't so sure. But she was beginning to think delivering a baby was a little less scary that the unexpected feelings towards Adam that had suddenly swept over her.

'Shouldn't I be boiling water or something?' she asked, to hide the growing sense of panic she was feeling. She'd never had much to do with babies. Her lifestyle as a private pilot meant most of her friends and acquaintances had been travellers. Single travellers. Men who left their wives and children at home. She had no close girlfriends with children. No nieces or nephews. Come to think of it, she'd never even changed a nappy.

'No.'

'But in all the movies—'

'You shouldn't believe everything you see in the movies, you know.' Outside the open window, the roar of an engine told them a car was entering the parking lot at a higher speed than was strictly necessary – or safe.

'Ah. That would be them.' Adam left to meet his patients.

Jess stood in the centre of the room looking at the tray of cold steel surgical instruments. They were quite terrifying. In her wildest dreams, she would never have imagined herself here. Doing what it seemed likely she was about to do. She glanced across at the open door, and any thought of running away vanished.

The girl looked young – like a teenager. She was tiny and she was terrified. Her mousy brown hair was dark with sweat and her brown eyes were wide with pain. She was holding tightly to the hand of a man – a boy really – who looked just as young and scared as she did, as Adam ushered them into the room.

'Nikki, this is Jess,' he said, by way of introduction. 'She's going to be helping me today.' He conveniently forgot to mention she was a pilot, not a nurse.

The pregnant girl looked up at her with pleading eyes. 'I'm so glad there's a woman here,' she said.

'It's going to be fine,' Jess said, as she helped the girl onto the bed.

'Now, Steve.' Adam looked at the nervous young man. 'I need you to sit next to Nikki. Hold her hand and help her breathe. Can you do that?'

Steve looked as if he was about to faint, but he moved to the side of the bed. He took the girl's hand and squeezed it tightly.

'That's good,' Adam said. 'Now, Nikki, just relax. This is going to take a while. I'm just going to check how you're doing. Okay?'

'Okay.'

'First babies are unpredictable,' Adam said, as he donned a pair of surgical gloves. 'Some of them come into this world in a rush. Others take their time. But you're here now, Nikki. You're safe with me and with Jess.'

Nikki nodded, and then she caught her breath as a contraction took her. She reached for Jess's hand. Jess saw the approval in Adam's eyes as she took the girl's hand in hers. Suddenly she was not quite so scared.

Adam finished his examination and looked at the three faces turned his way. 'Everything is fine. We've been preparing for this for a while. Remember everything we talked about. The baby is on its way, but won't be showing for a little while yet.'

If Jess wondered what Adam meant by 'a little while', she soon found out. Nikki and Steve's baby was in no hurry to meet the world. For the next few hours, she alternated between comforting the girl, and comforting the father-to-be. The harder and more frequent Nikki's contractions, the paler Steve's face became. He left the room several times to fetch more water for Nikki or to visit the bathroom. It was as if he were looking for reasons to escape.

Jess barely left Nikki's side. When Steve wasn't there, it was Jessica's hand she gripped when the contractions started. At times Jess felt as if her fingers were being crushed. Adam seemed the least concerned of them all. He spent most of the afternoon in the hospital room, leaving from time to time to answer a phone call or attend to some other piece of hospital business.

He was out of the room when a particularly strong contraction made Nikki scream for the first time. Steve's face turned a ghostly white and he leaped to his feet, letting go of Nikki's hand.

'I'll get the doctor,' he said, and fled the room.

'Just breathe, Nikki,' Jess said, taking the girl's other hand. 'Breathe.'

The contraction eased, and Nikki collapsed back onto

the pile of pillows. Jess offered her a glass of water, and wiped the sweat from her face with a cool cloth.

There was no sign of either Steve or Adam.

'Where did Steve go?' Nikki's voice trembled.

'He won't be far away,' Jess said. 'I'm sure they'll both be right back.'

Another few minutes dragged by, punctuated only by Nikki's laboured breathing. When the tears started forming in the girl's eyes, Jess decided she had to do something.

'Will you be all right alone just for a few moments?' she said. 'I'll go and look for Steve.' And Adam.

'Yes. Please get him!'

Jess left the room at a rapid walk. She didn't want to leave Nikki alone for long, but she had to find Steve. And when she did, she was going to say a few strong words!

She spotted him immediately. He was standing on the veranda overlooking the car park. Jess felt a rush of anger. He really was leaving! And at the moment Nikki needed him most of all. Well, not if she had any say in the matter. She took two strides towards the unfortunate teenager, but was stopped by a quiet but firm voice.

'Do you love her?'

'More than anything,' Steve said.

Jess realised Adam was standing just out of her view. 'Will you love the baby?'

'Of course I will. It's just ... this wasn't supposed to happen,' Steve said, his voice breaking with emotion. 'Nikki is only eighteen. We're not married.' The latter statement came out sounding so defensive that Jess wanted to put her arms around the boy.

'That doesn't matter,' Adam said. 'What matters now is how you treat her. And how you treat your child.'

'I know.'

'Then you treat them right.' Adam's voice was uncharacteristically hard.

Steve took a long steadying breath. He lifted his head and straightened his shoulders. Jess felt she was watching a boy become a man.

'I will,' Steve said in a much stronger voice.

'I'll be keeping an eye on you to make sure you do,' Adam said firmly. Then he stepped into Jess's view. She expected him to place his hand on the boy's shoulder, but he didn't.

Steve nodded.

'Right. Let's go back and see if your baby is about ready to make an entrance.'

Jess turned and darted back down the hallway towards Nikki's room. She didn't want either man to know she had been listening.

Nikki's face lit up when Steve returned. He walked straight to her side and took her hand. 'Sorry about that Nik,' he said. 'But don't worry. I'm here now.'

Jess looked at Adam trying to read his face as he watched the young couple. He caught her watching him. For a few seconds their eyes met. Jess wondered just what he was thinking, but then as he always did, he turned back to his patient.

'Nikki, let me just see how you're doing.' He reached for clean gloves. 'I think it'll all happen pretty soon.'

He was right. Nikki's contractions quickly became harder and stronger. Jessica's heart went out to the poor girl, and to the young man who never left her side.

Later, she couldn't remember exactly how it all happened.

All she recalled was that as Nikki bore down, Adam

asked Jess to hand him a towel. She turned to get one, and when she looked back, Adam was holding a small, squirming bundle of life in his hands. The baby was mottled and red and crying. She was damp with birthing fluids and she was the most beautiful thing Jess had ever seen.

Adam presented the baby to the young parents, both of whom were weeping unashamedly.

'You have an absolutely perfect daughter,' Adam said.

Nikki and Steve both reached out to gently touch their baby.

'She's so beautiful,' Nikki said softly.

Steve, too overcome with emotion, just nodded as tears streamed down his young face.

'I'll just get Jess to take her for a few moments,' Adam said.

He turned to Jess who held out the towel. Gently, Adam placed the baby in Jess's arms. As she carefully wrapped the towel around the newborn, Jess felt tears form in her own eyes. She held the tiny girl safe and looked at Adam. She blinked back the tears and nodded. Adam understood.

'I told you so,' he said, as he stroked the baby's cheek with one gentle finger.

Chapter Ten

Ellen would have screamed if it wasn't for the kids.

Beth and Harry were sitting at the table in the pub's big kitchen, happily downing home-made biscuits and milk. The biscuits, baked by Trish Warren of course, were a special treat because Ellen was about to leave them for the first night of her new job at The Mineside pub.

Except, she wasn't. She couldn't. Frustration washed over her again. Trish had found her a babysitter for the evening – a teenage girl Trish swore could be trusted. But the babysitter had called in sick just a short time ago and Trish had been unable to come up with a replacement. Ellen knew Trish couldn't watch the kids. Friday was the busiest night at the pub and Trish had work to do. There was no way Ellen would leave the kids alone. All of which meant she was going to have to call Pete, the manager at The Mineside, and tell him she couldn't come in. Ellen had no illusions. That conversation would end with Pete saying she no longer had a job. She couldn't blame him for that. In his place, she'd probably do exactly the same thing.

Ellen sighed loudly, causing Harry to look up.

'Is something wrong, Mummy?' he asked, his face creasing into a frown.

That frown just tore at Ellen's heart. She knew what had put that old look on such a young face. Whatever happened, she was never going to regret taking her precious children away from their old life.

'No, Harry,' she said brightly. 'There's nothing wrong. I'm just going to talk to Mrs Warren. You two finish your snack. I'll be right back.'

Ellen left the kitchen. She glanced at the clock. It was after five o'clock. She was supposed to be at work by five-thirty and stay there until eleven o'clock. She had run out of options. She had to call Pete. She was heading for the phone when she saw Jess Pearson walk in, with the strangest look on her face.

'Hi Jess,' Ellen said.

'Oh. Hi.'

'Is everything all right? You look a bit ...' Ellen searched for the right word and couldn't find it.

Jess laughed. 'Everything is fine. I've just had the most ... I don't know. I suppose it was an amazing experience.'

'What happened?' Ellen was glad of something to take her mind off her problems.

'I delivered a baby.'

'You what?'

'Well, all right. I didn't actually deliver the baby myself. Adam did. But with Sister Luke away, I had to help him.'

'And?'

'It was ... amazing.' Jess looked at Ellen. 'But I guess you know that, being a mother.'

'Yes, I do.'

'And Adam was just ... Well. He cares so much. Not just about the baby. The parents, too. They were so young and scared. He helped them so much.'

'He's quite something, that doctor, isn't he?'

'He sure is.'

Ellen couldn't help herself. She started to chuckle and was rewarded when Jess started to blush.

'Stop it,' Jess said. 'There's nothing like that.'

'There could be,' Ellen suggested.

'No. No there couldn't.' Jess sounded a little saddened by that thought.

Ellen had seen the way Jess looked when she talked about the doctor. She'd also met Adam now. He was a handsome man. Compelling and driven in his work. He wasn't her type, but she had no doubt that some women would find him very attractive. 'Are you sure?'

'Very sure.' The tone of Jess's voice made it clear the topic was closed. 'Anyway, what are you still doing here? I thought you were working tonight.'

Ellen explained her situation.

'But that's easy,' Jess said when Ellen finished. 'I'll look after the kids.'

Ellen felt a surge of gratitude, but her natural reticence made her shake her head. The kids liked Jess. And they would be safe with her. But Ellen wasn't one to impose. 'I couldn't ask you to do that.'

'You don't have to. I offered. That's if you trust me to take care of them?'

'Of course I do. After all, how many babysitters have delivered a baby?' They both laughed and Ellen felt a huge weight lift off her shoulders. She was more than happy to leave Jess in charge of her two. They didn't know each other well, but they were quickly becoming friends. They'd talked a little at the house, which Ellen was helping to turn into Jess's new home. Jess was better with the kids than she knew. The kids' well-being was the most important thing in Ellen's world. The second most important thing was to have a job so she could look after them.

After seeing the kids settled, Ellen set out on foot for The Mineside pub. She could have borrowed the car that Jess habitually used, but she didn't want to. She owed Jess enough for one night. And it was quite a pleasant evening for a walk. The sun had not yet disappeared from the sky, and a few clouds to the west were tinged with pink. The air had cooled a little and smelled fresh. Of course, she had to walk along the gravel edge of the east-bound highway. But there wasn't exactly a lot of traffic.

She didn't see another soul as she walked. Not even as she passed the houses where the married mine workers lived. She saw lights flick on in a couple of those homes and wondered about the women who lived there. Had they ever suffered as she had? Were there women behind those doors who needed to break away, too? Unconsciously she rubbed her arm where the bruise had now faded. She would never go back. Ahead of her, the pub beckoned. This was the start of her new life.

Her new life didn't look all that bright as she got closer. She could see the faded paint and the weathered boards on the veranda. The pile of empty kegs at the back of the pub had grown larger since her last visit. And a second drum now overflowed with empty bottles. A handful of cars had been parked haphazardly around the pub. They were, for the most part, old and battered and dirty. For a few seconds, Ellen felt the urge to turn around, collect her kids and head back east where at least she knew a few people. She rubbed her arm again. No. That wasn't an option. She took a deep breath, mustered all her courage and walked into the pub.

Five men were seated at the bar – and every one of them turned to look at Ellen as she walked in. One whistled. Ellen wondered why. She was no blousy barmaid. She had dressed carefully for the evening – in a pair of jeans, a button-up white shirt and flat shoes for comfort during the long evening. She wasn't wearing make-up. In fact, she didn't even own so much as a lip gloss now. There was no reason for anyone to whistle at her.

'Hey, Pete. She's here.'

Pete emerged from the cold room, looking just as thin and pale and tired as the last time she'd seen him.

'Hi, Boss,' she said, as she approached the bar.

'Glad you're here,' Pete said. 'The main crowd should be coming in about seven. Give you time to get things set up.'

'I'll be ready,' Ellen said.

'About bloody time.' The slurred comment came from the far end of the bar, where a large man was hunched on a stool, nursing a beer. The dust on his sweat stained shirt suggested he'd come to the pub straight from work. The way he swayed suggested he'd had more than just the one drink. 'I've been here all afternoon and I want some grub. Now!'

Ellen felt herself wince at the belligerent, drunken tone. She'd heard it too many times before, and knew where it led. Her instinct was to duck away and do whatever the man asked. That's how she'd survived in the past.

'I'll get right on it,' she said quickly, and darted through the door to the kitchen.

Once the swinging door had closed behind her and she was alone, Ellen leaned back against the big wooden table. She took a deep slow breath, gripping the table edge firmly to stop her hands from shaking with both fear and anger. She was afraid of the big man, and angry with herself for that fear. But there was nothing she could do about it. That was how the world was and more than anything else, all Ellen wanted to do was get out of the pub and find somewhere safe.

Before she could act on the thought Pete appeared.

'Don't worry about Mac,' he said in an offhand manner. 'He gets a bit drunk on Friday nights. He's harmless enough.'

'Oh, I wasn't worried,' Ellen said, forcing herself to move away from the table. 'I can handle him.'

'I hope so,' Pete said. He looked a little embarrassed. 'Look, you seem like a real nice person. You gotta know this pub is a bit rough. Are you sure you want to do this?'

'Oh, yes,' Ellen said with a bravado that was entirely false. 'I'm sure. Now why don't you take care of the bar and leave me to get things sorted out here.'

Pete hesitated for no more than a second, then left.

Ellen watched the door swing shut behind him. Could she handle the bully at the bar? Could she even handle this job? And if she couldn't do this, what was she ever going to be able to do?

Ellen glanced around at the unfamiliar kitchen. She knew how to cook, but this was different from anything she'd done before. Still, it couldn't be too hard. Pete had said his customers liked their steak. Steak wasn't hard – burn it or serve it still bleeding. That she could do. She headed for the cold room and looked inside. Yes, there it was. Steak. A lot of steak. And sausages, bacon and eggs. Next she checked the pantry. Potatoes. Onions. Carrots, many bottles of tomato sauce. And more potatoes.

'Well,' she said to herself, 'I guess I don't have to worry too much about the menu.'

As she was carrying bags of potatoes to the table, she noticed some cans and bottles at the back of one of the pantry shelves. Curious she pulled them forward for a closer look. Cans of mushrooms. A jar of crushed garlic. A bottle of virgin olive oil. A few cans of French beans. At some point someone had actually cooked in this kitchen.

Ellen decided not to check the use by dates on the bottles and jars. Whatever happened, she wasn't about to throw away those little bits of inspiration. This was a pub – and even a pub like this must have a bottle or a cask of red wine somewhere. If so, she could …

Forty minutes later, Ellen, wearing a hand towel tied around her waist as an apron, was back in the bar. A blackboard on the wall informed the patrons that they could have steak with eggs or mash or both. There was the option of bacon and sausage – also with the mash and eggs options. And a mixed grill, which Ellen assumed was all of the above. The board looked like it hadn't changed in years, but there was a piece of chalk on the wooden frame.

Ellen cleaned away the old menu, aware that every man in the bar was watching her. She was proud to see that her hand wasn't shaking as she started writing.

'What's that? Beef bog-ig-none. I ain't eating any foreign muck!'

Ellen took a deep breath, fixed a firm but friendly look on her face and turned to face both Mac, and her own cowardice.

'It's steak with red wine and if you tried it, I think you'd like it.'

'It's foreign muck, and I ain't having it.' His face turned a slighter darker shade of red. Ellen's heart plunged, and then another voice spoke.

'I think it sounds good. I'll have some. Please.'

Ellen felt a surge of relief. She turned to face the newcomer, and looked straight into Jack North's smiling eyes.

Chapter Eleven

Jack saw a series of emotions race across Ellen's face. Relief. Gratitude and something more. Could it be that she was pleased to see him?

'Hello, Jack. One beef bourguignon coming right up.' In the space of a second, her face changed. A look of friendly determination formed as she turned towards the end of the bar. 'And for you, Mac, there's always steak and the biggest one I've got has your name on it. All right?'

'All right.' The tone was grudging.

'How do you want it cooked?'

'Burn it!' Mac subsided back into contemplation of his half-empty glass.

'All right then.' Ellen cast another quick glance at Jack then vanished back into the kitchen.

Jack stepped up to the bar, and nodded to Pete, who set about pouring him a beer.

'G'day mate,' one of the miners raised his glass in salute from further down the bar.

Jack nodded. He wasn't often in The Mineside, but he knew most of the men here. As well as looking after the air ambulance and the hospital equipment, Jack spent some of his time maintaining machinery at the mine. Occasionally he'd join some of the men as they washed down the dust after a hard day's work. This was where they came. Jack seldom stayed for more than a single beer. For the most part the men were the single mine workers. Or the married ones who didn't want to go home. Jack preferred the company at the Warrens' pub, where families came for a meal out. Or he preferred a night at home, reading and listening to music.

Tonight, he'd felt compelled to come to The Mineside. He knew exactly why.

Jack paid for his beer and moved away from the bar. He wasn't looking for conversation with Pete or the other drinkers. He took a chair at a table with a clear view of the door leading to the kitchen.

A few minutes later, Ellen appeared. Her face was damp with sweat from the heat in the kitchen, her hair tucked behind her ears. She didn't notice Jack as she turned towards the end of the bar, and slid the plate onto the stained wood in front of Mac. The big man focused on the blackened steak and huge pile of mash, then looked up at Ellen and grunted something that might have been thanks.

Ellen caught Jack's eye as she headed back to the kitchen. 'You're next.'

The plate she brought out for him also held a goodly pile of mash. Jack smiled. She'd learned that bit fast. It also held a big serving of some sort of dark, meaty stew. Heads turned as the men caught the rich scent. There were green beans on the plate too, and Jack almost laughed. He would bet no one could remember the last time green vegetables had appeared on a plate in this place.

'That looks great,' he said. 'Thank you.'

Ellen almost blushed. She hesitated as if she was going to say something, but was interrupted by a call from the bar.

'Is that the foreign stuff?'

Jack saw Ellen tense a little at the words. The speaker was behind her, and Jack couldn't see him, but he did see the emotions that played over Ellen's face before she turned to answer the question.

110

'Yes – it's the beef,' she said.

'Well, it smells great! Can I have some?'

Jack could see the speaker now. He was smiling and Jack relaxed.

'Of course.' Ellen looked around the bar. 'Anyone else for beef bourguignon?'

A couple of men ordered the beef, and someone else played it safe by asking for a mixed grill. Ellen vanished back into the kitchen.

Jack watched her go, horrified by that flash of fear he'd seen on her face. He had a fair idea that fear had been put there by the same bastard responsible for the bruises on her arm. No one should feel afraid just at the sound of someone's voice. He looked at his own hands spread out on the table in front of him. Big hands. Hard hands. What sort of a man would raise his hands against a woman? Against a woman as beautiful and as kind as Ellen. It just wasn't right.

'Jack? Is there something wrong? You don't like it?'

Ellen was back, plates of the beef in her hands.

'No. I was just … No.' Jack picked up his fork and speared a piece of steak. He made quite a show of smothering it in the thick gravy before he ate it. He was determined to say something good about it, even if it tasted like mud.

The meat was so tender it almost melted in his mouth. As for the gravy …

'This is good,' he said. 'I mean really, really good.'

Ellen's face lit up as if she'd just won the lottery. Jack thought her blue eyes were suspiciously bright as she set off to deliver the meals to the waiting men. To him, that made them all the more beautiful, and he was absurdly pleased to think he had made her happy.

Friday nights at The Mineside had a pattern. Everyone knew what to expect. Gradually the bar filled. The men drank beer or rum. Most of them got a little drunk. A few got very drunk. Someone who'd had a bad day at work or trouble at home might go just that little too far. Sometimes a punch got thrown. More often, the offender would be dragged out of the bar by his mates, before he got into too much trouble. Tonight was no different.

Jack saw the trouble coming. He knew the man involved. He was called Bluey – a big, ruddy-faced, red-haired man with a temper to match. He'd only been at the mine a few months and lived alone in one of the company's family houses. Jack knew that his wife had taken their daughter and gone back east to her family. It seemed likely that she wasn't coming back. For most of the evening Bluey had sat alone at the end of the bar, throwing back drink after drink. The other men left him alone.

Just before ten o'clock, Ellen was behind the bar, collecting a couple of empty plates. Bluey looked up as she walked past him, as if seeing her for the first time. Ellen noticed.

'Can I get you something to eat?' she asked pleasantly. 'The beef bourguignon is all gone, but I could burn you a steak.'

'I want another beer,' Bluey said, pushing his empty glass forward.

'Pete can look after that. He's in the cold room, but he'll be back in a second,' Ellen said. 'I'm closing the kitchen in a few minutes, but I could do you a steak if you're hungry?'

'I don't want a steak,' Bluey's voice rose. 'I want another beer, and I want one now.'

Jack was on his feet as Bluey's fist thumped down on the bar. Ellen's face was frozen. She had backed away from Bluey and was pressed into the back of the bar as if she was trying to pass through the solid wall. Jack couldn't cross the bar fast enough.

'Hey, Bluey,' he said in a calming tone. 'I think maybe it's time you went home.'

'What's it to do with you?' Bluey asked, squaring up to Jack and clenching his fist.

'Nothing, mate. I'm just thinking that Pete threatened to ban you last time you got into a fight.'

'What if he did?'

'Well, unless you want to spend your nights at home, you might want to just call it quits tonight.'

Bluey looked down at his empty glass. 'And maybe I want another drink.'

He picked the glass up and slammed it down on the bar. The glass shattered and glass flew in all directions. A single shard of the glass sliced through Bluey's hand, and blood spattered onto the polished wood.

Jack heard Ellen's startled cry. He wanted to go to her, but he had to do something about Bluey. The man was too drunk to realise what he'd done. He was standing, swaying and staring at the steady stream of blood pouring from his hand.

'Get me a bar towel,' Jack called to Pete, who had darted back into the bar at the sound of Ellen's cry.

'Here.' Ellen pressed something into Jack's hand. He barely had time to acknowledge her, as he wrapped the cloth around Bluey's hand.

'Right, mate. Let's get you to the doc. Where are your car keys?'

Bluey was starting to turn quite pale, and his

belligerence had also faded. With his good hand, he fished some keys out of his pocket and handed them to Jack.

Jack looked back as he led Bluey from the bar. Ellen was still standing behind the bar. She looked shaken. He smiled and nodded to her, hoping in some small way that might offer some comfort and encouragement.

Bluey's car was parked next to the pub. Jack carefully manoeuvred his charge into the passenger seat and got behind the wheel. It didn't take them long to get to the hospital. The light on the front veranda was on, as it always was. And the door was unlocked.

'You here, Doc?' Jack called as he led Bluey inside.

Adam immediately appeared at the door to his office. 'What's up?'

'Beer glass.'

Adam nodded and indicated a doorway. Jack helped Bluey onto the exam table and then stepped out to let the doc do his work.

A few minutes later, Adam emerged.

'How's he doing?'

'They say God protects drunks and fools,' Adam said, shaking his head. 'A few centimetres more and he'd have lost some of the use of his hand. As it is, he's got some stitches and he'll be sore for a few days, but he'll be fine.'

'I can take him home?'

'Sure. But he's busy throwing up at the moment. You might want to wait a bit.'

'Sorry to disturb you this late, Doc.'

'That's what I'm here for,' Adam said. 'Anyway, I wasn't asleep. I was checking on a new arrival.'

'Steve's baby?' In a town where everyone knew everyone else, the young couple's pregnancy had set quite a few tongues wagging.

'Yep. A lovely baby girl.'

'Well good for him.'

'Jess helped me deliver her.'

Jack was surprised. Both by what Jessica had done, and by the look on Adam's face as he talked about it. 'How did Jess do?'

'She did great,' Adam replied.

Jack waited for him to continue, but he didn't.

'Jess is good people,' Jack said, just to watch the way the doc's face changed. 'I'm glad you hired her.'

'So am I.'

Jack had known Adam since he first flew into the Creek. Everyone liked the doc, but he didn't have a lot of friends. He was a bit of a loner. In fact, Jack was probably the closest thing he had to a friend. Apart from Sister Luke. Jack had never known the doc to have quite that look on his face when he talked about a woman before. In fact, Jack didn't think the doc had ever talked about a woman, other than as a patient. This was interesting.

Beside them the door opened and a pale and shaky Bluey emerged, one hand swathed in bandages.

'Jack's going to take you home now,' Adam said. 'Get some sleep and come back in the morning.'

Bluey murmured his thanks and followed Jack to the car.

By the time they had driven the short distance to Bluey's home, the injured man was almost asleep. And maudlin.

'She left me, you know,' he mumbled, as Jack helped him up the steps. 'It wasn't my fault. I didn't mean to hit her. She just made me so mad. You know.'

No, Jack thought, he didn't know. Or understand. He never would and Bluey's wife and daughter were probably far better off without him. Anyway, with that injured hand, Bluey wouldn't be hitting anyone for a while. Jack lowered Bluey onto the tattered old sofa and left the car keys by the door.

It didn't take him long to walk back to The Mineside. He stood outside for a few minutes, watching the shapes moving behind the lighted windows. Ellen's first night – and she'd had to face down Bluey. She'd been doing pretty well. He wished he had said something to her before he'd led the drunk away. But what could he have said that would have made it better? Nothing really. He shook his head and walked over to his ute.

The kitchen was probably the cleanest it had been in a long time. Ellen had finished a long evening by scrubbing the stove and the table and benches – the floor too – until they gleamed. As she cleaned, her mind went over and over the evening's events. Jack ordering the beef – and starting a trend that didn't end until the big pot was empty. Mac's grumpiness that had been so totally harmless. He'd even thanked her for the steak. Then there was the other one. The red-head. Jack had stepped in there, too. She, on the other hand, had fled to the kitchen like the coward she was. It took five minutes of hiding there, shaking like a leaf in the wind, before she'd been able to raise the courage to go back out into the bar. The rest of the drinkers acted as if nothing had happened, so she did too. At least on the outside. Inside she was still frightened.

And now she had to walk home.

The bar door swung open with a bang, and Pete appeared.

'Sorry,' he said, 'didn't mean to startle you.'

'That's all right,' she said, struggling to keep her voice steady. 'I'm done, so I'll head home.'

'All right. Good job. Here.' He placed a pile of money on the table. 'Your first night's wages. I hope cash is okay?'

'Yes. Yes. Of course.' Ellen looked down at the money.

'Sorry, the guys here aren't big on tipping,' Pete said. 'But there's a few dollars there.'

'I'm sure it'll be fine.' Ellen still hadn't moved to take the money.

'So, I'll see you tomorrow,' Pete said. 'And after that, if you're certain you want to stay; we can talk about ordering in whatever you need – food wise that is. These guys sure liked that foreign stuff.' Shaking his head, he vanished back into the bar.

Ellen waited until the door was closed, then picked up the money. She counted it, then folded it carefully and put it into her purse. It wasn't a lot of money, but it was money she had earned with her own hard work. It was hers, and no one was going to take it from her. Maybe the evening hadn't been so bad after all.

She left the pub by the kitchen entrance. It wasn't that she was afraid to walk out through the bar, where the last few drinkers were being served. She just didn't want to see anyone. Before she had taken many steps, she realised she wasn't alone. Someone was waiting for her, leaning against a battered white ute.

'Hello, Jack.'

'Hello.'

'I didn't expect to see you back here.'

'After I took Bluey home I had to come back for my car.'

Neither of them mentioned the hour that had passed since then.

'So, how was your first night?' Jack asked. 'I hope you won't let Bluey get to you.'

'I won't,' Ellen said softly. Then she took a deep breath. 'I can't afford to. I've got two kids to support. And I had better get back to them.'

'Can I give you a ride?' Jack asked.

'I'm not afraid to walk,' Ellen said, squaring her shoulders.

Jack just smiled. That gentle, warm smile that seemed to ease all the heartache she'd been carrying for so long.

'I know you're not. I was hoping you might just want to ride with me.'

Ellen thought for a moment. 'I think I'd like that,' she said.

Chapter Twelve

Babies were so fragile. So innocent. Adam looked down at the little girl in his arms. Just two days old. She was tiny. She was beautiful. She was perfect in every way.

'Hello, little one,' he whispered.

The baby opened her soft blue eyes and seemed to look at him, even though she was probably far too young to see him clearly. A wave of sadness washed over him and he planted a gentle kiss on her forehead. If only she didn't have to grow up. If only she didn't have to learn what the world was really like. What people were really like.

'It's a big and sometimes scary world out there,' he told her in the same gentle voice. 'But it can be a beautiful place. There are flowers. And music. There are glorious sunsets and a sky full of stars at night.'

The baby's eyes slowly closed. Adam carried her over to her crib and laid her gently on the well washed and faded yellow blanket that had already served several other babies. He stood up, and rubbed his left shoulder, feeling the rough texture of the scarred skin through the soft cotton of his shirt. The scars didn't hurt any more. At least, the scars on his body didn't hurt. But he still felt the pain when he held an innocent like this little girl. Or looked into the beautiful blue eyes of a woman he could never have.

'You just grow up strong,' he told the sleeping child. 'Then, when the world lets you down ... and when people try to hurt you ... you'll survive. You'll be able to take care of yourself. Be careful who you trust and never let them know when they hurt you. Never let the bad guys win.'

'That's not the sort of advice I would expect you to give a baby.'

Adam looked up. Jess was standing in the doorway, dressed in her uniform of blue jeans and white T-shirt. As usual she wore no make-up. Her hair was slightly tousled and unkempt, and it framed a face of rare natural beauty. She had a half-smile on her lips, but despite that she looked infinitely sad. Sad … but still beautiful.

'What advice would you give her?' Adam asked.

Jess crossed the room to stand beside him. She reached out as if to stroke the baby's fine dark hair, but instead she gently adjusted the blanket.

'I don't think I'd give her any advice – except to say be the very best version of herself that she can be, and never become one of the bad guys.'

'That also seems strange advice to give a baby.'

Jess looked away from the baby and her eyes met his. He saw something behind them that was a reflection of what she could probably see in his eyes. They were so alike. Two damaged souls. Every hour they spent together brought a unique mix of pleasure and sadness. Adam could feel the connection between them growing. Or trying to. But without sustenance, even the strongest shoot will wither and die. Did he want that to happen? Or did he want to build something with Jess? Was it even possible that he could take back a future the flames had stolen all those years ago? The silence was broken by the sound of a door opening as the baby's mother returned.

'Hello, Jess,' Nikki said, as she closed the bathroom door behind her. 'I'm so glad you came by. I wanted to say thank you.'

'She's so beautiful,' Jess said, as she helped Nikki ease herself gently back onto the bed.

Nikki didn't notice the shadow that lingered behind the smile. Adam did.

'Would you like to hold her?' Nikki asked.

Jess started to shake her head ... but hesitated. 'I'd love to,' she confessed.

She lifted the baby from the crib with great care and held her in her arms. The little girl stirred and wrapped her tiny fingers around Jessica's finger. Adam had seen many women hold babies – their own and other people's. Much as he loved this part of his job, his own strained relationship with his mother made it hard for him to feel moved by a mother's love. But looking at Jess with a baby in her arms made his heart ache. He wasn't sure why. Perhaps it was as simple as a desire for something that he would never have.

'Are you feeling all right?' His words were directed at Nikki, but his thoughts were with Jess.

'That shower felt great,' Nikki replied. 'Thanks for watching the baby.'

'You're welcome.'

'Does she have a name yet?' Jess asked, her voice so soft Adam could hardly hear her.

'I want to name her after my mum – Jan. Steve wants to name her after his – Mary. What do you think?'

'I think they are both nice names,' Jess said, her eyes still fixed on the baby in her arms. The baby began to wake. She squirmed a little and gave a faint cry.

'She's probably hungry again,' said Nikki, holding out her arms to take her daughter from Jess.

'You look after her, and don't worry about rushing home. I'd like you to stay here another night,' Adam said. 'Sister Luke is due back today and she'll be mad at me if I let you leave here before she sees the baby.'

'I'm in no hurry. This is such a lovely room. Much nicer than I thought a hospital would be.'

Adam had to agree with her. Not long after arriving in the Creek he'd decided that the cold hospital rooms were no place for sick people. And certainly no place for a mother with a new baby. The lovely polished wooden chest of drawers and the colonial-style double bed in this room had been in the doctor's house. When he decided to live in the resident's quarters at the hospital, he'd appropriated the nice furniture for this room. And was glad he'd done it. Except ... He felt Jess's eyes on him and mentally winced. Of course! This was the furniture that should have been in the home she was going to use.

He risked a look at Jess.

'It was very generous of you to set the room up so nicely,' Jess said sweetly. 'Where did you find such lovely things?'

The look on her face told him she had realised exactly where this furniture had come from. He guessed that he was going to be in trouble as soon as Jess caught him alone.

'Well,' he said. 'I had better get a move on. I have to ... do things.' He turned on his heel and tried to leave with some vestige of dignity.

Jess watched Adam go, feeling not the slightest bit annoyed at him. In fact, quite the reverse. His generosity and genuine concern for others were an essential part of him. Such an admirable part of him. And, of course, Jess was getting a house full of new furniture. She glanced at the bed, where Nikki was now feeding the baby. It was such a commonplace sight, but one that filled Jess with a storm of emotions.

Her thoughts flew to her own mother, a small and delicate woman who had held her head high every day in that courtroom. In the days following the seizure of the plane, she'd visited Jessica in jail, never flinching as the iron doors clanged shut behind her. She was waiting the day the charges against Jess were dropped and she walked free. Not once had her faith in her daughter wavered. Not one iota. A mother's love. There was nothing in the world stronger.

Last night Jess had slept more deeply than in a very long time. The voice in her head hadn't seemed quite so loud. The guilt not quite so overwhelming. Looking at the tiny baby she had helped to bring into the world, Jess wondered if perhaps she had taken another small step towards atoning for the lost lives she was responsible for. It wasn't enough. It would never be enough, but maybe it was a start.

Jess said a hasty goodbye to Nikki, who was so involved with her baby that she barely saw her go. As she left the hospital she saw Sister Luke approaching from the direction of the car park. Jess was eager to share her experiences.

'Sister Luke, it's good to have you back. Did you hear the news? Nikki had a baby girl.'

'Did she? And they are both well?'

'Yes. I helped Adam deliver the baby. It was an amazing experience …' Jess's voice trailed off. 'Are you all right, Sister Luke?'

'Of course, Jess. I'm just a little tired after the long trip, that's all.'

Jess wasn't so sure. Sister Luke looked … smaller. And older. Like someone who had lost a loved one. Or been given bad news. 'How did everything go?' Jess asked cautiously. 'At … what do you call it, the mother house? They're not taking you away from us, are they?'

'No. They aren't.' Sister Luke smiled slowly. 'It's not like you think. The order always does the best it can for the Sisters. They wouldn't take me away from somewhere I was needed and where I still had work to do.'

'That's good,' Jess said. 'Because we do need you. I mean, helping Adam deliver the baby was just the most wonderful experience. But I'm not a nurse. We really do need you.'

A shadow crossed Sister Luke's face, just for a moment. Then the older woman smiled. 'How did you find working with Adam?'

'It really was quite something. He was so good with Nikki. And with Steve, too. He said it's his favourite part of being a doctor.' As she spoke, Jess could feel just the smallest glow deep inside her. Small – but fierce and Adam was its cause.

'It is a wonderful thing to bring a new life into the world,' Sister Luke mused. 'One day it will be your turn.'

'I don't know about that,' Jessica said. With the turmoil of her life these past few months that sort of a future had been far out of reach.

'You should think about it,' Sister Luke said. 'Now I'd best go and meet the new arrival.'

'They're in that really nice room with the bed from my house.'

'I was wondering when you'd find out about that.'

'I should have guessed that was what he would do with the furniture,' Jess said. 'It's all right. He was just being generous.'

'He was just being Adam,' Sister Luke said, a whole world of affection in her voice.

'And I'm getting all new furniture now,' Jess said. 'Or I will when I move in.'

'When is that likely to be?'

'Soon, I hope. Jack and Ellen say it's almost ready.'

'I guess you'll be happy to get out of the pub,' Sister Luke said. 'The Warrens are lovely people – but that's not a home.' With that Sister Luke started towards the hospital steps. She hadn't gone far when she stopped and turned back. 'Jess, I'm glad you were here when Adam needed you,' she said.

'So am I,' Jess said. 'But I'm glad you're back, Sister Luke. He needs you more than he needs me.'

'I wouldn't be so sure about that,' Sister Luke said, so quietly Jess barely heard her.

Jess watched Sister Luke climb the stairs onto the wide cool veranda. There were only a few steps, but it almost seemed too much for her. Her thin fingers gripped the handrail as if she was afraid of falling. Jess felt she should step forward to help her. She wondered again how old the nun really was.

Jess walked down the side of the hospital building towards the house that should soon be her new home. As she did, Sister Luke's words played through her mind. When she was with Brian she had assumed marriage and a family somewhere in their future. That had been ripped away along with so much else. But she still wanted that future. She stopped walking and closed her eyes, thinking back two days to a hospital room and the start of a new life. She tried to put herself in that image. Tried to see herself as a mother. And by her side ... in the role of father?

No! That was crazy, she thought. Not Adam. That was never going to happen. Look at the distance he kept between them. She could still see the look on his face that one time she had touched him. He'd flinched away as if she were poison. That said it all.

The front door of her new home wasn't locked. She had a feeling it seldom was. There was no sign of Jack or Ellen, but the fruit of their joint labours was everywhere to be seen.

Every room sported a new coat of paint. The polished wood floors gleamed in the sunlight. The front room boasted a pair of big comfortable looking armchairs, and a sofa Jess guessed she could sleep on. It was certainly long enough. Walking through to the kitchen, Jess smiled as she saw the new fridge and stove. The cupboards were bare, but each was spotlessly clean. So was the en suite bathroom attached to the master bedroom. The enormous double bed looked just as comfortable as the one that Adam had purloined for use at the hospital. Walking through to the bright family room at the rear of the house, Jess saw the dining table and chairs – big enough for a family. She wouldn't be needing that, or the bed in the spare room. The third bedroom was empty. That made sense. She had no use for that either. It would make a good storeroom. But for what? She had brought so few things with her. She was going to have to go shopping just for pots and pans and knives and forks. Not that she would need many of those, living alone.

Jess left the house not feeling as cheered by it as she had hoped. She would have to check with Jack, but she guessed she could move in tomorrow. It wouldn't take long to buy the few things she needed. It would be good to have her own place. To have the privacy she lacked at the pub. Sometimes, when the nightmares woke her in the middle of the night, she wondered if Ellen, sleeping just across the hall, had heard her. She hoped not. It was pretty clear to her that Ellen had problems enough of her own. Life couldn't be easy for a single mum with two kids.

As she started walking back towards the pub, Jess's thoughts again turned to her own family. Her parents had opened their arms and their home to Jess when she was released from prison. Jess could still see her mother, all five foot nothing of her, standing on the top step, threatening the journalists camped outside the house. Jess had never doubted that her mother would have been after them with the fire irons if they had given her sufficient reason. Her mother hadn't wanted to see her daughter travel so far away. But staying away was the best thing Jess could do for them right now. Maybe, when enough time had passed, she could go back without dragging the media circus with her. In the meantime, phone calls and e-mails would have to do. In fact, she'd give her mother a call tonight!

Jess walked through the pub's back door into the rear lounge bar. The door to the kitchen was open and she could hear Trish Warren's voice inside. As she approached, the words slowly began to make sense.

'I hope you know what you are doing, Jack North!' This did not sound like the kind and gentle woman she knew. Trish sounded almost threatening. She was reminded again of her mother on the steps, facing down the reporters.

'I'm not doing anything,' Jack replied.

'I hope not. That poor woman and those two kids have been through enough. They don't need any more hurt in their lives.'

'I'd never hurt her.' Jack sounded outraged. 'I'm not that bastard, whoever he was. I would never hit a woman.'

'That's not the only way to hurt someone,' Trish told

him. 'She's vulnerable, Jack. Be a friend to her. That's all you can be right now.'

Jess didn't hear Jack's softly-spoken response. She hesitated for a moment as the impact of the words began to strike her. She had already come to suspect that Ellen had feelings for Jack. It seemed those feelings might well be returned. She was happy for Ellen, but determined to stay well out of their business. She was hardly qualified to give Ellen or anyone else romantic advice.

After a few seconds, Jess pushed a chair noisily into place under one of the tables. By the time she reached the kitchen, Trish and Jack's conversation had turned to that old outback standard – the weather.

'Hey, Jack,' Jess said. 'I was wondering when I can move into the house?'

'It's done,' Jack said. 'That's why I came by. To give you these.' He held out a set of keys.

'But I was just there,' Jess said, as she took them. 'The house isn't locked.'

'No reason to just yet,' Jack said. 'But if you're going to Birdsville and leaving your stuff there, you'll want to lock it.'

That was true enough.

'By the way,' Trish said, 'there's some stuff there. Cutlery, plates and so on. To help you get started.'

Jess glanced at the big box sitting on the kitchen bench. There was an awful lot of 'stuff' in it. 'Trish. Are you sure you can spare it? There's enough there for a whole family. I don't need that much.'

'Oh, you never know when you might have people drop by …' Trish's response was interrupted by a clatter of footsteps as Harry and Bethany ran into the kitchen, demanding cookies and milk.

'Where are your manners – say "please".' Their mother was following close behind. She was dressed for another night's work.

'Ellen, do you need me to watch the kids?' Jess asked. She had spent a pleasant evening playing games with them the night before, and suddenly realised that another similar evening wouldn't be a trial.

'Thanks, Jess,' Ellen said. 'But my babysitter is feeling better and she'll be here soon. I couldn't ask you to do it another night. Although I think the kids would prefer you.'

'Can Jack stay with us?' Harry asked.

'I promised your mum I'd drive her to her work,' Jack said, kneeling down next to Harry. 'Remember we talked about looking after girls?'

Harry nodded, his face becoming very serious.

'Well, I'm helping your mum. Is that all right by you?'

Harry nodded, then the grin came back and he turned his attention once more to the cookies.

'Jack, you don't have to drive me,' Ellen said. 'I can walk. Honestly.'

'I'm going that way,' Jack said casually, 'and I thought I might try some more of your cooking.'

Jess caught both the slight flush that rose to Ellen's cheeks, and the warning look that Trish cast at Jack. There it was again, she thought. That maternal instinct to protect. That's what she'd felt when she held Nikki's baby. She'd felt a bit of it while babysitting Harry and Bethany. She saw it in Ellen too, as she struggled to cope with two kids, living in a pub and a new job that must barely pay the cost of her room.

While she, with her good job and healthy bank balance, had a free house. A house big enough for …

Of course. It made so much sense.

'Ellen,' she said. 'Jack tells me the house is finished.'

Ellen looked a bit startled by the sudden change in topic.

'It is, but if there is anything else needs doing ... Jack has been generous in paying me, so I'm happy to come back and do some more.'

'I do want you to come back. But not to clean. Tomorrow, I'm moving in – and so are you and the kids.'

'What!' Ellen looked shocked.

'It's perfect,' said Jess. 'I've got more space than I could possibly use – and it's free.'

'I couldn't possibly ask you—'

'You didn't,' Jess said. 'I offered.'

'But ... the kids? You don't want them under your feet all the time.'

'Well, actually ...' Jess turned to look at Harry and Bethany who had stopped eating and were watching the adults closely. 'I think we'd do all right.'

'I ... I don't know what to say.' Ellen's eyes shone with unshed tears. 'This is just too generous of you. You are too kind.'

'No, I'm not,' Jess said. She could have said she was just beginning to realise she was lonely. She could have said she was trying to find atonement. Instead she said, 'We'll be helping each other out. Besides, I want a chance to taste that cooking of yours and I'm not going to The Mineside.'

'Speaking of which, I'll just grab my things. And ... thank you.' Ellen gave Jess a quick hug and darted from the room.

'Well, Jack. Any chance you'll be able to find some furniture for the kids' rooms?' Jess asked.

A long slow grin spread over Jack's face. 'You know. I just so happen to know somewhere I can lay my hands on a couple of small beds.'

Suspicion forming in her mind, Jess took another good look in the box of kitchen goods Trish had prepared. Enough for a family indeed!

Jess looked at the two beaming adults, suspicion turning to certainty.

'We were wondering if the two of you were ever going to sort it out for yourselves,' Trish said.

Chapter Thirteen

It seemed as if half the town wanted to be involved in Jess and Ellen's moving day.

Jack led the pack, with his dusty ute. The owner of the hardware store, a big ruddy-cheeked man Jess hadn't met before, suddenly appeared with two child-sized beds in the back of his truck. Smiling broadly, he dismissed questions about where the beds had come from, or who might be paying for them. Jack and Adam carried them into the large spare room and set about assembling them with screwdrivers and spanners.

Trish Warren was there with her box of kitchenware and a generous supply of food for the helpers. She and Ellen were in charge of the kitchen. Jess was happy to let that happen. She suspected Ellen was going to be doing a lot of the cooking in their new household, and she was fine with that.

Sister Luke arrived with a box of children's books. A house, she declared, was not a home if there were no books. And kids' books were the most important books of all. She didn't waste any time in enlisting Jack's support. She seemed pleased when he offered to build the kids some bookshelves, just as soon as he could 'borrow' some suitable wood from the carpenter's shop at the mine.

Looking at the elderly nun's face, Jess felt a twinge of concern. Sister Luke still looked tired. A few minutes later, Jess carried a box through to the main bedroom to find Sister Luke leaning against the bathroom door, her eyes closed as if she were in pain.

'Sister Luke. Are you all right?' Jess dropped her load and hurried to the older woman's side.

'I'm fine.' Sister Luke brushed aside her concern. 'Just a little tired, that's all.'

'Are you sure? Do you want me to get Adam?'

'No. No. I don't want to worry him. I'm fine. Honestly.' Sister Luke smiled and took a deep breath as if mustering her strength. 'So, how do you like your new home? It's starting to look rather good isn't it?'

'Yes,' Jess agreed. 'It's nice of everyone to help out like this.'

'That's Coorah Creek for you,' Sister Luke said. 'It's that kind of town. Everyone helps everyone.'

'Just make sure you don't help too much,' Jess admonished.

'I will be fine.' Together they walked back through into the bustling living room to find two new additions to the crowd.

Nikki and Steve had walked over from the hospital, their baby girl in their arms. They were about to go home, they said, but first they wanted to present Jess with a huge bunch of flowers. Steve, it turned out, was quite the gardener, coaxing the dry red earth to produce flowers that had graced many special occasions in the town.

'You didn't have to do this,' Jess said, as she took the bouquet of red, gold and yellow blooms.

'To say thank you,' Nikki said.

'I didn't do anything,' Jess replied, as she gently stroked the baby's tiny hand. 'It was Adam. All I did was stand there.'

'Having you there was such a help,' Nikki said, the suggestion of tears in her eyes.

'And besides,' Jack said, as he walked past, a cheerful

grin on his face. 'No one in their right mind is going to give flowers to the doc.'

Steve and Nikki stayed long enough to proudly show their new baby to everyone. It wasn't long before Ellen and Nikki were swapping baby stories and making offers of babysitting for each other.

Meanwhile, Jess found herself with flowers and nowhere to put them. Adam sent her to the hospital where she found an old vase. She was carrying it back to the house when a small blue sedan pulled up next to her gate. It wasn't shiny and new, but did show signs of having recently been given a wash – if not a polish. A thin, sour looking man got out.

'Can I help you?' Jess asked.

'These are for you.' He held out the car keys.

'I don't understand,' Jess said, as she took them.

'It's the car I promised you,' Adam said, emerging from the house. 'I know it's not much, but I've had the garage give it a good service. It should run fine. I hope it's all right?'

Jess looked at the car. It wasn't much, but it was hers. 'It'll do just fine,' she said. 'There's even room for the kids if Ellen needs to use it.'

'I know,' Adam said.

'So, you were in on the conspiracy too. Were you?'

Adam just winked and returned to bed construction.

Neither Jess nor Ellen had much in the way of personal possessions, so setting up their rooms didn't take long. They left Sister Luke in charge of the kids, and set off together to buy groceries. The town's only shop wasn't exactly a supermarket, but they managed to put together a fairly decent haul of essentials. When they returned laden with soap and toilet paper, several large boxes of foodstuffs and other household bits and pieces, the house was in order.

'Okay,' Jess said. 'I think we owe you all dinner. And by "we" I mean Ellen, because she's a far better cook than I am.'

It was a most unusual gathering in the big family room that evening. Returning from the kitchen where she was preparing tea and coffee, Jess paused in the doorway and looked at this group of people she had known for such a short time, but felt she could now call friends.

Adam, under Trish's watchful eye, was measuring the windows that looked out onto the backyard – garden was too fancy a word. Trish had some curtains that she didn't need and was trying to decide how much alteration they'd need to fit. Jack was sitting on the floor with Ellen's children. Harry had pushed up the sleeve of Jack's T-shirt and was carefully comparing the tattoo of the Disney duck on his arm with the drawing in a comic book. Bethany was just leaning against Jack's side, hugging the soft toy that had been his gift to her. Ellen and Sister Luke were both chatting at the big wooden table that still held the remains of an apple pie. Ellen had almost magically thrown together a wonderful meal for seven people, without batting an eyelid. The food had been very, very good; better than meals Jess had eaten in restaurants. And if the plates had been second-hand and mismatched, the company had been all she could ask for.

More than she could have asked for. Far more than she deserved.

What would these good, honest and kind people say if they knew who she was? Knew what she had done? Jess felt a lump rise to her throat, and turned quickly back to the kitchen. She busied herself with the teapot and mugs, pausing only to dash a tear from her eyes.

You killed my son!

No. I didn't know the drugs were on the plane.

'Jess?' Adam's voice chased the scream from her head.

'I'm just making the tea,' she said, without turning around.

'Jess? What's wrong?' Adam crossed the room to stand behind her.

He was so close she could hear the sound of his breathing. Sense the warmth of his body and even more the strength of his compassion and his desire to help her. More than anything in the world, at that moment she wanted to lean back against him. She wanted him to put his arms around her and tell her that everything was all right. That she was all right.

But that was just not going to happen. For so many reasons.

Hoping he wouldn't see the glint of a tear on her cheek, she shook her head. She didn't trust her voice so she just kept moving the mugs around on the worktop in front of her.

'Jess. Look at me.'

'I'm fine,' Jess mumbled as she turned to face him. 'Everyone has been so kind. I guess I'm just a bit over-emotional.' She brushed the tears away from her eyes.

He shook his head, denying her words. His eyes searched her face, and Jess felt as if he could see deep down inside of her. Deep into her soul. Asking questions that she wanted so desperately to answer. How she wished she could tell him everything. There would be no more secrets or lies between them. Those were becoming as hard to bear as the memories and the guilt.

But that was not going to happen. She broke eye contact and turned back to the teapot.

'Why did you come here, Jess?' he asked in a voice so gentle it almost broke her heart. 'What are you running away from?'

Maybe if she shared the past, the nightmares might leave her alone.

You killed my son!

She could never tell him that.

'What makes you think I'm running away from something?'

Because I've been there, Adam thought. I'm still there. Once you start to run, it's almost impossible to stop.

He wanted to put his arms around her and pull her close. To push her hair back from her lovely face and tell her she didn't have to hide any more. He wanted to tell her that whatever had happened to her in the past, Coorah Creek was a new start for her. He was a new start for her.

New starts didn't always work. No one knew that better than he. Some things could never be washed away. Never be forgotten. Whatever was haunting Jess, it had left a scar deep within her. Adam knew about scars. Not just those of the body. He understood how badly a soul could be scarred. He knew how she felt, because the pain in her eyes matched the pain deep inside him.

Maybe if he told her his truth? If he shared his past, maybe she'd feel safe enough to do the same. The temptation to tell her was so strong. But how could he? In all these years he had never been able to tell the full story to Sister Luke. What was it about Jess that made him feel as if he could place the very deepest part of his soul in her hands? Was it her innate kindness? Was it the sense that she knew what pain felt like? Or was it simply that Jess was a beautiful woman and he was a man who had been alone too long? Whatever it was, he couldn't do it. He wouldn't burden Jess with his pain. She couldn't heal his scars. But perhaps he could help her. If only she would let him. If only he knew how.

'Look at you,' he said. 'You're smart. Educated and beautiful. A jet pilot, no less. Why are you in a one horse town like this? Flying for someone like me? You could have the whole world, but you came to the Creek. There has to be a reason.'

Adam watched her eyes. He could see the memories passing behind them. He could see the intensity of the emotions – there was pain and something else as well. Guilt?

'You can tell me,' he said.

'No. I can't. I really can't.' The words were almost a sob.

His instincts told him to pull Jess to him and hold her until she felt safe again, but he knew he couldn't do it. He could never be the man she needed. All he could hope to do was to free her so she could be the woman she was meant to be. Then she could leave here and resume her life. Find a man who was worthy of her. The mere thought was like cold steel in his gut.

'Adam?' Trish's voice was hesitant, as if reluctant to interrupt. 'I'm sorry, but Syd has just called from the pub. He needs me back there.'

'I hope there's nothing wrong?' Jess stepped past Adam, as if anxious to get some distance between them.

'Not really. It's the mayor. It looks like he's having one of his nights.'

'I'm sorry … I don't understand,' Jess said.

'Geoff Coburn, our mayor,' Adam explained, willing

Jess to look his way. 'He's a good man most of the time, but once or twice a month he goes on a bit of a bender. He doesn't cause any trouble, but Trish is the only person who can deal with him when he's like that.'

'Really?' Jess questioned Trish, still refusing to look at Adam's face.

'Don't ask me why.' Trish shrugged. 'But I had better get back there. I was hoping Adam would drive me.'

'Of course—'

'Why don't I drive you?' Jess interrupted. 'I have this lovely new car outside. I've only driven it once. To the shop and back. It would be nice to have another run.'

Trish smiled. 'That would be great. Thanks, Jess.'

'It's the least I can do after I used your car so often,' Jess said. 'Let me go and get the keys.'

She walked out of the door without a second glance.

Trish bid Adam goodnight. Behind him the electric kettle bubbled furiously, then turned itself off with a loud click. He'd lost any appetite for coffee. He had a feeling he was in for a sleepless night, even without the caffeine. From the living room he could hear the soft murmur of voices. He should go back in there, but he didn't think he could face that either. Jack, Ellen and the kids had no idea of the darkness in his past. And Sister Luke knew far too much about it. It was time he went home to the hospital. It was empty now that Nikki had taken her baby home. Adam was comfortable with empty.

He headed for the kitchen door. He'd walk back to the hospital and maybe take this chance to do some work. Even for a tiny place such as this there was a surprising amount of paperwork, and he was always behind. Sister Luke would be pleasantly surprised if he did some of his own volition, rather than her dragging him to his desk like a reluctant horse. Just as he put his hand on the door handle, Sister Luke's voice stopped him.

'You're heading home?'

'I thought I might. I could get some of that paperwork done before you have to yell at me again.'

A faint smile touched the nun's lips. 'I never yell at you. I merely suggest.'

Adam started to smile, too, but it never reached his eyes. For the first time since her return from the east, he looked closely at his dear friend's face. 'Are you all right? You don't look well.'

'I'm just tired from the trip,' Sister Luke assured him.

'I think you should let me give you a check-up.'

'Adam Gilmore,' Sister Luke said with some of her familiar fire, 'don't you dare start fussing about me.'

'Absolutely not.' Adam held his hands up in acquiescence. 'Me? Fuss? Never!'

'All right then. In that case, I shall allow you to drive me home.'

Adam hid his surprise and the concern that followed. Sister Luke lived next to the church, just a short walk away. In all the years they had worked together in Coorah Creek, she had always walked home, whatever the hour of day or night. He made a mental note to talk to her again about her health. Soon.

'Should we say goodbye?' he asked, indicating the other room, from where Jack's voice could be heard.

'I think Ellen and Jack are doing just fine without us,' Sister Luke said. 'In fact, right now I think leaving them alone is probably the best thing we can do – for all of them.'

'Do I detect a hint of matchmaking?' Adam said, as he held the front door open for Sister Luke to precede him down the stairs.

'And what if you do?' Sister Luke challenged him.

'Nothing. Nothing.' Adam held up his hands as if to ward off evil.

'Ellen and Jack and those kids. They need each other.'

'I wouldn't have thought Jack needed anyone.' Adam followed Sister Luke down the stairs.

'Which goes to show how little you know about such matters.' Sister Luke fixed him with a steely glare. Then she smiled softly. 'But one of these days, Adam, you will learn.'

His car was parked in the driveway, and Sister Luke got in before he could respond. Adam shook his head. Sister Luke was right about so many things. She was probably right about Ellen and Jack. But in his own case …

Inside the house Ellen heard the car door slam and looked around. 'I guess everyone's gone home,' she said.

Jack was sitting on the big couch, Bethany tucked under one arm, sound asleep. Harry was sitting on Jack's lap, struggling to keep his eyes open as Jack read yet another one of the *Duck Tales* from the huge pile of comics he'd brought with him.

'I should go as well,' Jack said. 'And I think these two are ready for bed.'

'Well past ready,' Ellen said, with a fond smile. 'You have been so patient with them today. Thank you for that.'

Jack gently ruffled Harry's blond hair. 'My pleasure.'

'Now, Harry, you give Jack back his comics,' Ellen said. Her son's face fell, as he slowly closed the comic.

'No. You keep them,' Jack told the boy.

Ellen frowned. Jack's comics had each been sealed in individual plastic wrappers. There were a considerable

141

number of them, and she suspected some were quite old. She didn't know much about comics, but she had a feeling a collection like that had to be quite rare ... and valuable. 'Jack, you can't just give away your collection,' she said.

'I'll tell you what,' Jack said, looking down into Harry's face. 'How about you keep the comics here, and then we can read them together. That's if it's all right with your mum?'

Two sets of eyes fastened onto her face. Ellen wasn't sure which one swayed her. 'That will be fine,' she said.

While Harry carefully carried the box of comics through the door to the small bedroom, Jack gathered Ellen's sleeping daughter in his arms. He carried her through to join her brother. Ellen folded back the bedcovers, and Jack gently placed Bethany into her bed. His big hands gently pulled the bedclothes back over her as she curled into her sleeping position without even opening her eyes.

'Can Jack tuck me in too?' Harry asked.

Jack raised an eyebrow and Ellen nodded.

She stood in the doorway watching as her son settled himself down for the night. He slid up Jack's shirt sleeve for one more look at the tattoo. 'Goodnight Uncle Scrooge,' he said.

'Goodnight, Harry.'

Ellen almost giggled at Jack's really bad Scottish duck voice.

Jack stood up and joined her at the doorway. This close, in the half-darkness, Ellen was struck again at how big he was. She barely reached his shoulder. Those hands that had brushed her sleeping daughter's cheek could break up a fight in a pub, or move furniture or snap timber. But they could be gentle hands too. Ellen wondered what those hands would feel like ... gentle on her skin.

Jack looked down into her face and Ellen wished she were different. Wished she was the sort of woman who could invite a man to stay. Wished she were the kind of woman who could make a man want to stay. But she wasn't. She'd lost that many years ago. A man like Jack would want ... would deserve ... someone better than her. Stronger than her. Maybe she could have been that woman once, but too many years and a bad choice of husband had changed her. Jack would never want someone who was ... soiled. As she was. She dropped her eyes and turned back into the brightly lit living room.

'I guess I should go,' Jack said. 'Thank you for dinner.'

'You're very welcome,' Ellen replied, moving to open the front door. She stood aside as Jack stepped out onto the front veranda. He turned back and hesitated.

Ellen did not step through the door. 'Thank you for everything,' she said, from the safety of the living room.

'Goodnight.'

Ellen closed the door and leaned back against it. Her heart was pounding, but still she heard the long moments he waited, before he turned away.

Chapter Fourteen

'Are you busy next Friday?'

Adam turned as Jess spoke, looking startled by her question. 'Not especially. Well, not yet, but you know what it's like.'

'Yes, I do,' Jess replied with a smile. She swung her gaze away from her instrument panel to Adam who, as usual when they were flying, was sitting in the co-pilot's seat. 'It's either all go or else it's full stop.'

'Are you getting bored with us already? Missing the bright city lights?'

No and no, Jess thought. She certainly was not missing the bright city lights. And she wasn't bored. At least not at times like this. Flying with Adam was one of her greatest pleasures. If there was no patient to care for, he seemed most at ease when they were in the air. Less of a loner. Less reticent. His habit of sitting next to her was so very different from his earthbound tendency to avoid personal contact. Jess was honest enough to admit that she enjoyed the intimacy of their time alone at ten thousand feet.

But they didn't fly every day. When they were on the ground, Adam retreated back into his professional shell. She spent a lot of time alone at the hangar, waiting for a call to action. And there were only so many times a pilot could wash and polish her plane.

'I was talking to Sister Luke yesterday,' Jess said. 'She suggested I do a talk for the kids at the school. About being a pilot. Like a careers talk.'

'Sister Luke is always coming up with ideas like that,'

Adam said with a grin. 'If you let her, she'll have you helping with all kinds of projects.'

'I don't mind,' Jess said. 'It gives me something to do when it's quiet. And I want to feel as if I'm part of the town.'

'You're part of the town already,' Adam said. 'You'd be surprised how many of my patients ask about you – especially the single men,' he added in a teasing tone.

Almost as if he was flirting with her. Well, two could play that game.

'Sister Luke suggested we could do it together ... the talk at the school,' Jess said.

'Oh, did she?' Adam raised an eyebrow.

'Yes. If I didn't know better I would think she was trying to ...'

'Attention, all stations Birdsville ...' The harsh voice from the radio prevented Jess from taking the thought further. While she answered the radio call, she cast a quick glance at Adam. He was grinning to himself. That grin didn't appear often enough. It made him look a little younger and very handsome. Her heart skipped every time she saw it.

The radio crackled again and Jessica dragged her thoughts back to her job. It was not a good idea to get distracted when approaching a new airfield on one of the busiest days in the year.

Jess loved to see a new place for the first time from the air – an eagle's eye view of the towns and roads and rivers forming a patchwork so far below her. She liked to guess what crops grew in the farmlands, or what stock grazed the open paddocks. She would try to picture the people who lived and worked in the tiny matchbox buildings below her and wonder in what way their lives were different to hers. The day she had seen Coorah Creek from the air, her first thought was that she had fled as far away from her past as it was possible to get. That she had reached the very back of beyond. Looking down at Birdsville, she knew she had been wrong. The Creek was a thriving metropolis compared to Birdsville.

The biggest thing about the town was the airport – if such a description was valid for a couple of corrugated iron sheds and a long thin line of tarmac. There was a shorter dirt landing strip crossing at right angles to the tarmac. Either one was longer than the town's main street. If indeed it could be said to have a main street. Three roads – from the north, south and east – met at the centre of four town blocks, each with a handful of buildings. To the south, there were maybe twenty homes clustered near a large reservoir, filled with water that was deep green in colour. To the west, a thin line vanished among the sand dunes. That, she guessed, must be the famous Birdsville Track leading into the Simpson Desert; the vast arid heart of the country. That road had claimed more than a few foolhardy souls who had set out unprepared for what they would face. Around the tiny town there was nothing. Vast open plains baked so dry by the sun that she could not imagine any life there. Restless sand dunes that could obliterate a road in a few hours. A few steps from any front door, there was only desert.

It was probably the loneliest place Jess had ever seen.

Or it should have been. It would have been, except for the hive of activity below her as the town prepared for the race meeting, just two days away.

There were already several small planes parked in a neat line down one side of the airstrip. Vehicles scurried up and down the roads like ants. To the south-east of the town, there was even more activity. The sun glinted off the shiny new metal of a roof that hadn't even been up long enough

146

to accumulate a layer of dust. A faint oval outline in the yellow dust indicated this was the Birdsville Race Track. Her radio crackled as, not that far to the east, another light aircraft announced that it shared her destination.

'How many people did you say normally live here?' Jess asked Adam, who was also peering out of the window from the co-pilot's seat beside her, a wide almost boyish grin on his face. He was clearly looking forward to the next few days of madness.

'Maybe one hundred and fifty in a good year. A fair few tourists pass through heading into the desert too.'

'And for the next few days?'

'Usually about six thousand.'

'Where are they going to put them all?' Jess looked out of the window again. 'There aren't enough houses here for six hundred.'

'There's a caravan park. And a campsite. Most people bring tents. Some sleep in their cars or camper vans. Some sleep with their planes – in them or more likely under them.'

'Well, just as long as no one tries to sleep in or under this one!'

For the next few minutes, Jess was busy bringing the plane in for her usually gentle touchdown. She rolled the Beechcraft to a stop next to another air ambulance bearing the badge of the Royal Flying Doctor Service. Adam lowered the aircraft stairs and tossed their bags to a man who was waiting to greet them. He was wearing a white short-sleeved shirt and mirror sunglasses. Jess didn't need the wings on his collar to identify him as a fellow pilot. Everything about him said ex-military.

'Good to see you again, Doc.' The pilot briefly shook Adam's hand, but his eyes swung immediately to Jess. 'I guess you're the new pilot.'

'I guess I am. Jess Pearson.'

'Greg Anderson. Welcome to the team.'

She couldn't see his eyes through her own reflection in his sunglasses, but Jess could feel Greg's close scrutiny as they shook hands.

'Right, I'll let Greg show you the ropes here,' Adam said, as he slung his rucksack onto his shoulder. 'I'm going to check in at the hospital. I'll see you later at the pub.' With a quick smile he set out across the dusty earth towards a small cluster of low buildings that was the town. Jess watched him go. He walked quickly with such energy and bounce to his stride. He had the air of a child encountering a fun fair. Did nothing ever give him pause, she wondered.

'So, Jess, let's get your plane squared away and I'll show you around,' Greg offered. 'A lot of people fly in for the races, but we get priority at all times. The apron is all ours ... the civilians have to park out of the way along the side of the dirt strip.'

As he spoke another aircraft appeared, turning for its final approach. Jess and Greg watched it touchdown in a neat and controlled landing. The pilot waved at them as he taxied past, close enough for his face to be visible through the window glass. Jessica's heart skipped a beat. He looked familiar. The world of private pilots was a small one. It wasn't unreasonable to think that someone she knew – or more importantly someone who knew her – might be on their way here. Might be here already.

Jess felt the familiar urge to run, then she almost laughed. Where would she go? She couldn't run any further than this. She was as far from that courtroom as it was possible to get and not just in terms of distance. She looked around at the dust and the desert and the tin sheds. If she wasn't safe here, she wasn't safe anywhere.

'The medical team all have rooms at the pub,' Greg said, as they waited for the newcomers to join them. 'The private pilots have to camp, but they usually hang out with us. We're all on duty, so we can't drink much – if at all. But you'd be surprised how much of a party a hundred odd pilots can have with a couple of cans of coke and a few packets of Twisties.'

'I'm not much for parties,' Jess said quietly. All it would take was one of those pilots to recognise her. Someone based in Sydney. Someone who read the papers. Someone who'd heard her name mentioned ... No, she would keep her distance.

'You'll like this one. We're a pretty tight knit bunch, the outback pilots,' Greg said. 'We look after our own.'

There was something in the tone of his voice ... Jess turned to look at him. He'd removed his sunglasses, and one look at his face told her. 'You know who I am,' she said quietly.

'I know you're a good pilot. I know you drive an air ambulance. That's all I need to know. All anyone needs to know,' he said in a gentle tone.

Jess closed her eyes and took a firm grip on her composure. She wasn't ready for this.

'You know, we're just the pilots here,' Greg continued. 'Everybody ignores us. The press are too busy with the visiting celebrities and the drunks doing foolish things to pay much attention to the likes of you and me.'

He was telling her she was going to be safe. She wanted to believe him. She really did ... but it wasn't easy.

'I didn't do it,' she said. 'I didn't know the drugs were on my plane.'

'Jess, you don't have to explain yourself to me, or to anyone out here for that matter,' Greg said. 'In the outback, you're judged by what you do – not what people say about you. You work with the doc. You help people. Out here that means a lot. And it's all anyone needs to know.'

How she wanted to believe those words.

Jess heaved a small sigh of relief as the new arrival approached. She didn't know him. Maybe, just maybe this was going to work out all right.

That thought stayed with her for a while. She met some other pilots, learned the layout of the town. Greg took her for a drive to see the stretch of flat land that once each year became a racetrack. Teams were hard at work setting up temporary stalls for the horses, and a bar, and railings around the course. Like most people, Jess had seen other horse races on television. The smooth green grass. The bright jockeys' silks and fashionable ladies wearing big hats. She equated horse racing with the clink of champagne glasses amid carefully tended rose beds. This dusty group of people building something out of almost nothing was totally beyond her wildest imaginings. As the tour ended at the pub, Jess was beginning to enjoy the experience.

Greg introduced her to a harried publican who tossed her a room key as he dashed past clutching glasses of beer. Promising to join the pilots later, Jess took the key and headed for the long low line of motel-style rooms behind the pub. She found the right door and opened it. She slowly looked around the room. Saw the rucksack that had been tossed casually onto one of the two double beds.

Oh, no, she thought as she recognised it. Surely not?

'Can I give you a lift, Doc?'

'No thanks. I'm good.' Adam waved the driver on. He was enjoying a chance to stretch his legs. He loved the feel of the activity all around him. The energy of dozens of people who were building a wonder out of a bare patch of sand. And these races were a wonder. Thousands of people gathered where normally there was nothing but dust. Horses running where normally lizards lay soaking up the sun. A community built on the edge of nowhere.

He loved the energy and excitement of the place and he was looking forward to showing it all to Jess. He wanted to watch her face, waiting for that smile. The one that seemed to light up the whole world. It was rare, but it was worth the wait.

Adam raised a hand in greeting to another vehicle, waving the driver on as he passed. Out here people seldom walked anywhere. The heat and the burning sun made sure of that. But today was relatively mild and the afternoon was drawing to a close. The sun was low on the horizon, adding a lovely golden glow to the bare earth. Adam liked to walk. He liked to feel that gentle warmth on his skin.

He'd been to check the medical facilities at the racetrack. Well, medical facility was too grand a description for a newly constructed shed. But it had power, water and air-conditioning. The shelves were stocked with a good selection of medical supplies. Enough to deal with the drunken foolishness and the small accidents that always brought people to his door. Anyone with real injuries would go to the Birdsville clinic. It was smaller even than his little hospital in Coorah Creek, but for these few days it was supplemented by enough supplies and people to deal with all but the most severe emergencies. And for those ... well, that was what the air ambulances were for. Jess could get them to a major hospital in just a couple of hours.

Jess.

Less than a kilometre ahead of him was the cluster of buildings that made up the town. Jess would be there somewhere. No doubt the other air ambulance pilots had shown her around the airstrip and the town. They would have given her some idea of what the next few days would be like. From a professional point of view. Now both of them had done what their jobs required, Adam wanted to show Jess what he loved about this place and this event. To the left of the track he was walking along, Adam could see the campsite taking shape. Although the bulk of the visitors would arrive tomorrow, there were already dozens of tents set up. Barbecues were already burning and when the wind wafted in the right direction, he could smell the steak cooking. The makeshift bars were also in place. There'd be a few drinks taken tonight – but not too many. Most of the people already here were the workers and would take it easy. The real party would start tomorrow when the punters arrived. He'd be tied to his work then. But tonight he wasn't needed. Tonight the desert waited … and so did Jess.

Adam quickened his steps.

'G'day, Doc!'

The greeting came from several of the crowd at the bar when Adam entered the Birdsville pub. He greeted those he knew, but all the time his eyes were searching for one person. By the jukebox, easily identified by their white shirts and badges, several pilots were talking over glasses of what looked suspiciously like orange juice. Jess wasn't among them. Perhaps she'd gone to find her room. Adam pulled his own key out of his pocket. That wasn't such a bad idea. He was sweating after his walk. He'd have a quick shower and find Jess. Maybe they could eat together.

His room was dark, the curtains drawn against the sun. He tossed the keys onto the dresser and crossed to the window. He flung the curtains back – and was rewarded with a flood of gentle light from the setting sun. He unbuttoned his shirt and was slipping it from his shoulders as he turned, only to be frozen in the act by the sight of a golden woman, almost naked, lying on his bed.

'What …?'

Jess was asleep. Her long legs curved graciously across the bedcovers. Her skin was gilded by the setting sun and looked as soft as satin. She was wearing a tiny tank top and a pair of white lacy briefs. Her body curved in all the right places. Her hands, so strong and competent in the cockpit of her plane, lay open on the bedcover, the fingers curved slightly as if trying to hold on to some fragile thing. Her hair framed a face softened by sleep. She looked tranquil and young and vulnerable.

And so very, very sexy.

Adam's body shook with a wave of pure sexual desire. He wanted to stretch his body beside her. To run his fingers up the golden satin of her thighs. To press his lips to the curves of her breasts. To taste the rosy lips. He hadn't felt a need this strong for years. No. He had never felt desire this strong. And to feel it now for someone so beyond his reach made him want to cry out with the pain of it.

Jess stirred sleepily, raising an arm to protect her eyes from the sunlight. Then with an intake of breath, she rose into a sitting position, her legs folding under her, her hands grasping her top to pull it downwards, in a vain attempt at modesty.

Suddenly aware of his own body, Adam pulled the shirt back on, swiftly buttoning it.

'Adam?'

Adam knew he should avert his eyes. He would, if he had conscious control over himself. But the sight of Jess's body like this was more than any man should be expected to ignore.

'What are you doing in my bed?'

Jess lowered her hand as her eyes became accustomed to the light. 'Actually,' she said in a voice blurred by sleep. 'This is my bed. You can have the other one.'

'I don't understand.' Adam's wits had scattered to the four corners of the earth.

'I'll explain, but first, would you mind?'

'Mind ...? Uh. Yes. Sorry.' Adam turned his back. He stared out of the window at the dry brown earth, while behind him a creaking of bed springs suggested Jess was getting off the bed to dress. Adam felt a flash of regret.

'You can turn around now.'

Jess had pulled on a pair of blue jeans, but the image of her lovely body was seared into his brain. He wasn't likely to forget that for a while. He took a slow breath and pushed it aside. 'What's going on?'

'Apparently, you neglected to mention to anyone that you now have a female pilot. They have put us both in one room as they did—'

'Last year,' Adam finished the sentence for her. 'Jess. I am so sorry. I'll go talk to the publican and organise another room for you.'

'I already talked to him. There is no other room. Some wit suggested you could sleep in the jail cell. I thought that was a pretty good idea, but the police sergeant says he'll probably need it.'

He hoped she was joking. 'Don't worry, Jess. I'll find somewhere else to sleep.'

'But there isn't anywhere.'

'I'll find something. A spare sleeping bag in someone's tent. A bunk in a camper van—'

'No you won't. You're here to do a job. You need a proper bed and a real bathroom and this is the only one available. We can share. After all, we're colleagues. Right? There's no reason why two colleagues shouldn't share a room?'

No reason at all, Adam thought, except for the image of Jess's body burned into his brain. 'No,' he said, swallowing the lump in his throat. 'None at all, if you're sure it's okay.'

'I'm sure.'

'But ...' Adam said, 'it might be a good idea if you refrained from lying around in a state of undress.'

Jess blushed. 'I'm sorry about that. I decided to have a shower and ... well ... we were up and on the way very early this morning. I guess I just fell asleep.'

She looked so good when she blushed. This sharing a room was not going to be easy. Well, not for him at least.

'I'll tell you what, if you're up for it, why don't you head down to the bar. I'll wash off the worst of the dust and buy you dinner.'

'But ... according to Greg the pilots and doctors eat for free,' Jess grinned mischievously, 'so I guess you're going to have to buy me a lemonade instead.'

He'd happily buy her anything she wanted, Adam thought after she'd gone. He just hoped her afternoon nap hadn't left her too rested. He wanted her tucked up in bed early this evening, If he was going to get any rest at all tonight, there was no way he was going near their shared room until she was safely asleep – *under* the covers.

Chapter Fifteen

The Birdsville races always left a new layer of dust at Coorah Creek.

There were several unfamiliar cars parked in front of the pub. Of the crowds who flocked to the annual race meet, quite a few came by car. And many of those chose to break the long journey from the east coast by spending a night at places like the Creek. All of the rooms at the pub would be full tonight, and the campsite would be doing a brisk trade, too. Jack knew that Syd and Trish Warren were more than happy to take the extra income this weekend. In fact, that was why he was here … to help Syd change the kegs. Not that he'd asked. Syd didn't like to admit that he wasn't as young as he used to be. But Jack knew if he just dropped by, the older man would be pleased to accept a hand with the heavy lifting.

'G'day Jack!' The publican walked past, a tray of drinks in hand. 'I think there's a seat at the bar.'

There was, but only one. The crowd was mostly racegoers, but there were a few familiar faces.

'Jack. We don't see you in here so much these days,' one of the locals greeted him.

'That's because he's usually down at The Mineside,' another offered with a leer and a wink. 'I guess the food down there is better.'

'In that case, I guess you won't be wanting this steak then, Steve Doohan?' Trish Warren walked into the room, two steaming plates in her hands. 'You can go down the road any time.'

'Aw, Trish, I was just teasing him.' Steve looked suitably abashed

'Teasing, eh.' Trish put the plate down in front of him. 'If I was dating two girls at the same time, I'd be careful about doing any teasing.'

Steve ducked his head as the men around him started to laugh. There wasn't much went on in Coorah Creek that Trish Warren didn't know about.

'You pay no attention to that lot,' she said to Jack, as she ducked behind the bar to pour him a beer. 'They're just jealous.'

'There's nothing to be jealous of,' Jack said, as he reached for his wallet. 'I'm just helping out. That's all.'

'Of course it is.' Trish patted his hand. 'And when she's ready, Ellen will realise the reason why.'

Jack blinked. It seemed like just a few days ago that Trish was warning him to stay away from Ellen. Now she was matchmaking? There were some things he would never understand.

'Now, speaking of helping,' Trish continued, 'there are some kegs need lifting in the cold room. I'd appreciate it if you could give Syd a hand with them. He's pretty busy tonight.' Like her husband, Trish would never admit to advancing years, but she was the practical one and not too proud to ask for help if she thought her man needed it.

'Sure thing.'

'And you can put that wallet away, Jack North. Can I fix you a steak?'

'No thanks.' Jack felt almost embarrassed as he said it. Not that Trish didn't cook a fine steak, but he was looking forward to dinner later tonight down at The Mineside. The pub didn't offer accommodation, but the town's packed campsite was just a short walk away and business would be brisk.

'Ellen's working tonight, then,' Trish guessed. 'That pub's likely to get a bit rowdy with the crowd from the campsite. I'll tell Syd to get those kegs done right away then, so you can get down there.'

She set off back to the kitchen.

Jack took a deep drink from his glass, his thoughts as they so often were, on Ellen. She was quite something. Considering what he suspected had happened to her in the past, she had taken control of her new life with a strength that amazed him. She'd made a home for her children. Enrolled them in school and given them a new life. The reservation he'd had about her job at The Mineside had proved unfounded. She had somehow managed to turn that place around too. That pub was more popular than it had ever been, but somehow the rough edges had been smoothed away. There were fewer fights. Some of the miners had even started bringing their wives and girlfriends to the pub. Mind you, some of them hadn't. Jack's forehead creased into a frown. Some of them wanted to appear single at the bar, so they could flirt with Ellen. Not that she ever flirted back. Well, not seriously anyway.

There were times when he still saw a flash of fear in her eyes. She hid it well, but he knew she still carried the scars of her past. She kept the men at arm's length because she wasn't ready yet. Jack had to believe that one day the fear would vanish, and when it did, he wanted to be the man waiting for her.

'G'day, Jack.'

'Sarge,' Jack said, as the policeman fronted up to the bar next to him. 'Busy?'

'Pretty much. Same as every year about this time.' Sergeant Max Delaney wasn't an outback man. He'd been raised on the coast, where the weather was kinder and the work of law enforcement a whole lot harder. He'd been assigned to the Creek four years ago and fitted right in. There was an art to policing a small town. A good outback copper knew when the law was perhaps less important than the community. There were times he had to be blind. And there were times he had to make his own rules. Max had sorted that out within a couple of months of his arrival. That wasn't to say he was ever less than a cop. He was just the right sort of cop.

'How're things with you?' the Sarge asked in a voice so casual that Jack knew there had to be a reason.

'Not bad.'

'I heard you're spending a bit of time down at The Mineside.'

'I guess I am.'

'Well, you're not the only one. I hear the food is pretty good these days.' Max nodded his thanks to Syd who had placed his usual, a soda water, on the bar in front of him.

'It is. You should drop by for a meal one night.'

'I might just do that.'

'In fact,' Jack said in an offhand manner, his eyes on the half-empty glass of beer in his hand, 'it's likely to be a bit busy there this weekend. Maybe a bit rowdy, too. Strangers mostly… It might be worth dropping by.'

'I was planning to keep a pretty good eye on the place,' Max said, sipping his drink. Both men sat in silence for a minute before the policeman spoke again. 'I've had a report in from the coast. To be on the look out for some missing persons.'

'Oh, yeah?' Jack forced his voice to remain calm and casual, despite the sudden pounding of his heart.

'Yeah. Woman and two kids. Seems there's a question of custody. Also a suggestion of stolen money.'

Jack turned to look at the man sitting next to him. One look at the policeman's face told him everything he needed to know. The alert was about Ellen and the kids. The Sarge knew it and now so did he.

'When she got here, there were bruises all over her arms. She was terrified. The kids too,' Jack said in a quiet voice so none of the other men at the bar could hear.

The policeman's face darkened. 'That so?'

'She just needs time to get on her feet,' Jack said. 'And she's a great mother. Those kids need time with her to forget whatever happened before.'

The Sergeant didn't say anything. He took another low slow drink of his soda water. As he put the glass back on the bar he turned to look at Jack. The two men's eyes met and Jack could see the policeman was weighing up every word he'd said.

'You know, these bulletins take a while to get to us out here,' Max said. 'And I am pretty busy what with the races and so forth. I might get a bit behind with some of my paperwork. But at some point, I am going to have to talk to her.'

Jack nodded.

'Right. See you later.' Calling his thanks to Syd for the drink, Max left.

The policeman's words stayed with Jack as he hefted kegs for Syd in the cold room. He didn't stay around after that. He left the noisy bar and still deep in thought, got into his car. He was planning to go The Mineside, but instead found himself driving towards the hospital where a single light was glowing through the office window.

'I knew I'd find you here,' he said to Sister Luke, as he walked into the office.

'Well, with Adam and Jess down at Birdsville, I thought someone should man the phones,' the nun said in her gentle voice. 'Besides, the peace and quiet gives me a chance to catch up on paperwork.' She gestured to the piles of paper spread across the narrow metal desk.

'Have you heard from Adam or Jess?'

'No. I imagine they are too busy to call home.' Sister Luke folded her hands and leaned back into her chair. 'Did you want to talk about something, Jack?'

Jack almost smiled. Sister Luke could see through anyone.

'I was wondering, you must know about ... well ...' He picked up one of the many pens that littered the desk, twisting it around in his hands as he struggled to find the right words. '... helping women who have ... you know ... had a tough time.'

Sister Luke smiled a small, sad smile. 'A little bit. I've seen it happen far too many times.'

'Well, how does a woman get past something like that? Can she ever ... well ... you know... be with a man again?'

'Oh, Jack.' Sister Luke leaned forward to remove the pen and pat his hands gently. 'It's not easy for a woman who has been hurt to learn to trust again. But they can. It takes a lot of time ... and good friends.'

'How can I help her?' He raised his eyes to look at Sister Luke's lined face.

'Just keep doing what you have been doing, Jack. Let her find herself again. Let her learn to like herself. Be her friend.'

Jack wanted to believe Sister Luke was right.

'But what if ... well. What if the man who hurt her is looking for her? If he went to the police and made accusations against her? The police will believe her, won't they? They wouldn't take the kids away?'

'Jack.' Sister Luke's voice was suddenly sharp. 'What's happened?'

'I was just talking to Max. There's some sort of bulletin out for her as a missing person. And accusations too.'

'Then she needs a lawyer.'

'She can't afford a lawyer,' Jack said. 'But I can help her with that, if she'll let me.'

Sister Luke nodded. 'But don't expect anything, Jack. This may not end the way you want it to.'

'I know,' Jack said, his heart nearly breaking. 'Just as long as she is safe and happy.'

'Will that be enough for you?'

'It might have to be.'

Sister Luke rose from the chair and came to rest a comforting hand on his shoulder. 'You're a good man, Jack North. Now, do you think you could do an old lady a favour and give me a lift home? It's late and I'm tired.'

The sudden weakness in her voice dragged Jack away from his own problems. 'Of course, Sister Luke.'

He leaped to his feet and led the way to his car. As he did, he took a careful look at Sister Luke's face. This was the second time she'd wanted a lift home. Adam had mentioned he'd driven her home after the house-warming party. That was so unlike her. He'd been so caught up in his own problems, he hadn't noticed how tired she looked. He'd have to talk to Adam when he got back and make sure the Sister wasn't working too hard.

Jack dropped Sister Luke at her small house next to

the town's Catholic Church. The town had no priest. A visiting priest came by once a month to hold services in the church which Sister Luke cared for. Jack made a mental note to see if he could take some of that burden off her shoulders.

Without thinking, he then turned towards The Mineside. As he approached, it was pretty clear that this pub was also sharing the fruits of the weekend's extra traffic. It looked crowded. Climbing the stairs to the front door, Jack guessed he wouldn't find his usual table waiting for him. He opened the doors and walked into the bar. His eyes immediately found Ellen, who had just emerged from the kitchen carrying two big plates of food. Her face was flushed with the kitchen's heat and her hair was a mess. She was so beautiful.

Ellen looked across the room and the smile that was his alone lit her face. Jack knew then that he could wait forever, if that's what it took.

Chapter Sixteen

Adam lay in bed listening to Jess breathing.

She slept deeply. Every breath was almost a sigh … long and deep and soft. She was so close. He could almost feel the warmth of her body. He knew he could stretch across the gap that separated their two beds and touch her. He also knew her skin would be warm and soft.

It was a very long time since Adam had shared the night with another human being. He'd spent many a long night watching over his patients, willing them to take one more breath as he tried to heal them. But to share a night's rest with another person – that was an intimacy he had long denied himself.

Women found him attractive and there had been a time he'd been glad to welcome them into his bed. When he was young, the pity in their eyes when they saw his scars mattered far less than the sex that would follow. But that had changed. The pity had become too hard to ignore. He began to avoid casual encounters. And a deeper relationship meant getting close to someone. Giving them the power to hurt him. He avoided those, too.

He had forgotten what it was like to share the gentlest hours of the day with someone else. To share one's most vulnerable moments.

He hadn't planned this, and his main thought was to get through the next few days without Jess discovering his secret. He just couldn't stand the thought of pity in Jessica's eyes.

But still, the desire was there. How could it not be? She was a beautiful woman. The image of her body, golden in the sunlight, was burned into his mind. He wanted to run his hands up those long shapely legs. Press his lips against the curves of her body. Feel her flesh against his. Feel the warmth of her breath …

Jess sighed and moved in her sleep. She gave a little moan.

Adam shifted uncomfortably in his bed. He kept his eyes firmly fixed on the faint line of light at the edge of the curtains that covered the window, wishing the sunrise would come. He had no business feeling like this. For so many reasons. He could never have a life with Jess. There were too many secrets he couldn't share. And with Jess, it would be all or nothing.

Jess had her own secrets too. He didn't know what they might be, but he knew that she had come to Coorah Creek to escape. To heal. Then she would leave the outback and go back to the life she deserved. Back to the bright lights. To the people who must be waiting for her. To the people who would be more to her than he ever could. An icy dagger slipped silently between Adam's ribs and pierced his heart. He didn't want her to leave. But he could give her no reason to stay.

Jess moved again, her even breathing broken by a short, sharp cry.

A nightmare. Adam recognised the signs. God knew Adam had survived more than his share of nightmares. As a boy he'd woken every night screaming into the darkness, the pain in his mind as real as the pain in his body. The nightmares had faded as the boy became a man, but still sometimes came to haunt his nights. What ghosts, he wondered, came to disturb Jessica's sleep?

Another cry from the other bed caused Adam to turn his head. Jess thrashed her head from side to side.

All other thoughts fled before the wish to simply comfort her. Should he go to her? As a tortured child he had welcomed Sister Luke's touch to ease his fears. Jess was no child, but Adam had no doubt that something tortured her. He wished he could go to her and put his arms around her. Make the pain go away.

With another cry, Jess suddenly sat up in bed, looking wildly around her.

Instinctively, Adam closed his eyes and feigned sleep.

After a few minutes, he heard Jess's rapid breathing begin to slow. The bedclothes rustled as she got out of bed.

'Adam?' The whispered word was not to wake him, but rather to ask if he was awake. Adam didn't reply. Jess didn't need to see pity in his eyes either.

He heard her moving around the room in the darkness. There came the sound of running water from the bathroom, then finally the click of the room door as it opened – then closed again behind her.

Adam opened his eyes. The faint light of dawn seeped around the edges of the curtains. The bed next to his was rumpled and empty and cold. He was alone.

The sun was just beginning to peep above the horizon, and the light was soft and gentle. Despite this, Jess could hear noise and movement. Today would see the vast influx of people and horses for the races that would begin on Friday. Although she supposed everything was in place, there were still last minute preparations going on, even this early in the day. Jess did not want company right now. She turned north, away from the activity and towards the airport.

Her Beechcraft was parked where she had left it, next

to the other air ambulances. There were a few more planes parked around the airstrip. One or two had tents pitched under the wings. The sounds of light snores suggested the occupants slept more soundly than she had.

Jess walked round the aircraft, running her fingers lightly over the paint and performing the routine checks she did every morning. The routines always soothed her and made her feel in control of something – even if she could not control her nightmares.

You killed him. You killed my son!

She had thought the nightmares were fading. These weeks in Coorah Creek, sharing her life with Ellen and the kids; with Jack and Sister Luke … and most of all with Adam, had brought something very close to happiness. But last night the nightmares had returned. She was only glad that Adam had slept through them. She didn't know what she would have done if he'd woken and asked her what was wrong. Adam was an important part of that tentative happiness she felt. Working with him was like a balm to her soul. Watching a baby being born. Helping the sick and injured. Even sharing stew around a campfire with the stockmen. The thought that something might rip apart those fragile feelings was more than she could bear.

She looked down at her hands. They were shaking ever so slightly. They hadn't done that for a while. It must be the crowds. The knowledge that there were journalists and cameras here. She told herself firmly they were here for the races. Not for her. It was time she got past the fear.

She pulled the keys from her pocket and unlocked the plane. Spending a few minutes checking the interior steadied her hands, but did not make her more inclined to face other people. She climbed back down the aircraft stairs. The sun was above the horizon now; the day starting to feel hotter. Soon a new influx of aircraft would begin. In the town, there would be cars and buses and trucks of horses. There was no way she could avoid people. Nor could she forget what had happened. All she could do was try to ignore the past and look to the future.

She turned her steps in the direction of the pub.

She walked through the pub door to find breakfast in full swing. The pilots she'd met the day before were all there, feasting on bacon and eggs and sausages, along with a few of the race organisers and officials. There were pots of coffee on the tables and the noise was pretty substantial. She grabbed some toast and coffee, and joined Greg Anderson and his colleagues from the Flying Doctor service.

'Hey, Jess. Where's the doc?'

'Still asleep, I guess.'

A strangled laugh came from somewhere in the vicinity of the coffee pot. Another of the group waggled his eyebrows at her in an exaggerated leer.

Determined not to blush, Jess shrugged. 'Well, guys, how would you like sleeping with your boss?'

The laughter that followed told Jess she had deflected the potential embarrassment, until she glanced up and saw Adam standing in the doorway. His eyes were on her, a slight question on his face.

'At least I don't snore,' he said quickly, responding to the curious looks cast his way.

'Yes, you do,' Jess shot back. 'Like an elephant with a bad head cold.'

Under cover of the roar of laughter that followed, Jess looked closely at Adam. He had appeared asleep when she got out of bed, but what if her nightmare had woken him too? He showed no sign of tension as he collected a huge plate of food and an equally large mug of coffee and joined her table. Talk soon turned to the day ahead and who was to be on duty at the airport and at the racetrack and the town's medical centre. Jess decided that everything was all right. Today was Thursday. The races were held on Friday and Saturday. Sunday evening, once the town had emptied of visitors, they would head back to the Creek. Surely she could keep her nightmares under control for just three more nights?

Jess had been expecting a busy day. She was surprised to find the reverse was true. There was plenty of activity, but no need for her services. Cars and trucks and buses roared down the road towards the racetrack. There was a steady beat of aircraft landing at the airport. Hotel staff and campsite workers were rushing about as the trickle of incoming racegoers turned into a flood. Tents were springing up at the campsite. The temporary food and drink stands were in full swing. There was music and laughter and, of course, there was dust. Great clouds of it stirred up by thousands of feet.

In all of this activity, all Jess had to do was wait.

Adam and the two other doctors were already on duty, tending to minor scrapes among the workers, and minor escapades among the crowd who seemed to start drinking the moment their feet touched the dusty ground. Jess was on standby. But there'd be nothing for her to do unless some emergency called for an airlift. She waited at the town's tiny medical clinic, reading and watching the passing parade of arrivals. By mid-afternoon she was restless. When it was Greg's turn to be on call, Jess set out for a walk, grateful for a chance to stretch her legs.

She hadn't gone very far when she heard the wolf

whistle. She ignored it, but a second following close behind caused her to turn her head.

'Hello, darling!'

Some young men standing near the makeshift bar were waving to attract her attention. 'Come on over here and let us buy you a drink.'

Smiling, she shook her head and walked on. It wasn't the first such offer she had received. Like so many outback events, the population attracted here was mostly male and out for a good time. They meant no harm, but Jess made a mental note not to stray too far on her own late at night, after a long hot and thirsty day ... when the beer had been flowing a little too freely for some.

She kept walking, enjoying the sights and sounds around her. This was like nothing she had ever seen before. There was laughter and music and the smell of burgers cooking. A large part of the growing crowd were city folk walking around clutching beer cans and slowly being turned a lobster red by the sun. They wore jeans and running shoes. The girls wore skirts and flat sandals ... their feet quickly disappearing beneath a layer of yellow dust. The rest were outback people come in search of a couple of days respite from the loneliness and hard toil that was their daily lot. They wore broad-brimmed Akubra hats already stained with sweat and faded by the sun. Their elastic-sided riding boots showed signs of hard wear. Their skins were brown and toughened by exposure to a harsh climate.

Whatever their origin, the racegoers were all there for the same reason – to have some fun.

Jess stepped aside to let a truck roll past. She smelled, rather than saw, the horses in the back. That was what this event was supposed to be all about. Horse racing, but she had a feeling some of the revellers might not actually get as far as the track. A second horse van followed the first, and as Jess stepped out of the way, she saw the cameras.

A small crowd of media people were walking her way, pausing now and then to snap photos or take videos of the spectacle that was unfolding. Jess's heart started to pound, and she turned her head. She began to push her way through the crowd which had suddenly turned into some sort of impenetrable wall. She glanced back over her shoulder. The media scrum had turned in the direction of the bar. Good, she thought. Put those cameras away and go get a drink. One of the group turned her way and just for an instant their eyes met. Jessica prayed she would see no recognition there as she tried to lose herself again in the crowd.

By the time she was back at the medical centre, Jess had convinced herself that she had escaped unnoticed. But, just in case, she decided she'd spend a quiet night in her room. There was plenty of time over the next two days to experience the excitement of the races. Right now, she needed a little peace and quiet. The sun was setting and so she was off duty. The airstrip had no lights, so no aircraft would be leaving now. She strolled over to check her plane one last time. There were a lot of aircraft parked by the side of the airstrip now. Jess searched the line for any that looked familiar. There were none, and that left her feeling relieved. She still felt a little exposed. Anyone seeing her around the Beechcraft would guess she was a pilot. It wasn't a great leap from there to …

No. That wasn't going to happen! Chiding herself for being paranoid, Jess walked back to the pub. She guessed Greg and the other pilots would be there. She would join them for dinner. Adam would be on call most of the night. At least she might have the room to herself for a while.

Jess stretched to ease her muscles. She felt as if she was wearing a layer of dust.

'A shower would feel pretty good,' she said to the sinking sun. 'Yes. A shower then dinner.'

She slipped the key into the door and pushed it open. The first thing she saw was Adam clad only in a towel. He was standing by the window, his arms raised as he towelled his wet hair. Jess barely noticed the fine lines of his torso, or the muscles in his bare legs. All she saw was the terrible ruin of his back and shoulders. Her breath froze in her throat as the meaning of those scars struck home.

A custody battle ... the father sprayed petrol on the family home and set it on fire. The boy was badly burned.

That night at the restaurant in Mount Isa, when she had asked how he had met Sister Luke.

Sister Luke sat with him, day after day. The doctors may have healed his body, but she brought his soul back from the darkness.

Himself! Adam had been talking about himself. He was the boy accidentally burned by his father. The boy who had grown up to be a doctor so Sister Luke would be proud of him.

Adam had his back to her. He had not noticed her. Jessica stepped back and silently closed the door. Tears filled her eyes as she leaned her forehead against the wood. Oh, Adam! To have known so much pain. Her heart ached for him. Her mind flashed back to the day after they met. Unknowingly, she had placed her hand on Adam's shoulder, only to have him flinch away. Now she understood. Slowly she turned and walked away from the door. He had obviously kept that secret for many years. Jess knew about secrets and how to keep them. She would keep this one too. For Adam.

With the click of the door, Adam lowered his hands. The closed door was reflected in the glass of the window. He didn't see it. He could only see the look on Jessica's face when she saw his back. The horror. The pity. He'd seen that look before. On many other faces. But somehow, it was just that much harder to take on hers. A tiny spark of hope – or was it perhaps a dream – that lay hidden in the deepest recesses of his heart flickered and died. He lifted his hand and ran his fingers along his shoulder, feeling the puckered skin. The scars had faded a little over time, but were still horrible to look at. If ever he and Jess were to … he would want her to look at him with passion and desire. Not pity. Never that.

Chapter Seventeen

From where Adam stood outside the first aid hut, the pounding of hooves was like approaching thunder. The jockeys' silks were distant flashes of colour against the brilliant blue sky. The horses' coats shone like polished copper and bronze as they hurled themselves at breakneck speed down the track, while all around people screamed encouragement to their favourites.

Adam wasn't having fun. Well, not as much as he should have been.

The Birdsville Races were his favourite event of the year. Adam loved the colour and energy of the crowd. He loved the optimism of people who would organise a race meeting in the middle of nowhere and the sense of adventure of the people who came from all over the country – all over the world – to join the fun. As someone who worked alone most of the time, he enjoyed the camaraderie of being part of a medical team. And if the hours were long, the work for the most part wasn't hard. Minor scrapes and the occasional mishap caused by overindulgence. There was always the potential for a more serious medical emergency, but, so far, things had gone pretty well.

Professionally, that was. He couldn't say the same thing about his personal life.

Adam wasn't sure what he had expected would happen between him and Jess during these few days. Not romance. Never that. But he had hoped their friendship would continue to grow. She had become such an important part of his life. The days he spent with her were the best days. Days when he didn't see her, even if just for a few minutes, seemed somehow wasted.

He just hoped yesterday hadn't spoiled everything.

Sharing the room had been a genuine oversight on his part. Now he had to live with the consequences of that mistake. He just wished Jess had returned to the room a few minutes later. He wished she had never seen the scars on his back. If she ever tried to talk to him about those scars, he would have to lie and once that lie was between them, nothing was going to be the same. Most of all he wished he had never seen the pity in her eyes. Of all the things he might want from Jessica, pity was not one of them.

Maybe she wouldn't ask about the scars. When she backed out of the room, she must have assumed he hadn't seen her. It was not an unreasonable assumption, given he'd been towelling his hair dry. He could hope she would just forget what she saw. It was a vain hope, as was the hope that the horror in her eyes would not change their relationship. It was already happening. Adam had spent the evening in the medical centre, dealing with a few minor injuries among the revellers. When he'd returned to the pub, Jess was in bed, the bedding pulled up high over her shoulders. Her regular breathing told him she was asleep. He'd lain awake for a while listening to her breathing and wondering if she was really asleep, or just pretending. Was the sight of his scars so hideous that she just couldn't bring herself to look at him again? He knew just how ugly his body was, but he believed Jess was a better person than that. Given time, he hoped their relationship would resume its former footing. But any hope he had of something more between them was now irretrievably lost.

'Hey, Doc, picked a winner yet?' a passing local asked.

'Not yet,' he replied, pulling himself out of his reverie.

'Today is my day,' the man continued, his voice just a little blurred by beer. 'The bookies weep when they see me coming!' The man vanished into the crowd, his step as unsteady as his voice.

Adam smiled. That man had the right idea. He was out to enjoy himself, and that was what Adam should do. He wasn't about to spoil the big event by useless dreams.

The next race was the biggest race of the day. Leaving one of his colleagues at the first aid station, Adam set out for the parade ring, his emergency medical kit in the rucksack slung over his shoulder. The horses made a spectacular sight as they danced past the crowds towards the starting line. Adam wasn't a betting man. Money wasn't important to him, but he did like to try to pick the winner. He ran his eyes over the thoroughbreds as they trotted towards the starting position. Long and lean, full of energy and fire. They were a beautiful sight. Adam's eyes fixed on a dark blood bay mare. She wasn't the tallest horse on the track, but there was something about the way she held her head. She was a fighter. That was something he could relate to. The jockey's silks were bright red and yellow. The colour of a desert dawn. He liked that too.

For a couple of minutes, the horses milled around at the starting line. Then they were set. A silence descended on the crowd as they waited for the moment ...

'They're off!' The commentator's voice over the loudspeakers was drowned out by the roar of the crowd when the horses leaped forward as if shot from a starting gun. Caught up in the excitement of the moment, Adam leaned forward over the rail. All around him people were yelling their encouragement.

The blood bay mare was in the leading bunch of horses. Slowly she started to pull forward, a rangy grey at her side.

'Come on, girl!' Adam whispered. 'Come on!'

It happened too fast to truly comprehend.

The grey horse seemed to stumble. It staggered sideways and collided with the bay mare. She fell to her knees and somersaulted over the top of her rider. The next two horses rose like a wave to jump the fallen horse and rider, but the ones behind had no chance. They appeared to run right over the top of the red and yellow figure. The jockey was dragged forward several yards. The last few horses were steered around the fallen figure and the pack raced on leaving two horses and two riders sprawled in the dust.

Adam was over the railing and running before the announcer had time to call for medical aid.

He passed the bay mare, now on her feet and limping slowly away, obviously hurt. The grey horse was still down, its rider kneeling next to it. Adam reached him first.

'Are you all right?' he asked.

'I'm okay,' the jockey replied, stroking his injured mount's neck. He slipped off his helmet and Adam could see the tears in his eyes. 'But we need a vet.'

There was nothing he could do here. Adam turned his back on the dying horse and started to run towards a small crowd gathered a few metres away.

'Let me through!' he shouted. The crowd parted and Adam dropped to his knees next to the fallen rider.

Someone had removed the rider's helmet, or it had been lost in the fall. With a start Adam realised the jockey was a woman. She was conscious, but her face was white with pain.

'I think she's broken her arm, Doc,' someone said next to him.

It wasn't a difficult diagnosis. The arm lay twisted across the girl's body. Blood was oozing from a long gash in her forearm, but Adam was relieved there was no bone protruding from the wound. The break would heal.

'Get the ambulance here,' Adam said to the people milling around. 'And someone alert the airport. We'll need to get her to Mount Isa.'

'On it, Doc.'

'Now, can you tell me your name?' Adam asked the jockey.

He ignored the responses from the people standing around, some of whom obviously knew her. He needed to hear the girl speak. He needed to know she was aware of herself and what was going on around her.

'Carrie Bryant,' the voice was just a whisper.

'Okay. Carrie. I'm Adam. I'm going to look after you.'

Carrie tried to nod, but winced in pain.

'No moving,' Adam said. 'You took a really bad fall. Your arm is broken.'

'Tasha …?'

Adam looked up at the people around him.

'The horse,' someone said.

He didn't know how badly the horse had been injured, and he wasn't about to give Carrie any bad news. 'She's being taken care of.' He knew that, at least, would be no lie. 'Now you have to let me take care of you.'

Carrie opened her mouth as if to speak, but no words came out. Her breathing was becoming laboured. This wasn't a good sign. Adam reached into his bag for a stethoscope. He listened to the girl's chest for a few seconds, during which time, her breathing became noticeably harder.

The broken arm was the least of her problems.

'Carrie, listen to me,' Adam said, taking the girl's good hand in his. 'You've got what we call a pneumothorax. That means you probably took a couple of hard hits from some of those iron horseshoes. Your lung is damaged. Air is escaping into your chest. Now, that's not as bad as it sounds,' he went on, when he saw the fear flash in her eyes, 'but I have to get some of the air out of your chest before we can move you. Okay?'

The fear-filled amber eyes held his.

'All right. So, I'm going to drain some of the air from your chest. I'm going to use a syringe. It's sort of like drawing blood, but we'll take the air out instead.'

The girl opened her mouth to speak. Adam leaned close so he could hear her. '... hate needles ...'

Adam's heart went out to her. Such bravery in the face of that terrible pain and fear.

'To tell you the truth, I'm not that fond of them myself.' Adam laid a hand gently on her forehead. 'But I have to do this. All right?'

Someone had placed his bag right to hand. He opened it up and found the syringe he was looking for. He attached a large needle. He tried to keep it out of the girl's sight, but knew that just wouldn't be possible.

'All right,' he said. 'I'm going to have to rip your shirt open. I hope there's no jealous boyfriend here going to hit me for that.'

Her skin was already starting to darken with bruises. Carefully Adam slid the large needle between the girl's ribs, hearing a moan of pain as he did so. She was too short of breath to cry out. Slowly he withdrew some of the air from her chest cavity. Almost immediately her breathing became a little less laboured. He sucked more air and she took a deeper breath.

'You're doing great,' he told her. 'Now I'm going to give you some painkillers, get this arm secured with a splint and then it's off to hospital we go. I've got a plane standing by.'

'I don't like flying.' Even through the pain she sounded stronger already.

'Ah – but I have a great pilot. She'll take good care of you, just wait and see.'

Jess was alone at the airport. She had left the rest of the medical team at the hospital, claiming the need to run some small checks on her plane. The reality was that she just wanted to be alone. She needed to figure out what to do with the shocking truth she had learned about Adam.

Sitting at the small desk inside the hangar, she relived those few seconds in the hotel room. Again and again.

The terrible scars had revealed so much about his past. She couldn't begin to imagine what he had been through. Something deep inside her cried for that horribly injured boy. The pain he must have suffered! No child should ever know that sort of pain.

And what about the man that boy had become?

Adam's father could not have known his child was in the house when he set it on fire. That past was a tragic accident. But Adam still had to live with the knowledge that his father had caused his injuries. How difficult must it have been growing up with that knowledge? How did anyone live with that? She wondered how his relationship with his family was now – he never spoke of them. Not his mother and certainly not his father.

Not only that, she wondered how he had come to terms with such a difficult past to become the man he now was. How had he maintained the compassion for others that was such an important part of him? She imagined Sister Luke had a lot to do with that.

She had run from the hotel room before Adam had seen her. He didn't know that she had seen his scarred body or learned his secret. How could she tell him? But how could she ignore what she had learned? She was a little afraid to face him. Afraid that he would read the knowledge on her face. She knew now why he kept himself distant from others. Why he didn't like to be touched. If he learned that she knew the truth, would he become even more distant? The mere thought was like a hot knife in her heart.

The phone on the desk began to ring.

'There's been a fall at the race.' The caller didn't identify himself. He didn't need to. His message was the important thing. 'You need to get to the Isa. The ambulance will be there in a few minutes. One injured female jockey.'

'I'll be ready.' Jess ended the call and got to her feet.

Her plane was ready for a fast take-off. By the time she had opened the doors and completed her pre-flight checks, she could hear the ambulance approaching. A small convoy of other vehicles followed in its wake. Jess ignored the other vehicles as the ambulance pulled up close to her aircraft. The driver walked swiftly to the rear and opened the double doors. Jess looked inside to see Adam seated next to the stretcher, one hand on his patient's shoulder.

The driver slid the stretcher forward. Adam stepped out and smiled down at the terrified girl in torn and bloodstained jockey's silks.

'Carrie, this is Jess, our pilot.'

'Hi, Carrie,' Jess said gently. 'Let's get you on board.'

As the driver started to manoeuvre the stretcher, Jess became aware of other people milling around. She heard an all too familiar sound ... the whirring of a camera shutter. She spun to face the noise. A man with a large camera was pushing his way towards them, his finger on the shutter trigger. Not far behind him was another man with a video camera. She knew them – or rather she knew their type. They were press out for a story. Her first instinct was to duck away, to avoid their stares and their lenses. But she had a job to do. Adam and his patient needed her. Besides, it wasn't her they were chasing. It was the injured girl. She was their victim this time. But Carrie was in her care now, and Jess wasn't going to let them have her.

She immediately moved her body to block their shots. Behind her, she could hear some pushing as the two men tried to get through, but she had a feeling there were others around who shared her desire to protect their injured jockey.

As the ambulance driver carefully slid the stretcher onto the plane, Adam took Jess to one side.

'She's got a broken arm and a punctured lung,' he said quietly. 'We need to get her to Mount Isa pretty fast. She needs a smooth flight, but don't go too high. We need to watch the pressure.'

'Got it,' she said. 'Will she be all right?'

Adam nodded.

While Adam turned to collect his bag from the ambulance, Jess quickly climbed aboard the plane. Carrie's stretcher was strapped in and ready for take-off. Jess's heart went out to the girl who was pale with pain and fear.

'You'll be fine,' Jess said, as she moved forward towards the pilot's seat. 'Adam is an amazing doctor and he'll take good care of you.'

'He said the same about you,' the girl whispered back.

Chapter Eighteen

'Are you sure you don't mind?' Ellen asked for the tenth time.

'Mind? Of course I don't mind. I'm looking forward to it.' The look on Jack's face made her believe he meant every word he said.

'Well, thanks. You saved my life.' That was a bit of an overstatement but he had certainly saved her some heartache. Her babysitter had set off this morning to the Birdsville Races – and only remembered to tell Ellen about it at the very last minute. Ellen hadn't been able to find another sitter, and that meant she was going to have to call Pete and tell him she wasn't coming to work. It wouldn't have been quite as bad as it might once have been. In just a few short weeks, Ellen had established herself firmly as a fixture on Friday and Saturday nights at the pub. Her cooking had proved so popular that she was no longer afraid of losing her job. But losing a night's wages was a big deal. Despite the job and her new home with Jess, money was still tight and every cent mattered. Then Jack had stepped in with an offer of babysitting.

'Of course, I will miss my favourite meal of the week.'

Ellen almost blushed as he smiled down at her, his brown eyes twinkling with humour. He was just being kind, she thought, just as he was being kind when he showed up at the pub every Friday night for dinner. And Saturdays, too. She'd overheard some of the regulars comment on his sudden liking for a pub he'd seldom patronised before. One or two had cast speculative looks her way, which she had ignored, just as she'd tried to ignore the little lift in her heart every time Jack walked into the bar.

'No you won't. Come with me.' She led the way through to the kitchen.

It was the same room that Jack had so carefully repaired just a short time ago – but it wasn't. There were wildflowers in a vase in the centre of the big wooden table. Bright curtains hung over the window and the door of the fridge was decorated with colourful finger paint pictures. In short, the kitchen had become what it was always meant to be – the warm centre of a home. And right now, it smelled great.

'Beef bourguignon?' Jack asked

'Yes. It's in the oven. And this time I've been able to make it with all the proper ingredients.'

Jack shook his head. 'I don't know. It would have to be pretty fine to top that first one you made. I'll never forget how good that tasted.'

Ellen would never forget that first night at The Mineside either; but it wasn't the beef she would remember. It was Jack, quietly slipping into the bar. Jack ordering that first meal. He'd helped her find her feet and then let her take those first few important steps on her own. Would she ever be able to tell him how much that meant to her? How much he ...

Ellen felt something contract deep inside her. She wasn't brave enough to look at Jack. Afraid he would see something in her face. Afraid that the light in her eyes would not be reflected in his. Afraid that it would.

For a few very long seconds there was absolute stillness in a small world she shared only with Jack. She could almost hear her heart beating. Could Jack hear it too?

'Jack!' The high-pitched yell and the sound of running feet forced Ellen to breathe again.

Harry dashed into the room, his face lighting up as he laid eyes on Jack.

'Hello, Harry,' Jack said, as the boy slid to a stop in front of him.

'Mum says you're going to stay with us tonight.'

'That's right I am. Where's your sister?'

'She's watching TV,' Harry said. 'Something with girls in it.' The boy's face wrinkled in disgust and Jack chuckled. It was a deep soft sound that curled around Ellen's heart.

'Well then, she'll miss out on our special treat,' Jack said.

'Did you bring them?' Harry's face shone even more brightly.

'I did. There's a box by the door. But you'll have to wait until your mum has left for work,' Jack said.

With an excited squeal, Harry vanished again. Ellen looked at Jack and raised a questioning eyebrow.

'Uncle Scrooge comics,' Jack explained.

Of course. Harry's fascination with the cartoon tattooed on Jack's arm had led to his discovery of the Disney comics. She'd been able to buy him a couple, but comics were few and far between all the way out here. And she didn't have the money to buy him more. Jack had been generous with his collection. It seemed a strange thing for a grown man to collect comics but watching Jack and Harry together, Ellen had come to be grateful for it. Jack managed to turn each comic into a learning experience for her son. Based on the Duck family adventures, Harry had discovered the Incas, and the Egyptian pyramids. He'd also learned about keeping promises and telling the truth.

Ellen knew that most of what her son was learning came not from the comics, but from the man who read them.

'He'll love that,' she said. 'It's really good of you to share them with him.'

'My pleasure.'

Ellen glanced down at her watch. 'It's getting late. I'd better go.'

'Here.' Jack was holding out the keys to his ute. 'Take my car.'

'No. Jack. You are already helping by looking after the kids. Thanks for the offer, but I can walk.'

'Yes, you can. But why don't you take the ute.' He lifted her hand, placed his keys into her palm and gently folded her fingers around them. His fingers were strong and rough with hard work, but oh, so gentle. These hands would never hurt her. She looked up into his face and she saw something there. Just a flash in the dark brown eyes that held hers. Just the promise of something so unbearably sweet that she felt a lump in her throat.

'Jaaaack …' The childish voice was dripping with impatience.

'You had better go to work … and I had better open that box of comics before Harry explodes.'

Relief and disappointment in equal measure washed over Ellen as he let go of her hand. 'If you need me …'

'I know where to find you. Don't worry; the kids are safe with me.'

Yes they were, Ellen thought as she walked out to the dusty white ute sitting in her driveway. The kids were safer with Jack than with their father. And not just the kids. She opened the door and slid into the leather seat, feeling where it had moulded itself to the shape of the man. The cab smelled of dust and engine oil and perhaps a hint of sweat.

It smelled of Jack. She slipped the key into the ignition and turned it. The engine leaped into life. How typical of Jack that even a beaten up old ute would purr like a Rolls-Royce in his care. She slipped the vehicle into gear and reversed out of the driveway. As she headed towards the pub, it occurred to her that Jack hadn't given her any instructions about driving his car. He hadn't warned her not to leave the lights on. Or forget the handbrake. He had simply assumed she knew what she was doing. Why must some men always assume the opposite?

When Ellen entered the pub, she was greeted with enthusiasm by the patrons already seated at the bar, quite a few of whom she now knew by name. She fended off queries about what was on that night's menu and made her way through to the kitchen. As she walked through the door, it struck her that this kitchen, just like the one in her new home, was a different place to that of a few weeks ago. Regular cleaning had given the wooden surfaces a dull sheen. Behind the gleaming steel doors, the cold room was overflowing with food. And not just steak and potatoes. Since that first unexpected beef bourguignon, the patrons at the pub had been subjected to an ever-changing menu, featuring items like quiche and couscous and, heaven forbid – spinach. Even a salad or two had slipped onto the menu. Every single dish had vanished amid much acclaim. She still served steak and potatoes – but these days, it usually came with a brandy mushroom sauce rather than tomato ketchup. She wondered what tonight's crowd would think about her prawn risotto. The prawns were frozen of course ... but it still should work out all right. She reached for the packet of rice.

The risotto was half done when a voice interrupted her in her work.

'If you keep that up, I'll have to give you a second job.'

'Keep what up?' she asked Pete.

'That singing.'

Ellen blinked in surprise. She hadn't even realised she was singing.

'You've got such a pretty voice. And you are ... well. I mean ... You could ...' His words trailed off.

Ellen busied herself over her pots, wanting to spare her boss further embarrassment. If she turned around, she knew his face would be flushed as he stammered out the words. She had glimpsed him earlier in the evening, wearing what was obviously a new shirt. She could still see the creases from the packaging. It was the second new shirt he'd worn in the past fortnight. His hair was freshly cut too – and washed. Ellen had a feeling she knew why.

'Thanks – but no thanks,' she said. 'I am more than happy with my pots and pans.'

'Sure. Sure. And you are doing a great job. Really. I'm so glad you came here.'

She had to say something. Slowly Ellen turned around. Pete hovered near the door, as if ready to flee.

'I'm glad I did too, Pete,' Ellen said gently. 'I enjoy my job – now go away so I can get on with it.' She smiled to take any sting out of the words.

'Okay.' He was gone.

Ellen felt a wash of relief. She hoped Pete would understand what she really meant was 'no thanks'. 'Please,' she whispered under her breath. Not only did she need this job – she was also starting to enjoy it. She didn't have a lot of experience with working. She had lived with her parents right up until her marriage, helping her father in his small corner store. That hadn't been like a real job at all. When Harry and then Bethany had come along, she'd been more than happy to be a stay at home mum. Until it all went so terribly wrong. But there was much to be said about working to support her kids herself. She liked the feeling of independence. For the first time in many years, she felt as if she had some control over her life. That was such a good feeling.

Ellen was singing again as she carried the last of her risotto into the bar later in the evening. The dish had been a resounding success and she was wondering if perhaps a curry might be a good idea. At the end of the bar, a man wearing a police uniform was waiting for his dinner.

'That looks great. Thanks,' he said, as she placed the steaming plate in front of him.

'Enjoy,' she said.

'This place has changed a bit,' the policeman said, as she turned to go. 'I guess that's your doing.'

Ellen stopped. 'I don't understand.'

'I used to get called down here fairly often on Friday and Saturday night,' he said. 'When things got a bit rough. Hasn't happened for a while.'

'Well, surely that's a good thing,' Ellen said.

'I'm not complaining.' The officer took a mouthful of the food. 'And I'm not complaining about this either.'

Ellen flashed him a quick smile and headed back to the kitchen. She wasn't sure if the policeman was right. Her presence and her food might have had some effect on the pub's patrons, but she was pretty sure that Jack's presence at his corner table was also a factor. His size and his willingness to step in when someone looked like they were spoiling for a fight had to count for something. She glanced over at the table she had come to think of as his. It was empty. Despite being grateful that he was sitting with her kids, Ellen missed seeing him there. Despite the compliments for her cooking and the success of her new recipe, the evening lacked something.

It was a little later than usual when she left that evening. Pete had lingered to chat to her, getting underfoot as she cleaned the kitchen. He had even offered to help, an offer she had declined with thanks. It didn't take much to figure out that he'd chosen tonight to linger with her – because Jack wasn't waiting outside. Anxious to avoid any awkward moments, Ellen waited until Pete was in the bar sorting glasses before calling her goodbyes and quickly slipping out the back door to where Jack's ute was parked. As she drove off, she caught a glimpse of Pete watching from the lighted window. She hoped he would recognise the ute. She didn't want any awkwardness at work. And she certainly didn't want to get involved with her boss. The easiest way to discourage him was to let him think that she and Jack were …

But they weren't.

Not that she wanted too, of course. She had sworn off men. For life. If her past relationship was anything to go by, she only attracted losers anyway. And Jack was not a loser. Far from it, she thought as she drove home through the dark and empty streets. Jack was anything but a loser. Jack was – well pretty amazing.

She just loved Jack's face. It wasn't handsome, not in the traditional sense, but it said everything about him. It said that he was strong and gentle. It lit up when he was with her kids. He was so good with them. She was beginning to believe that he really did care for Harry and Bethany.

And what about her?

Jack was her friend. There was no doubting that. He'd helped her find a place to live. He'd been there to watch over her that first night in The Mineside. But at the same time, he hadn't taken charge of her life. He was allowing her to be the person she wanted to be. She wasn't that person yet, but she was getting closer.

And when she was that person – what then? What would Jack be to her then? What did she want him to be? The answer to that question lay in the slow soft ache deep inside her body and her soul.

Ellen turned off the road into the driveway that led to the house behind the hospital. That led to her home. She could see the glow of light in the window. Ellen was careful not to slam the door as she got out of the ute. She didn't want to risk waking the kids. She tripped lightly up the stairs, happier than she had been for a long, long time. Too long.

She walked into the living room, and stopped dead in her tracks. Jack was asleep on the big sofa, his feet, clad only in socks, were propped up on the coffee table. Snuggled up against him and even more soundly asleep was her son. Harry's hand rested on a colourful comic that was lying in Jack's lap. Ellen couldn't stop herself. Tears welled up in her eyes. This was all she had ever wanted. Arms stronger than hers to keep her children safe from harm. Hands to hold – not to hurt. If only she had met Jack a long time ago. Things might have been different. But it was too late now. Too late for her. Wasn't it?

Jack opened his eyes and smiled at her, a long slow smile.

'Hello,' he whispered.

'Hello yourself,' she whispered right back.

Jack raised one hand and laid it gently on Harry's hair. 'I did put him to bed when you told me to. Honestly. But he wouldn't go to sleep. I thought if I read to him for a while that might do the job.'

'Well, it worked. On both of you, it seems.'

'I guess so.'

'I'll just put down my things and I can put him to bed.'

'Let me.' With effortless strength and great gentleness, Jack rose to his feet, cradling the sleeping boy in his arms. He padded softly into the kids' room. Bethany was curled tightly around her dolly, sound asleep and as beautiful a sight as any mother had ever seen. Ellen waited until Jack had laid Harry in his bed, then she carefully pulled the covers up. She brushed her son's hair back from his face, and gently kissed his soft forehead. Jack watched from the doorway.

She took a step back and for a few moments they both just stood there, watching the children sleep. It was almost, Ellen thought, as if they were a family. As if she and Jack were like any other couple, putting their children to bed. She was very aware of Jack standing so close to her. She could hear him breathing. She could almost feel his warmth. If he was to just reach out his hand, he could touch her skin. If he lowered his head, his lips would touch the skin of her throat. If they were really a family, he would take her in his arms and they …

'They are great kids,' Jack said. 'Harry is so good to his sister. They didn't even fight over the comics. He was perfectly happy to share with her.'

'He's always been good with her. He even tried to protect her …' Ellen's words stuck in her throat.

'Protect her from what?' Jack's voice was still a gentle whisper.

How she wanted to tell him. It would be so easy. To let go of the terrible secrets she'd held inside for so long. If she told him now, she wouldn't see his face. Wouldn't see the disgust on it. Or the pity. But it would be there when she finally looked him in the eyes.

'From ... the scary dog who lived in our street,' Ellen lied, as her dream came crashing down around her. She turned, forcing Jack to step back out of the doorway and led the way to the kitchen. Her mind was racing almost as fast as her heart. What had she been thinking? She and Jack would never be a family. She was older than him in more than years. He deserved someone better than her. If he knew the truth, he would never feel about her the way she wanted him to. And with a lie between them, she was lucky to have him as a friend.

'Thanks for looking after them,' she said. 'I would offer you coffee or something, but it was a really long night, and I'm tired. I think I need to go to bed.'

'Of course.' Jack's brow creased in a little frown. 'I understand. I'll drop by tomorrow afternoon and see if you need me again.'

She wanted to say no. She wanted to tell him to stay away. But she couldn't. Her babysitter was spending the whole weekend in Birdsville. She needed Jack. But just to help with the kids. She wasn't going to let herself fall into the trap of believing in anything more. 'Thanks Jack. Goodnight,' she said, as she opened the front door. She closed it quickly behind him. She didn't want him to see her tears.

Chapter Nineteen

Adam loved flying with Jess. He'd flown many times before with a variety of other pilots. Good pilots, all of them. He'd seen the splendour of the outback in all its moods. He'd watched the vast red plains roll away beneath him, and marvelled at the beauty of it. But it was all fresh and new now he was seeing it with Jess at his side. Everything was better with Jess at his side. There were times when he almost forgot ... everything.

He loved to watch her hands. Her long slim fingers gripped the controls firmly, but with a gentleness that was almost a caress. Yet her movements were so precise ... a minor adjustment here or there as the plane flew. Her touch was sure. They could have been the hands of a surgeon, but at the same time they were uniquely Jessica's hands. She wore no rings. Had no shadow of a line to indicate she had ever worn a ring – on either hand. Some small part of Adam was absurdly pleased about that. He had never seen her with painted nails. And he really didn't want to. No long fake nails or brilliant red nail polish could make Jess's strong, yet gentle, hands any more beautiful than they were.

She was never still when she flew. Her eyes were constantly moving across the incomprehensible – at least to him – array of dials and glowing displays in front of her. When she wasn't checking her instruments, she was looking out at the sky, reading the weather patterns or watching the endless earth passing beneath them. Occasionally she would look across at him. Her eyes had a special sort of a shine when she was flying. He could sense that she was happy. He liked to think part of her happiness was because he was there to share it with her – just the two of them soaring across that vast brilliant blue arc.

Sometimes when she reached for a map, or to check something, her hand would brush against his shirt sleeve. Or if she twisted to look down at something passing beneath them, her shoulder might brush his in the tight confines of the cabin. Just the faintest touch. Accidental and meaningless, but Adam felt it as acutely as he felt the sun on his face or the cool caress of icy water. He didn't flinch away from her, as he did most others, even though her every touch brought him the pain of longing for something that could never be. Part of him wished that just once she might reach out to touch him because she wanted to. But that would never happen now. She'd seen the scars on his body. What woman would ever want to touch him?

But they talked. How they talked. They talked about books and movies and music. They talked politics and religion. They talked about places they had been or dreamed of going. They talked about people. Ellen and Jack. Sister Luke and Adam's patients. They talked about anyone and anything except themselves. They never talked about the past ... or the future. They were content to live in the now.

And this now was their return to Birdsville after leaving the injured jockey in safe hands at the Mount Isa hospital.

'So what do you think so far?' Adam asked, as Jess began their descent into Birdsville.

'I've never seen anything quite like this,' she said, with a nod to the activity below them. 'It's really something.'

'It is,' he agreed, 'but I was thinking in more general terms. Are you happy here?'

The question surprised him as much as it obviously surprised her.

'Yes.' She spoke without the slightest hesitation.

'I'm glad. I'd hate to lose you.' He spoke the words without thinking, realising as he did that they were true. He wanted her to stay. Maybe even needed her to stay. And it wasn't just about flying the air ambulance.

'I was worried a bit at first,' Jess continued in a teasing tone. 'You see there was this madman of a doctor who almost decapitated himself running under a spinning propeller.'

Jess turned to look at him. Her eyes were shining – at him.

'But despite his failings,' she said with the hint of a grin, 'especially in the area of accommodation, he turned out all right.'

Adam felt a queer tightness in his chest. For once in his life, he didn't have a ready answer, but luckily Jess didn't seem to expect one. She reached for her radio and with a call to any other pilots in the area; she turned for her final run. Adam was spared conversation as Jess brought the plane to a standstill in front of the hangar with her customary ease.

'I guess I had better check in at the clinic,' he said reluctantly, unwilling to give up the easy companionship just yet.

'I'll get refuelled, just in case.'

'And I want to call Sister Luke at the Creek and make sure everything is all right there,' Adam said. He hesitated, unused to sharing his thoughts. But this was Jess. 'I am a bit worried about her. She seems ... tired, I guess.'

'I know,' Jess agreed. 'She didn't look well after that trip back east. I thought she was just tired from the journey, but she still isn't back to her old self.'

'I'll try to talk her into a check-up when we get back,' Adam said. 'But it won't be easy. She can be stubborn at times.'

'Look who's talking,' Jess teased.

Adam set out to walk to the town's medical centre, wishing he'd had the courage to stay. The courage to give voice to the tiny seed of hope that was beginning to take root in his heart.

This flight should have put his relationship with Jess firmly back where it had been. The need to help the injured woman had initially overcome any awkwardness he felt about Jess seeing his scars. Jess had said nothing, but it was as if something between them had changed. Not in their professional life, but on a personal level. Could it be that there was a chance for something between them? He knew that Jess was carrying her own burdens. Sometimes, when she thought she was alone, shadows crossed her face. Shadows put there by whatever secret she hugged so close to her. But Coorah Creek had a special sort of magic. It had worked on him when he flew into town five years ago, and now it seemed to be working on Jess, too. Those shadows came less often. If that magic could make her forget her emotional scars, maybe it could make her blind to his physical scars as well …

Of course, beyond those scars was the lie he told the world. The lie he had lived with all his life and would carry to his grave. He'd never told Sister Luke the truth – yet she had remained his mentor and his best friend. Could he tell Jess the lie and still have a relationship with her, too? Or was she the one person he could tell the truth? Was he even capable of speaking the words, after so many years?

'Hey, Doc!'

Adam was so lost in his thoughts; he hadn't seen the man approach until he spoke. Adam shifted his focus from a hoped-for future to the present, and a man who seemed vaguely familiar.

'Yes?'

'I was just wondering about the accident and the mercy flight ...' As the man stopped in front of him, Adam saw the camera dangling around his neck and realised where he had seen him before.

'You're a reporter,' he said. 'I saw you taking photographs.'

'That's right. John Hewitt. I'm a local stringer for the east coast papers.' The man held out his hand.

Adam took it reluctantly. 'John, you need to be a bit more careful about getting in the way when a medical team is working,' he said in a measured tone.

'Yeah. Sorry about that. I wanted to be sure I got the story. It went national, you know.'

Adam heard the pride in Hewitt's voice. He tried to tell himself that the reporter was just doing his job when he photographed the injured girl yesterday. But that didn't work. Carrie Bryant was his patient and his desire to protect and heal her hadn't stopped when he settled her in the Mount Isa hospital yesterday.

'So, I was wondering,' the reporter said, 'about doing a story on the air ambulance. I was surprised to see your pilot was a woman. What was her name again?'

'Jessica,' Adam said.

'Yes, that's right, Jessica Pearson.'

'Yes. By the way, the injured jockey is going to be fine, in case you were wondering.' Adam was liking this man less and less by the minute. He particularly didn't like the sudden light that had come to the man's eyes when he spoke about Jess.

'What? Oh, yes. Great. Good news. Now, about this story. I was hoping I could interview Jess ...'

Adam's uncertainty was rapidly turning into active dislike.

'I don't know. I think if you want to do a story, you should really go to the Royal Flying Doctor Service. They do such good work. We work for a private company and are just on loan for the races. So we probably would prefer not to do any interviews.'

Adam knew he shouldn't be speaking for Jess, but his every instinct told him she wouldn't want to be involved with the reporter. The desire to protect her was very strong.

'Well, yes of course.' Hewitt beamed at him in an ingratiating fashion. 'But it's the angle of a woman pilot that I think my readers would really like. Where can I find her?'

Adam felt his hackles rise. 'I really can't say. I have to go now.' He stalked off, very aware of Hewitt's eyes on his back as he did. The next time he saw Jess, he would warn her. Just in case the man was persistent.

After refuelling and locking her plane, Jess set off to walk back into the centre of the town. She hadn't walked very far, when a man approached her. It was as if he had been lying in wait for her. She recognised him instantly.

'Jessica. Can I talk to you for a minute?'

Jess's steps faltered and she almost stumbled. He knew her name! Then she caught herself. Any one of more than a dozen people could have told him the name of the air ambulance pilot. It meant nothing, but she still wanted to get away from the reporter.

'Sorry, I have to get back and report in,' she said

walking on. It was a lie, but she didn't feel so much as a blink of guilt. This was the reporter who had been pushing his way forward to photograph the injured jockey yesterday. Her dislike for the media had hit new heights when he did that.

'I only want a minute of your time. I just want to get my facts right before I send my story in.' He moved as if to block her path.

'I can't tell you anything about the patient or the flight, sorry.' She brushed past him.

'It isn't the mercy flight I want to talk about, Jess. It's the drug running.'

Jess stopped in her tracks. It wasn't just her name – he knew about her past! The memories and the fear rushed back at her like a slap in the face. She had become so involved in her new life, in her job and in Adam's fight to save a life; she had forgotten to protect herself. And now ...

'I think you are mistaking me for someone else.' Even as she spoke the words, Jess had no hope that the reporter would simply go away.

'I don't think so. You're Jessica Pearson. You were the pilot flying heroin into the country on a private jet. You avoided prosecution by testifying against your lover. Now you're flying an air ambulance. That's quite a story.'

'No. It's not.' Jess fought to keep her voice steady against the panic rising inside her. 'It's all history. No one is interested in it anymore.'

The reporter was smiling at her. It was the kind of smile she would expect to see on the face of a snake, just before it devoured a petrified mouse. 'What did the good doctor say when you told him his new pilot was a drug dealer?'

Adam! Jess's heart contracted. Oh, no ... he hadn't ... 'You talked to Adam?'

'Only briefly, I was hoping …' the reporter's voice trailed off. His eyes narrowed. 'He doesn't know.' He said slowly.

Jess struggled to take the next breath as fear settled icy cold around her heart.

'You haven't told him.' There was something very like joy in the reporter's voice. 'You lied to the air ambulance. Considering your history, I guess that's not surprising.'

He was goading her, trying to make her lose control and say or do something that would add to his story. Jess was quivering with anger, and fear, and the effort to say nothing. She simply shook her head and forced her way past the man.

'I'm not going to give up. There's a story here and I'm going to get it.'

Jess tried to block her ears to the triumph in his voice as he shouted at her retreating back.

Please, no. This can't be happening. It can't. Please.

The refrain echoed through Jess's head as she walked. She didn't see the people or the buildings around her. She didn't hear the distant roar from the racetrack, or the music from the campground stage or the excited voices all around her. All she could hear was a woman's voice. *You killed my son.*

Adam was going to find out what she had done.

After the guilty verdict, the prosecutor has turned to where she was sitting in the public gallery. She could barely hear his voice over the uproar in the court.

Thank you. Without your evidence, he might have gone free.

She had done the right thing. But she was still the one at the controls of the plane that had brought the drugs into the country. Her plane. Her responsibility. That was how she saw it. Adam would see it that way too and that would be the end of something that had become very precious to her. He would never understand or forgive what she had done.

The second he found out she would lose him forever.

Even in the blackest times ... as the armed men stormed her plane, during police interrogation and even when walking into that prison cell, she had never been as scared as she was at the thought of Adam's reaction when he learned the truth.

'Hey, Doc, where's that gorgeous pilot of yours?'

'As far away from you as she can possibly get,' Adam tossed back with a smile he didn't feel. Around him the men at the bar erupted into gruff laughter. Unabashed, the barman handed Adam a beer, waving away his attempts to pay.

As Adam carried his first, and only, beer of the evening out onto the wide veranda that fronted the pub, he couldn't help but echo the barman's thoughts. Where was Jess? He hadn't seen her since they parted company at the airport. Had that reporter found her? And if so, what had happened? With every fibre of his being, he knew that the reporter was bad news. He didn't know why ... or what the man was going to do. He just knew he was a threat. A threat to Jess.

He wasn't going to let that man hurt her. The races were nearly over. Just one more day. Then they'd be on their way back to Coorah Creek. Away from whatever threat the reporter posed.

Adam thumped his clenched fist onto the veranda rail.

This weekend should have been memorable for so many good reasons. Instead, it had been a disaster from start to finish, and it was mostly his own fault. Starting with the shared room. The image of Jessica's golden body curled so seductively on the bed flashed to the forefront of his brain. That image would never leave him. Just as he imagined the horror of his scarred back would never leave her.

Strange that they should share the very things that kept them apart.

As he leaned against the veranda post, his drink forgotten in his hand, Adam let his eyes wander towards the western sky. The sun was sinking in what was going to be another spectacular outback sunset. In all his years out here, he'd never tired of those moments when the sun hovered on the edge of the world. Those sunsets always lifted his spirits – it was part of the magic of this hot dry and dusty plain. He dragged his eyes from the sky back to the crowd of racegoers milling around the pub. In couples and in groups, they were making the most of the last night of the races. A young couple almost waltzed past, dancing to their own music, holding hands and sharing the promise of the night ahead.

How he would love to do that with Jess.

And … why couldn't he? He shook his head, but the thought didn't go away. Jess had seen the worst of him. She had seen the ruin of his body. The worst moment was past. They both still kept secrets. Things he didn't know about her. Things she could never know about him. But did that make it impossible?

And if something was possible. What better place than here? A place with its own magic. As if to answer him, the crowd moved and he saw Jess walking towards him, her face dark in thought. She looked up and saw him, and began to smile. That smile was enough.

Adam turned and stuck his head back into the bar.

'Can I borrow your car?' he said to the barman. The man shrugged and tossed him a set of keys. Adam turned and quickly intercepted Jess.

'Come on. I've got something to show you.'

Jess hesitated. 'Aren't you on call or something?'

'No. I've got a break. Come on, we haven't much time. The sun is almost gone.'

The barman's car was a new four-wheel drive ute, with spotlights attached to the roof and a fresh layer of dust all over it. Adam slid behind the wheel and as soon as Jess was beside him, he gunned the engine. The vehicle shot forward, bouncing across the rough ground. There was no road. He didn't need one.

'Where are we going?'

'Just you wait and see.'

Adam drove for about ten minutes. There were no hills around Birdsville, but that didn't really matter. He just needed to go far enough that the sounds of the party were lost. And the lights were far, far away.

He slid the vehicle to a stop and climbed out. He swung into the flat tray of the ute and sat back against the roof. With a shrug, Jess swung herself up beside him.

'Watch,' was all he said.

They were facing west where the sun was sinking into the horizon. The world seemed to hold its breath as the golden orb dropped slowly lower, changing as it did to a red molten ball. Invisible wisps of cloud flared orange and yellow, turning to purple as the sun dropped lower.

Adam could hear his own heart beating. Could Jess hear it too?

The sun touched the dark line of the earth, sending bright yellow flares to all the corners of the compass.

Then, suddenly, it was gone. The sky darkened to a deep velvet blue as the first stars appeared. Bright pinpoints of light. A few, then more and more until the whole sky seemed to glow.

Beside him, Jess let out a long deep sigh. He wanted so much to reach out and take her hand. That was still a step too far for him. But the desire to touch her. To feel her touch him. That was a start.

Tomorrow the great exodus would begin. The thousands would desert Birdsville, heading back to their homes and lives. He and Jess would return to Coorah Creek. That town was a very special place. He'd made his home there. Jess too seemed content. Maybe Coorah Creek could continue to work some more magic in their future.

He had a long way to go to exorcise his demons, but for the first time he believed he could do it. For Jess.

Chapter Twenty

The nightmare was different this time.

You killed my son! The woman outside the courtroom ... her face contorted with anger and grief. It's your fault!

Adam, his eyes questioning hers. His handsome face cold and distant. Why Jess? Why did you do it?

I didn't know, Jess said in her dream. I didn't know he'd put drugs on the plane.

How could you not know? It was your plane. Your responsibility. You had to know. It is your fault. And Adam turned away – a look of disgust on his face ...

'I didn't know ...' Jess sat bolt upright in her bed, her breath coming in short ragged gasps.

The room was dark and she was alone. She glanced at the clock. Dawn was not all that far away.

Jess slipped out of bed and crossed to the window. Across the moonlit expanse of dried grass, the Coorah Creek hospital was clearly visible, a dark shape against the star-studded sky. There was a light in one window. Adam was awake too. Had he been awake all night, or did his own nightmares wake him in the early hours? Or was it loneliness that robbed him of his rest?

Had he been lonely that last night in Birdsville? Was that why he had taken her to share the sunset with him? When darkness fell, he had simply driven her back into town and returned to his shift at the medical centre. Without saying a single word. What was she supposed to read into that?

Of course, she'd been just as bad. She'd watched that

sunset, so very aware of the man sitting next to her. And she had also said exactly nothing. They were two of a kind, she and Adam. Neither of them brave enough to take the first step towards ... whatever it was they were both searching for.

Jess was so glad to be back in Coorah Creek, where troubling moments of intimacy could be avoided.

The light in the hospital window went out. In her mind, she pictured Adam going to bed. Tonight, instead of sharing a room with her, he'd be sleeping alone. Would he miss her as she had missed him? Missed the sound of his breathing. Missed knowing he was close. Missed the longing that she felt.

She thought for the thousandth time about the scars on his back. Everyone had their secrets. Adam had been an innocent victim. He had a secret – but he had no guilt. Her burden of guilt was almost overwhelming.

Feeling lonely now that the light was gone, and just a little claustrophobic, Jess left her bedroom and walked quietly through the house. Ellen and the kids were sleeping, and she didn't want to wake them. She softly opened the front door and crossed the wide veranda to sit on the top of the steps leading to the front yard.

The night was still. Jess took a deep breath of the warm air. She could smell the dust. The trees. The fading heat from yesterday bringing the promise of another hot day tomorrow. She could taste and smell everything about the outback that had seemed so strange to her the day she arrived. Now these things, this place and most of all these people were so much a part of her life that she wondered how she would live without them. The thought she might have to do that was almost enough to break her heart.

But she might, because her past had found her.

She heard soft footsteps and a moment later Ellen sat down beside her. For a few minutes the two sat in silence.

'I would have thought that after the weekend, you'd be exhausted and sleeping like a baby,' Ellen said.

'So did I,' Jess said bitterly. 'But I've got something on my mind, I guess. What about you?'

'I must have something on my mind, too.'

They sat in silence for a few more minutes, listening to the sounds of the night.

'Jack,' Jess said. It wasn't a question.

'Adam,' Ellen countered.

'You first,' Jess said. It hadn't escaped her notice that Ellen and Jack were becoming ... close. She was glad for her friends. And right now, a little happy ever after for Ellen might just cheer her up a bit.

'Jack is ... wonderful.' Ellen's words were almost a whisper. 'He's so good with the kids.'

'Yes he is,' Jess agreed.

'Ever since Harry saw that tattoo on his arm, he's become fascinated by the duck comics. Jack reads to him all the time. But it's not just the stories ... he talks to him. Teaches him.'

'He's a good role model for Harry.'

Beside her, Jess felt rather than heard Ellen catch her breath. There was a few seconds silence before Ellen continued, in a voice that quivered.

'Harry hasn't had much of a father figure. His own father ...' Ellen stopped speaking and Jess could feel her fear. We all have our demons, Jess thought. Every one of us.

'My husband has a temper.' Ellen's words came out in a rush.

'He hit you?' Jess was horrified.

'Yes.' There was a whole world of pain and fear and guilt in just that one word.

'Oh, Ellen.'

'He seemed so wonderful when we met. I didn't have much experience with men. I was still living at home with my parents. He seemed kind and loving. Our wedding was the happiest day of my life.'

'What happened?'

'Everything was fine at first. We were happy when I became pregnant with Harry. But after he was born, we started fighting. My husband said I was neglecting him because of the baby.' Ellen's voice broke. She paused for a few moments before continuing. 'I tried to make it work. I really did. Everything seemed better for a while, then I fell pregnant with Bethany. He said he didn't want another baby. That it was all my fault.'

'It wasn't your fault.'

'I know. I think I knew then that I had made a terrible mistake in my marriage. But what could I do? He started going out drinking. Sometimes he'd come home drunk and angry. He never hit me when I was pregnant though. He pushed me, maybe, a couple of times. The hitting didn't start until after Bethany was born.'

'He had no right to hit you,' Jess said quietly.

'I know. But with the baby crying all the time. He wasn't getting any sleep. And I was so busy with the kids …'

'That doesn't excuse him.'

'When Harry saw his father hit me, he tried to step in. You should have seen him. So small and so brave. And I was terrified that he'd be next. So I had to leave. I waited until my husband was going to be away for a couple of days on business, then I took what we could carry and came as far away as I could get. I felt like a coward. Running away. But I couldn't go to my parents. He would have followed me. I had to come somewhere he'd never find me.'

Jess reached out to squeeze her friend's hand. 'I'm so sorry.'

'At least I got them away.'

'At some point, you might have to deal with him,' Jess said hesitantly. She knew from bitter experience that avoiding an issue does not make it go away.

'I know. But not right now. I needed … I needed to find me first. I needed to make sure the kids were safe. And I didn't want Harry to grow up thinking it was all right to hit a woman. I'm just so glad he's got Jack to show him how a real man behaves. He's strong, but he's gentle too. Bethany adores him.'

'And what about you, Ellen?'

In the darkness, Jess heard the quietest sound; a sound that could almost be a sob. She squeezed Ellen's hand tightly. 'Ellen?'

'He doesn't want me.'

'Why would you say that? You're a warm and wonderful person. You are a good mother. If you're worried that you are older than him, don't be. I've seen the way he looks at you. You're beautiful – and he thinks so too.'

'Jack would never want someone who … who would let a man do what my husband did. I'm … I'm not good enough.'

'Don't you say that!' Jess said with quiet vehemence. 'What he did was despicable. It wasn't your fault. You did nothing wrong.'

Ellen was silent.

'And don't sell Jack short,' Jess added. 'He's not the kind of man who would judge you. He's better than that.'

'I know.' Ellen's voice was so quiet Jess could barely hear her. 'And sometimes I imagine what it would feel like to ... well ... you know.'

Jess could almost feel the heat of Ellen's blush.

'Maybe he just needs a bit of encouragement.'

'Oh, I couldn't.'

'Yes, you could. But don't do anything you're not ready for. He's a pretty smart guy. He'll wait for you.'

The two of them sat in silence for a while, then came the words Jess had been dreading.

'So, what about you and Adam?'

What indeed? 'It's complicated.'

'Isn't everything?'

Ellen was right. Every person had their own issues. Things from the past that still haunted them. Scars inside ... and out.

'Adam is very driven. His work is so important to him. I sometimes don't think he sees past that.'

'He does, you know,' Ellen said. 'He sees you.'

'He sees ...' Jessica's voice faded.

'It's all right. You don't have to talk about it if you don't want to.'

Ellen sounded like a cross between her mother and her best friend. Here, in the safety of the home she'd made, wrapped in the comforting darkness, Jessica found she did want to tell Ellen.

'It's a long story. I chose the wrong man too. Brian was – oh – he was everything. Handsome. A self-made millionaire. He hired me to fly his private jet and we fell in love. It was a dream for me. The gifts he gave me. The beautiful clothes. The five star hotels. We flew everywhere together – but mostly into Asia where he had business.'

'What sort of business?'

'I was a fool, and too blinded by Brian to ask. He said he was an importer. What I didn't realise ...' Jess stopped. Once the words were out, there was no going back. 'I didn't realise that he was importing drugs.'

'Oh!'

Jess felt Ellen stiffen beside her. She didn't need the sharp intake of breath to tell her that her friend was shocked.

'I didn't know. Looking back there were signs that maybe should have told me something was wrong. Maybe I was too busy being in love. I just didn't see what was happening.' It was important that Ellen understand.

'Of course you didn't,' the support was immediate. 'How did you find out?'

'I found the drugs on the plane. I went to the authorities. They made me ... they made me pretend that everything was all right.' A simple phrase that went no way to describing that last terrible day and night. Watching Brian, trying to smile at him. She'd pleaded a headache and slept in the spare room of their hotel suite. The mere thought of sleeping beside him on that last night ... of him touching her ... Even now she felt the nausea. 'They set up a sting. When we flew back to Sydney, the federal police were waiting. They boarded the plane. Found the drugs and arrested Brian. I was arrested too. I spent a few days in custody, but they didn't charge me. I gave evidence against him at the trial.'

'That must have been hard.'

'It was horrible. Sitting in that courtroom. With Brian so close. He'd look at me and smile. That same smile I fell in love with.'

'You did the right thing.'

'I know. And I knew it wouldn't be easy. The newspaper headlines were so vile. They claimed I was just as guilty as Brian. That I had escaped prosecution by giving evidence. That just wasn't true.'

'Jess, you did nothing wrong. You have nothing to be ashamed of.'

Jess wanted to believe her, but deep down, that cold rock of guilt remained untouched.

'My parents took me in. They were so supportive. Then the media found them. They were prisoners in their own home. That's why I had to leave. I had to give them their lives back.'

Jess's voice trailed off. Talking about the past was so very hard. Talking about the future was too. 'If Adam knew ...'

'He would understand.'

'But kids died taking the drugs I helped bring into the country,' Jess cried. 'Adam is a doctor. Look how he fights for his patients. He will never forgive that.'

'Now, don't you sell Adam short,' Ellen said firmly. 'He's a pretty smart guy too. You are a good person, Jess Pearson. He knows that. And besides,' Ellen said with a wide grin, 'he obviously fancies you like crazy. I've seen the way he looks at you too, especially in those tight jeans. Adam is a man after all.'

Jess grinned back, but her heart wasn't in it. She appreciated Ellen's attempt to lighten her mood, but Ellen couldn't know that she had unwittingly raised another obstacle.

How could any physical relationship exist with a man who did not like to be touched? By anyone. Now she knew about his past, she could understand Adam's reasons for flinching away from her. There was so much more to Adam than his damaged body. She could see past that to the man he really was. She could accept the scars, perhaps more easily than Adam did. But that wasn't enough. The flames that had burned his body had also left other scars. Jess knew those were the ones Adam would find hardest to overcome.

And she couldn't talk to Ellen about this. It was not her secret to share.

She was excused any further need to explain by the sudden arrival of both the sunrise and Harry, at pretty much the same moment. Ellen went to put her son back to bed, but Jess knew there was no more sleep for her. She was too restless. There was only one thing to do – the thing that always helped.

Jess was inside her plane, cleaning the windscreen, when she saw movement outside. In her hangar. It was only just past eight o'clock – far too early for most people to be around. Maybe she was needed. Jess backed out of the cockpit and turned towards the stairs, only to be startled by flashes of blinding light and the click and whirr of a camera.

'What the …?'

'Hello, Jessica. John Hewitt. Remember me?'

It was the reporter from the races. He hadn't given up.

'Get off my plane.'

'Now, Jessica. I don't want this to be unfriendly.'

'I said get off my plane.'

Holding a hand up as if to ward off her anger, the reporter backed down the stairs. But he didn't go far. Jessica had no choice. She walked down the stairs to confront him.

'I told you. I don't want to talk to you.'

'Have you told the doc yet?' Hewitt asked, his voice eager.

'This is none of your business. Just leave me alone.' Jess bit back the word please. This man did not deserve the courtesy.

'You haven't, have you?' The reporter's glee was obvious. 'I can't wait to break the news to him.'

'You wouldn't ...' But even as she spoke, Jess knew that he would.

'I'll do you a deal, Jessica.' The man's voice was slimy. 'If you give me an interview, I won't talk to the doc. If not, I'll just have to interview him.'

Jessica went cold all over. 'You wouldn't.'

'Yes, I would. I'd have to. I need to interview someone for this story. If not you ...' Hewitt let the threat hang.

'Just get out of my hangar.' Jess's hands were starting to shake. She didn't know how much longer she was going to be able to control her anger ... or her fear.

'All right. I'll tell you what. I'm staying at the pub. I'll wait there until four o'clock – then I'm going looking for the doc. It's your choice, Jess.'

Jess watched him walk away, realising that she had no choice. Whatever she did, Adam was going to find out about her past. And when he did ...

A sudden pain wracked her as if someone had driven a spear through her heart. Her legs felt weak and she grabbed the wing of the plane to steady herself.

Adam.

The thought of losing him was more than she could bear. The thought of a life without seeing him. Without hearing him laugh. That wasn't any sort of life at all. She didn't care about the scars on his body. She didn't care about the ghosts that so obviously haunted him.

The realisation hit her like a physical blow.

She was in love with Adam.

What she felt was so different to her time with Brian. That had been all about fancy hotels and fine living. They made such a beautiful couple. She might have thought she loved Brian – but she hadn't. She had simply been dazzled by him.

Adam wasn't dazzling. He wasn't rich. He took her to outback pubs, not five star hotels. But he was ten times the man Brian could ever dream of being. He was caring and honest. He was gentle, but at the same time he was the strongest man she had ever known. When he looked at her with those deep brown eyes, it was as if the sun shone more brightly. He made her feel more alive than she had ever felt in her life.

And she loved him.

They had never kissed. Never made love. Never even touched. All that was still ahead of them, but Jess knew she needed him as much as she needed to breathe. She wanted him more than anything else on earth.

And she was about to lose him.

Adam would never forgive someone who harmed another human being. And if he heard that journalist's version of events, that's what he would think Jess had done. The journalist would paint Jess as some sort of criminal. As part of a drug ring, preying on the young and those who Adam would seek to help. That's not who she was. Having the rest of the world believe that was hard enough. If Adam believed it, she would be destroyed.

If she had any hope that he would understand, he had to hear it from her. Adam would believe her if she told him the truth – the whole truth. He had to!

Quickly, she locked the plane and walked to her car.

She had to go now, before her courage failed her. It took just a few minutes to drive to the hospital. Jess almost ran inside and headed for Adam's office.

'Adam …' She pushed the door open.

'He's not here,' said Sister Luke, who was sitting at the desk, patient files spread in front of her. 'What is it, Jess?'

'I need to talk to Adam. Right away,' Jess said.

'He and Jack are on their way to the national park,' replied Sister Luke. 'Someone is trapped underground, in one of the caves.'

Chapter Twenty-One

'I wouldn't go in there.'

'Claustrophobic, Doc?' Jack raised a questioning eyebrow.

'Look at it,' Adam said. 'There's no way of knowing what's down there.'

The cave was set low in the side of a tall, red sandstone cliff. The opening was only shoulder high, and immediately inside the opening, the rock-strewn floor of the cave sloped sharply downwards. The roof also sloped down, giving the impression that the cave was only a few metres deep. But that was a misconception. According to the park ranger, this opening led to a cave system that stretched a great distance inside the cliff ... with dozens of caves and tunnels and steep shafts.

'It's not that different to when I was working at the mine,' Jack said.

'Yes it is,' Adam declared. 'There aren't any beams holding up the roof. No air shafts either. And a person could get lost down there.'

'Well, let's just hope they didn't,' said a voice behind them, accompanied by the clank of metal.

Park Ranger Dan Mitchell was laden with ropes and buckles and other paraphernalia that Adam couldn't even begin to guess at. He was also carrying hard hats with lights built into them. The ranger was a tall, lean man who gave the impression of great strength. His skin was tanned dark by the sun, and lined. Adam guessed he was probably younger than he appeared. He looked the sort of person who would be very good at pretty much everything.

'We're going to need ropes to get down into the main cave,' Dan said.

'How did those kids get down there?' Adam asked.

'It's really only a moderately difficult cave – and they had experience. But there was a problem with their gear. They both fell, but the girl is trapped down a cleft in the rock. The boyfriend couldn't get her out. He came for help.'

'How badly hurt is she?' Adam wanted to know.

'He said she was conscious. She's hurt her arm. It may be broken.'

'Then you are going to need me down there,' Adam said. The mere thought almost made him shake. He hated to be trapped in enclosed spaces. But there was someone down there who needed him.

'No we don't, Doc.' Dan was firm. 'You won't know what you are doing down there. We can't help her and you at the same time. You need to wait here. Jack and I will bring her out.'

Adam was torn between his desire to get to his patient and the realisation that Dan was right. He'd be useless underground. Perhaps even worse than useless.

'The boyfriend's over there.' Dan nodded in the direction of his Land Rover. 'He's got a few cuts and scrapes and he's pretty shaken up. I need you to stay with him, Doc, while Jack and I go get the girl. Stop him from doing something stupid like coming after us.'

'Shouldn't you wait for more help?' Adam asked.

'I think we can do it,' Jack said calmly. 'But if we need more help, I'll call the mine.'

Adam fought back his frustration. 'When you get to her, ask her what her name is and where she is. The date. That sort of thing. Make sure she's not concussed. If she has any head or neck or back injury, tell her to remain still. Don't move her. Come and get me, no matter where she is.'

'All right,' Dan agreed.

'I'll give you a support for her arm. Jack knows how it works.'

Adam pulled a small emergency pack from the back of his ambulance – in reality a big four-wheel drive Jeep that had been equipped for the purpose by the mining company. He gave the pack to Jack then stood back to watch Dan and Jack enter the cave. He wanted to go with them, but at the same time was relieved that he wasn't. Jack may have been joking about the claustrophobia, but he didn't realise how right he was. Adam had been trapped in a small place once before, many years ago, and it had almost cost him his life. His dislike of enclosed places was just another legacy of that day ... another scar that had never healed.

If he couldn't get to the girl to help her, there was someone else who needed him.

The young man sitting in the park service Land Rover was still in his late teens. His clothes were covered in red dust, and there was blood trickling across his sweat-streaked forehead.

'Hello. My name's Adam. I'm a doctor.'

The young man started forward. 'Doctor. It's Andrea. You've got to get to her. She's still in the cave.' He started to get out of the car, and then hesitated. His face turned a deathly pale and he began to sway.

'Whoa.' Adam pushed him gently back onto the seat. 'You're not going anywhere just yet.'

'I'm fine.' The young man angrily wiped the dampness from his forehead. 'It's Andrea we have to help.'

'You can't help her like this.' Adam lifted the young man's hand, which was smeared with blood. His fingers closed as he checked the pulse. 'So, tell me, what's your name?'

'Lachlan. Lachlan Collins.'

'All right, Lachlan. You've got a bit of a cut on your forehead. I need to deal with that first.'

'But, Andrea? She's hurt.'

'They're on their way to get her now. They'll bring her out of the cave. I need to make sure you're all right, so that when she arrives, I can help her. Okay?'

Lachlan took a breath as if to protest. His face contorted with pain, and a moment later, his shoulders sagged. 'Okay.'

Lachlan wasn't badly hurt. Adam used butterfly bandages to close the gash in his forehead. He'd need a couple of stitches when they got back to the Creek. Once the blood was cleaned away, the young man looked far less likely to faint. His hands were badly scraped and Lachlan fidgeted constantly as Adam washed the scrapes and applied antiseptics.

'How long are they going to be?' Lachlan asked for the hundredth time, as Adam packed his gear away.

'They are both good men,' Adam said. 'Andrea couldn't be in better hands.'

'It's all my fault,' the young man's voice was filled with anguish. 'This holiday was my idea. I wanted to see the caves. If something happens to her ...'

The stress wasn't doing Lachlan any good at all.

'Tell me about her,' Adam asked, just to distract him. Adam handed him some painkillers and a flask of water. 'Where did you meet?'

'At college. We were in the same tutorial. She was so

smart and so pretty. Funny too.' Lachlan's voice softened. 'For a long time I didn't think there was anything there. Then suddenly one day. Bam! You know how it is?'

No, thought Adam. I don't.

'It's the best thing in the world. Suddenly there's a reason for everything. It's her. Our parents think we're too young to know – but we do. This is it for us. The once in a lifetime thing.' The young man's face started to crumple. 'If anything happens to her … I just don't know what I would do. Without her …'

Adam was at a loss what to do. This was something he wasn't equipped to deal with. He could mend physical wounds. Stitch flesh and set bones. He could apply a tourniquet to a bleeding wound … but he could do nothing for the boy's aching heart. If he were someone else, like Jack, he'd probably put his arm around the boy's shoulders and reassure him that everything was going to be all right. But he wasn't like Jack. He couldn't do that.

Adam walked away from the car towards the mouth of the cave. He crouched down and inched a little inside. Now he could see the steeply sloping passage leading down into the cave system. Into the darkness. He could almost feel the weight of the rock above him. He listened intently. Not even the smallest sound could be heard in the cave. There was no sign of Jack and Dan. Adam felt his shoulders start to tense. He sat down on a rock just inside the cave mouth, where there was plenty of daylight and he could still smell the fresh air.

He glanced down at his watch, wondering how long Jack and Dan had been gone. It seemed like a long, long time. He turned his eyes back towards the darkness, willing some light to appear. Just a faint glimmer that would tell him the rescue team was on the way back.

That his patient was coming. That he had a reason for crouching on the edge of the blackness.

A light …

That's what he wanted to see.

A flickering light.

The light of a flame, held in his father's hand. Adam frowned. His dad wasn't supposed to come to the house any more. His mother had told him that if he ever saw his dad, he had to lock the door and tell her. But his mother wasn't here. His father was moving around on the veranda. There was a sound like splashing water and Adam smelled something sharp. It made his throat feel funny. Maybe he should open the door. Talk to his dad.

'Is there any sign of them?' Lachlan's voice dragged Adam back to the present. The boy stooped to peer in the mouth of the cave.

Adam wiped the sweat from his forehead. 'Not yet.'

'Damn it! What's taking them so long?'

'It's all right,' Adam said, knowing whatever reassurance he could offer would not be enough. 'It just means that they're being careful. They'll bring her out soon. You'll see.'

His words were truer than even he suspected. Just a few minutes later, Adam saw a light in the darkness inside the cave. Then Jack and Dan appeared, carrying a stretcher. Adam started to move forward, and then backed away, pulling Lachlan with him. They needed to get that stretcher out of the cave before Adam could do anything to help its occupant.

Jack and Dan emerged into the sunlight, covered in dirt and sweat. Both were breathing heavily, but they gently laid the stretcher on the ground with the utmost care.

Adam crouched down beside the girl who lay there, her brown eyes huge in a face white with pain.

'You must be Andrea,' he said, with a gentle smile.

'Yes.' It was the faintest whisper.

'Well, I'm Adam. I'm a doctor.' Adam ignored the noise behind him as Lachlan darted forward. Someone, Jack maybe, held the young man back a few steps, to give Adam room to do what he needed to do.

'So, Andrea, can you tell me your last name?'

'Geroldi,' the girl whispered.

'Lachie …?' Her eyes darted past Adam's shoulder, seeking her boyfriend.

'I'm here.' Lachlan pushed past Jack and dropped to his knees beside the stretcher. There were tears in his eyes.

Adam took a moment to wonder at the strength of the young man's emotions. Then he turned back to his patient. 'Okay, Andrea. Let's have a look at you.'

His examination was brief. The girl's arm was indeed broken, but Jack had done such a good job with the temporary splint that Adam decided to leave it in place until they reached his hospital. There was a large scrape on the girl's thigh. He attended to that, and to the rope burns on her hands. She whimpered with pain, and tears poured down her face.

'All right,' he said, after giving the girl a pain killing injection. 'You're going to be fine. We have to get you to hospital so I can set that arm.'

The ashen-faced girl nodded. Both her hands were bandaged, but that didn't stop Lachlan cradling one of them in his own battered hands.

'It's a long ride, but we'll make you as comfortable as we can in the back of the Jeep.'

'I want to stay with her,' Lachlan said firmly, as if expecting an argument.

'That's fine,' Adam said. 'You can ride in the back together.'

The Jeep's rear had been modified to take a stretcher and there was room for a passenger to ride with the patient. Lachlan took that seat. After making sure both his patients were fine, Adam climbed into the front beside Jack and they set out on the long haul back to town. In the rear-view mirror, Adam saw the park ranger lift one arm in farewell, as he was lost in the dust kicked up by their swift departure.

They rode in silence for a while. The road out of the national park was graded dirt and very rough. Despite Jack's best efforts, all of them were jostled about, and from time to time Andrea cried out in pain. Adam glanced back. His patients seemed to be coping. He couldn't give Andrea any more painkillers yet. Lachlan just sat and stared into the girl's face, as if his salvation lay there. Every now and then she smiled up at him, seeming to take some strength from his presence.

'This is a bit unlike you, Doc,' Jack said, as they pulled off the rough dirt park road onto the smoother surface of the highway leading back to town.

'What is?'

'Riding up front. You're usually in the back with the patient.'

'They're both going to be fine. They don't need me there.' Adam glanced back again at the young couple. 'In fact, I think they are both better off this way.'

'Really?'

Adam looked at Jack, whose eyes were firmly glued on the road as he drove. Was Jack smirking?

'Being together reduces their stress,' Adam said defensively. 'And that keeps their blood pressure down.'

'Sure, Doc.'

Jack was definitely smirking. 'What's got into you today, Jack?'

'Nothing, Doc. I was just thinking how nice it is to see a couple of kids who care like that.'

'If they took a bit more care, I wouldn't be about to set a broken arm,' Adam said tersely.

Jack took no notice. Adam wasn't entirely sure the man wasn't humming softly to himself as he drove. Jack was certainly cheerful these days. Adam wasn't blind. He'd noticed how often Jack seemed to be at The Mineside of late. He'd noticed how Ellen seemed to almost blush whenever Jack was around, not to mention the number of small repairs Jack seemed to find at the house where Ellen and her kids lived. Sister Luke didn't need to send him there any more – he went for reasons of his own. Well, good luck to them both, Adam thought. It must be nice to feel like that.

He couldn't, of course. There would be no 'bam' moment for him. That chance had been lost to him a long time ago.

They were entering Coorah Creek when Adam saw her. He'd turned around to reassure Andrea and Lachlan that they were just minutes from the hospital. When he turned back, there she was … just walking along the road towards them. She was wearing pale blue jeans and another of her seemingly inexhaustible supply of plain white tops. Her face was a little red from the heat, but her arms swung loosely at her side as she walked with that lovely long, free stride. There was something about the way she moved. Adam could watch her walk all day.

Adam smiled, as he always did when he saw Jess. She turned at the sound of the vehicle.

'Pull over,' Adam told Jack. 'I need to tell Jess we won't need her this time.'

Jack did as he was told, and Jess's face creased in question as she drew near.

'Do you need the plane?' she asked.

'No. I just wanted to let you know that everything is fine. We don't need a transport.'

Adam loved the relief that flashed across her face. It showed how much she cared. It was just another thing they had in common.

He nodded to Jess as Jack slipped the vehicle back into gear. As they pulled away, Adam glanced in the rear-view mirror ... and saw Jess looking after them. She was frowning. Adam wondered why. He instinctively wanted to wipe that frown away. He could do that. That was the great gift she had given him – that he could make her smile.

And he understood now – that smile was for him.

There was no 'bam' moment. The sudden pounding of his heart was something that had been creeping up on him for weeks. Since the day he'd run up those aircraft stairs and come face to face with a woman who was smart and sexy and just as strong and difficult as he was. It wasn't just that she was beautiful ... although she was. It wasn't just the memory of her body lying soft and golden in the sunlight. It was watching the sunset together in silence. It was laughing together as they flew. It was desire and so much more. Jess knew about the scars on his back. She knew about his past. But when she looked at him, she just saw him. The man he was. And she looked at him just the same way that Andrea looked at Lachlan. Those

227

kids shared a love strong enough to ease the pain of a shattered bone. What he and Jess shared was stronger than that. It was strong enough to wipe away his scars. Strong enough to wipe away whatever haunted Jess. He had been clinging to a slowly building hope. Hope had now become belief. And certainty.

Adam started to hum along with Jack.

Chapter Twenty-Two

There were clouds on the horizon when Adam emerged from the hospital. The air had that crisp electric feel that comes right before a storm. He could almost feel the hairs on his arm tingling. A storm was strange for this time of the year, but Adam wasn't in the mood to question it. He was in a good mood. Since coming to Coorah Creek, he'd been content with his life. Now he was more than simply content. For the first time in a long, long time, he was happy. Actually happy.

He'd set Andrea's arm. The break was clean and the girl was going to heal just fine. He'd left the young couple getting settled into the room where they would both spend the night. Sister Luke was there to take care of them. As long as there were no other emergencies, he was free for the rest of the day. Please, he thought raising his eyes to the sky, can no one do anything stupid or dangerous for the next few hours.

He glanced down at his watch and was surprised to find it was only midday. Could it be that he had been involved in the rescue, set a broken arm, treated a multitude of scrapes and bruises all in just a morning? He pursed his lips and tried to whistle. It sounded a bit strange – music was not his talent. But it sounded good all the same. He sounded like a happy man.

He glanced towards Jessica's house. She might be there – or she might be down at the airstrip with her aircraft. She just loved that plane. Either way, he had something to do before he went looking for her. He would stroll over to the pub and see if Syd or Trish had a nice bottle of wine they could let him have to share over dinner tonight. Maybe he could convince Ellen to cook something special. He was due to check on Steve and Nikki's new baby later today. The one he and Jess had delivered together. Perhaps Jess would want to go with him. She seemed to like the baby and her young parents. Then if Steve still had flowers in his garden ... Or would flowers be too much? It was a long time since Adam had ... what was the word ... courted a woman. He really wasn't sure what he was supposed to do.

He had a feeling, a hope at least, that Jess wouldn't judge his efforts too harshly.

He was halfway to the pub when the smile on his face suddenly faded.

'Hello, Doc,' John Hewitt said, as he drew near.

'Hello.' Adam was not at all pleased to see the journalist. He angled his steps to avoid the man, but John held up a hand to stop him.

'Can you spare me a minute, Doc?'

'Well, actually, I am on my way somewhere.' Adam brushed past.

'It's about Jess,' the voice behind him spoke the only words that would stop Adam in mid-stride.

Adam took firm control of himself, and slowly turned to face the reporter. He didn't like the look on Hewitt's face.

'I was wondering just how well you knew her.'

Adam felt his gut clench. He didn't know what was coming, but his intuition told him Hewitt was out to make trouble.

'I know everything I need to know,' Adam said firmly. He turned around and kept walking, hoping deep down inside that he could still avoid what was coming. He'd taken three steps when Hewitt spoke again.

'So you do know about the drug smuggling?'

Adam stopped. With every fibre of his being he wished he had never heard those words. He wished he could keep walking. But it was too late now. Slowly he turned to face the journalist. The look of triumph on the man's face made Adam clench his hands into fists. The desire to hit the man was almost overwhelming. He'd always known that something haunted Jess. That she was keeping something secret from the people who had become her friends. From him. He'd thought it had something to do with a man. A past lover. But this? Drugs?

No. Not Jess!

'I don't know what you're talking about,' he said. 'You've made some mistake.'

'I'm not the one who is mistaken,' Hewitt said, unable to hide the glee in his voice. 'Didn't you ever wonder why someone like her was flying an air ambulance way out here in the middle of nowhere?'

Adam couldn't answer – because he had asked himself that very question more than once.

'Let me tell you about Jessica Pearson,' Hewitt continued. 'Her boyfriend was Brian Hayes. You must have heard of him. Heroin Hayes they called him. It was in all the papers. Jet-setting playboy – and drug smuggler. He imported the drugs on board his fancy private jet. And his pilot was – you guessed it – none other than your Jessica.'

'If that was true she would have been charged,' Adam said.

'But she turned him in. Maybe they had a lover's spat. She handed him over to the feds in return for immunity. How's that for loyalty?'

'You're lying,' Adam said, turning away, trying hard to believe that it really was a lie.

'Really?' The reporter pulled a piece of paper out of his pocket. He unfolded it and waved it triumphantly in front of Adam. 'Then I guess this is a fake?'

Adam didn't want to look. He wanted to go back in time and erase the last few minutes from history. Take back the words that were now seared into his brain. But he couldn't do it. Any more than he could stop his eyes from turning towards that piece of paper. It was a printout from some internet news page.

Drug Baron GUILTY screamed the headline, but it was the name that leaped off the page. Jessica Pearson. The photo wasn't very clear. The woman's face was hidden behind an unexpected mane of long dark hair, but he didn't need to see her face to know it was Jess. His Jess. Nothing as simple as changing her hair or where she worked would ever disguise the woman he had come to ... The words began to dance in front of him – drug plane pilot ... escaped charges ... evidence against her lover ...

'So, Doc. Have you got a quote for me about your pilot?'

Adam looked into the man's face. For the first time in a very long time, he hated another human being. Anger, disappointment and above all an overwhelming sense of losing something indescribably precious boiled over. He clenched his fist and swung at the sneering mouth. Pain shot up his arm as his fist connected, but that was nothing to the satisfaction of seeing Hewitt fall flat on his back in the red dust.

'If I ever see you anywhere near my hospital, or the houses on the hospital grounds or the airport, I will call the cops. So why don't you just crawl back under whatever rock you came from.'

Adam was shaking as he spun on his heel and walked away. He never lost his temper. Never. He knew only too well what happened when a person lost control. But that reporter had been asking for it. Telling lies like that. And enjoying it! What sort of a person took glee from destroying another person. Or trying to. A drug smuggler? Jess would never get involved in something like that.

If he repeated the words often enough, it might take away that horrible doubt that was roiling in the bottom of his gut.

He glanced over to see Jessica's car pull up outside her house. With his anger driving him, he strode across the parched earth. He would put an end to this right now. He'd tell Jessica what the reporter was up to. Then he'd help her stop that story being published. Because it was all lies. It had to be lies.

When he reached the house, Jessica was on the veranda, digging in her pockets for the key to the front door. She was wearing those same blue jeans and white top that such a short time ago had sent his heart pounding. She turned as she heard him approach, and as always her face broke into a smile when she saw him. Then the smile faltered. She frowned.

'Adam?'

In two quick leaps he was up the stairs, standing in front of her. Her eyes grew wide as they searched his face, and her face went a deathly shade of white.

The suspicion he'd been trying to deny suddenly grew into a monster.

'Jess ... tell me it's not true?'

Jess opened her mouth to speak, but the words just would not come. She tried to draw a breath, but couldn't. All she could see was Adam's face. He was begging her to deny something he already half-believed. Part of her died because she couldn't deny it.

For an eternity they stared at each other – so close Jess could reach out and touch him, but for the wall between them that was growing higher with each passing second. Adam's face changed. The question vanished and she saw an emotion that may have been disappointment ... or anger ... or hate.

'It's true?' His words were little more than a whisper, but the depth of feeling in those two words tore a hole in her heart.

'I was going to tell you, Adam. I went to the hospital this morning, but you weren't there.'

He shook his head. 'That was today. What about yesterday? And last week. All this time, Jess, you were lying to me.'

'No. Not lying.'

'You didn't tell me the truth. That you were part of a drug ring.'

'I wasn't ...' The words caught in her throat. She couldn't deny it. Her plane. Her responsibility. The look on Adam's face was destroying her. She felt her knees start to give way.

Adam reached out and grabbed her. As she felt his strong fingers grip her arms so tightly it hurt, she realised this was the first time Adam had ever reached out to touch her. The first ... and the last.

'You weren't what? Jess. Talk to me. I'll believe you, Jess. Just tell me you didn't do this. Not drugs, Jess. Anything but drugs.'

She could hear the pleading in his voice. He wanted her to deny it. Almost as much as she wanted to speak the words.

But she couldn't. She was who she was. In coming to Coorah Creek she had been running away. There was nowhere left to run. She had to face up to what she had done.

'Adam, I am so sorry.'

His hand dropped away. 'It's true. You brought drugs into the country on your plane?'

Her throat was too constricted to form words. She nodded.

'And you gave evidence to save yourself from prosecution?'

It wasn't like that, she wanted to say. But she couldn't find her voice. She could barely breathe. She nodded again.

'And this drug baron – he was your boss? He was your ... lover?' As he spoke the last word, his voice broke.

She nodded again and watched as his face closed over and became like stone. He took a step back, opening a gulf between them that Jess knew could never be crossed.

Of all the moments in the nightmare of her life, this one hurt the most.

The day she found the white powder. The drug agents tearing apart her beautiful plane. Not even the nights in prison had hurt one fraction as much as the look on Adam's face right here and now.

It was over. Jess knew in her heart of hearts that there was no coming back from this. In a moment, Adam would speak the words that would send her away from Coorah Creek. Away from the friends who had come to mean so much to her. Away from him. He was sentencing her to a different kind of prison.

His chest rose as he took one long, deep breath.

'Adam!' The loud shout came from the direction of the hospital. 'Jessica!'

235

They both dragged their eyes away from each other and turned to find Sister Luke hurrying in their direction. 'You need to get in the air. There's been a shooting.'

Adam was the first to speak. 'Where?'

'Clifton Downs.'

Jess saw Adam's shoulder's sink. She had no idea where Clifton Downs was, but she knew what was coming. Adam turned back towards her.

'Go to the airport. I'll get my gear and be right behind you.'

She nodded. Whatever problems lay between the two of them, the job came first. Someone needed help and that was her job. Once she was in the air, in that vast blue expanse where everything had always seemed so easy, she might find an answer. A way to talk to Adam and tell him that he was wrong. Because if she didn't this would be their last flight together.

And that thought was just too terrible to bear.

Chapter Twenty-Three

The cabin of the Beechcraft was a little less than ten metres long. Jess could feel Adam's presence as keenly as if he were right next to her. But he wasn't. When they had boarded the plane, Adam had chosen a seat as far away from Jessica as he could be. Apart from the necessities of their work, he hadn't spoken to her. He had even avoided looking at her. The co-pilot's seat seemed very empty without him in it.

The storm that had been building all day over Coorah Creek broke as they flew away. She'd seen the lightning fade into the distance behind them. It hadn't lasted long. Outback storms were quickly spent. But the storm she was facing would not be so easily diffused. Nor could she leave it behind. It was right there in the aircraft with her.

On this flight there was no easy conversation. No shared laughter. The only noise was the steady hum of the engines. Jess kept her eyes steadfastly ahead of her, fixed on her instrument panel or the endless blue sky.

Sister Luke had joined them on the flight. She was seated in the middle of the aircraft, her eyes darting from Jessica to Adam and back again. Her face was creased in a small, tight frown. She could obviously sense the tension between the two of them, but had no idea about its cause. Soon, Jessica was going to have to tell Sister Luke everything. To explain why she was leaving. Because leave she must. Adam didn't want her to stay. That much was very clear.

She would tell Sister Luke the truth. The whole truth. Jack, too. These people who had become her friends deserved the truth. Ellen knew the whole story, and hadn't judged her. She was sure Jack and Sister Luke would be equally understanding. And Adam? He wasn't ready to hear it. Maybe one day. Long after she'd gone and Adam had let go of his anger, perhaps one of them would tell him her side of the story. It would be too late for her, but she hoped he would hear it any way.

The radio crackled. Clifton Downs was calling. It was the third such call since they'd left Coorah Creek.

'Reading you, Clifton Downs.'

'How far out are you?'

Jess didn't need to check her instruments. Without Adam by her side to talk to, she had been tracking their progress in minute detail, hoping it would stop her from thinking. It hadn't.

'Clifton we'll be there in about thirty minutes.'

'Can we talk to the doc again?'

Jess turned in her seat. 'Adam …'

Adam's eyes were hooded and unreadable as he made his way forward. He slipped into the co-pilot's seat, taking extreme care not to even brush against her shoulder. It seemed he wanted the gulf between them to be as physical as it was emotional.

'Doctor Adam Gilmore here, Clifton Downs.'

'Doc. He's not good. We did everything you said when we called earlier. But it's not good.'

'He's still breathing?'

'Yes. But Doc, it's really ragged. And the head wound …' Even over a radio, it was clear the person on the ground was deeply distressed.

'Just make sure he doesn't move,' Adam said. Then to Jess, 'Can we go any faster?' He didn't look at her as he asked.

'I'm doing the best I can, Adam, but this plane can only go so fast. I'll get you on the ground as soon as possible.'

'Clifton Downs, make sure there's someone at the airport waiting for me. Every second counts.'

'Roger, Doc. There'll be someone there.'

Adam turned away without another word and returned to his seat at the back of the plane. Jess fought back the tears that threatened and checked her instruments to see if there was even the tiniest fraction more speed she could safely coax from the Beechcraft. No one was ever going to say she didn't try hard enough!

When she finally saw Clifton Downs, she banked and lost height as fast as possible. She may have shaved a few safety standards, but she also shaved a few minutes off the flight. A dusty brown station wagon was waiting at the end of the airstrip, and as she pulled up next to it, Jessica knew she had done everything humanly possible to get Adam to the injured man in time. No one could have done better. A sudden wave of pain lanced through her with the realisation that next time Adam hurried to help a patient, there would be someone else at the controls of the Beechcraft. Someone else at Adam's side. Tears pricked her eyes at the thought, but she brushed them away. Tears would change nothing.

While she was still shutting down the engines, Adam was on his feet, handing his medical bags out to the eager hands outside. He leaped down the aircraft stairs without even a glance at Jessica. Sister Luke was close behind, but she took the time to ever so briefly lay a comforting hand on Jessica's shoulder.

A few seconds later, the sound of a racing engine told Jessica they were gone. Slowly she slumped forward, rubbing her hands over her face. Her shoulders ached with tension. That had been the most difficult flight of her entire life. The day she flew back from Vietnam, with Brian and a load of drugs on board the plane had been difficult. But she'd had a co-pilot sitting next to her. And Brian was in the back of the plane with his associates, far away from her. Knowing that police and arrest were waiting for them in Sydney had made that flight hard. Knowing she'd been betrayed by Brian had made it even harder. But that flight was nothing compared to the difficulty of the past couple of hours. She had come to really love this job. To believe in the importance of her work. Ellen and her kids, Jack and Sister Luke had become like family to her. And Adam ...

Sitting at the controls of the plane, knowing he was behind her. Hating her and wishing her gone. Nothing in her life had ever been harder than that.

The sound of another car engine caused her to lift her head. They couldn't be back already? Quickly she unstrapped herself from the pilot's seat. She climbed down the aircraft stairs to be greeted by an Aboriginal stockman just emerging from another dusty car.

'Do you need to refuel?' the man asked.

Jessica glanced at her watch, and at the position of the sun. There was enough daylight left to fly back to Coorah Creek. Or to Mount Isa – which had landing lights on the strip. If the injured man was as seriously hurt as he sounded, she had to be ready for another fast departure.

'Yes, I do.'

The man led the way to a small rusty tin shed. Inside were several forty-four gallon drums of aviation fuel. With a powerful heave and a deep grunt, the man tipped one over and began to roll it towards the Beechcraft. Jess picked up the hand pump and followed.

When Adam needed her, she would be ready.

As soon as he walked into the room Adam knew there was nothing he could do. He crossed to the bed and looked down at the man who lay there. A rough, bloodstained bandage covered half his face and the back of his head, but it couldn't hide the damage the shotgun blast had done. The man's breath was ragged. As each shallow breath stuttered to its end, it seemed he would not take another. Then slowly his chest would rise again. Adam placed his medical bag on the end of the table and opened it. He was a doctor. He would do what he could, but he knew he was going to fail. This man was going to die, and there was nothing he could do about it.

He heard footsteps behind him. Sister Luke took up position at the other side of the bed, ready to assist. She looked at Adam and raised an eyebrow in question. He shook his head slowly. He saw acceptance cross Sister Luke's face. She gently reached for the man's large calloused brown hand and cradled it in hers. In the other hand, she grasped the plain wooden cross that hung around her neck. Her eyes closed and her lips began to move in prayer.

Adam lifted the bloody bandage, wincing as he saw the extent of the man's injuries. The shooting had been a terrible accident while the station staff were culling wild pigs. It was such a tragic loss of life, made even more so by the fact that the man had a young family. Adam carefully covered the wound with a new dressing. Taking some cotton wool, he began to gently clean the blood from the man's face. Not that it would matter to his patient. The man would never wake. But his wife and children didn't need to see him like this.

He was disposing of the soiled dressing when he realised that the room had fallen silent. One glance at his patient's face told him it was over. He looked at his watch to note the time for the death certificate he would soon have to sign. Sister Luke crossed herself, and then gently placed the man's hand back on the bed. A cotton bedcover lay on a chair in the corner of the room. Adam helped Sister Luke to lay it over the dead man, then took a deep breath and went to tell the family.

The station manager drove them back to the airstrip.

'Are you sure about heading back, Doc?'

'Yes. I have patients in my clinic back at the Creek,' Adam said. He'd given the distressed widow some sedatives. Beyond that, there was nothing more he could do here.

'All right.'

'The police will be here soon,' Adam said. 'I reported the shooting from the plane. I know it was an accident, but that's the law. I had to do it.'

'I know. We had word the sergeant is on his way. He won't get here until later tonight.'

'He'll take it from here.'

'Okay. Thanks Doc.' The man parked the vehicle beside the Beechcraft.

Adam slowly got out of the car. Jess was waiting in the shade of the aircraft wing. He saw the understanding in her face as she watched him approach. And the sympathy. He wanted none of it.

'Do we have time to get back to the Creek before dark?' he asked. The words came out harsher than he wanted, but that was not something he could change now.

'Yes.'

'Then let's go.'

He walked past her and climbed the aircraft stairs. Again, where once he would have taken the co-pilot's seat, he turned towards the rear of the aircraft. He dropped into the seat and clipped his seat belt tightly. Then he leaned back and closed his eyes. He was exhausted, but he knew he would find no rest on this flight. The rhythms of take-off and the gentle hum of the engines used to easily lull him into sleep. In the past, he'd slept away many a long, dull flight. Since Jess came, though, the flights hadn't been dull. Nothing with Jess was ever dull, and he'd loved every minute spent in that co-pilot's seat. Talking to Jess. Laughing with Jess while the great western plains had rolled away below them. She had a way of lifting the darkness inside him. She might even have been able to take away some of the pain that filled him on days like today – when his skill had not been enough to save someone.

But he'd never know, because that Jess was gone.

The Jess he thought he'd known cared about people. She was funny and caring and a good friend. All this time he'd known she had a secret ... but he had not even begun to suspect it was drugs. Drugs! The healer in him hated drugs and everything and everyone connected with them. It wasn't the illegality of it that shocked him so much as the disregard for the poor souls who lost themselves. How could Jess be involved in drug dealing?

He obviously didn't know her at all.

It was going to be a very long flight back to the Creek. And then Jess would leave ...

'You're not fooling me, you know.'

Adam opened his eyes as Sister Luke slipped into the seat across the aisle from him. He couldn't help but glance towards the front of the plane. He could see the outline of Jess's head moving slightly as she did that thing she always did – the constant rotation of her eyes from the window to her instruments and back again. There had been a time when she'd looked at him too. But that was gone now.

'I don't know what you mean,' Adam said, with very little hope that Sister Luke would leave him alone. The nun was like a dog with a bone sometimes.

'There's something wrong between you and Jess,' Sister Luke said.

It would do him no good to deny it. She knew him too well. 'She's leaving as soon as we get back.'

'What? Why?'

Sister Luke looked genuinely shocked. Adam felt his heart clench. Sister Luke deserved to know, but she should hear it from Jessica. If Jessica didn't have the courage to tell Sister Luke ... well ... he'd make sure she did what she had to do. Sister Luke deserved that.

'You'll have to ask her to explain,' he said.

'Do not let her go,' Sister Luke told him, her voice firm. 'Whatever it is, you need to fix it.'

Adam shook his head. 'It can't be fixed.'

Chapter Twenty-Four

'So, if you need me, I'll just be a couple of minutes away.' Ellen smiled at the young couple.

'Thank you so much.'

The girl, Andrea, was almost asleep. Ellen couldn't blame her. She'd been through so much. The accident in the cave. The journey back to Coorah Creek with a broken arm must have been terribly painful. Not to mention having her arm set. Then her doctor had been called away. Normally Sister Luke would look after anyone at the hospital, but she'd gone on the plane too. Ellen didn't know many details about the emergency. Adam had simply called her and asked her to look after the young couple until he and Sister Luke returned. It had been obvious from the tone of his voice that something was very wrong and she guessed that meant his patient was badly hurt. Ellen had been more than happy to make sure everything was all right at this end.

Lachlan was sitting on the side of his girlfriend's bed. The two of them would spend the night in the hospital. Apparently their camping gear and car were still out at the national park.

'I'd like to say thanks to the guys who got Andrea out of the cave,' he said. 'They were pretty amazing. The ranger ... and Jack.'

'Yes. I imagine they were.' Ellen smiled. 'The doctor will probably want you to stay in town for a few days and I'm sure you'll get the chance to say thanks. In the meantime, just relax. Try to get some sleep. I'll be back later with something for you to eat.'

'Thank you,' Andrea whispered. Lachlan just settled more comfortably on the bed, taking his girlfriend's good hand in his as she closed her eyes again.

Ellen smiled as she walked down the hallway. They were such a nice young couple. And so very much in love. It was beautiful to see. It was almost enough to give her hope that one day she might find someone to love her that way. She opened the back door of the hospital and stepped outside. A short storm had passed through the town a few hours earlier. The rain had already soaked into the ground, leaving no trace of where it had fallen. But the air still retained a sharp sweetness. She closed her eyes to take a long, deep breath. When she opened them again, she saw Jack walking towards her from the direction of the house. He looked up and saw her in the doorway. Then he smiled. Ellen's heart did a little backflip. That boy was right. Jack was pretty wonderful. They hadn't had much time alone lately – ever. Maybe Jess was right. Maybe she should just say something ... if only she could find the courage!

'G'day, Ellen.' Jack wasn't wearing a hat, but still he gave the impression of tipping one at her. She felt her lips start to curl into a smile ... and reached inside her and found her courage.

'Hello, Jack.'

'How are the patients doing?'

'They're fine. I'll be back later to bring them some dinner.' Ellen took a deep breath and before her courage could slip through her fingers she made a decision. 'Would you like to come around for dinner tonight? With Jess and Adam gone it will be just us and the kids.'

If only she was one of those women who could flirt. A toss of her hair. A flutter of eyelashes. Anything to let Jack know that this was more than a dinner invitation.

'Sure. I can keep an eye on the kids while you look after the patients.'

Ellen took a deep breath. She looked down at her hands. 'Thanks. But that wasn't what I was thinking. I thought it would be nice if you and I could ... spend some time together.' Ellen raced to the end of the sentence before her courage failed her. Fearfully, she glanced up at Jack's face. He looked surprised ... and ... pleased?

'That would be great,' he said softly, and smiled. Ellen felt her heart race. Was it fear or pleasure? Or something entirely different?

'Good,' she said.

For a few seconds they both stood there in silence. Close enough to touch – but not touching.

'I'd better pick up the kids ...'

'I have gotta get to the strip ...'

They said at once. Then they both laughed. Ellen thought she was going crazy, but Jack sounded almost as nervous as she felt.

'I had best collect the kids,' she finally said again.

'And I have to get down to the strip,' he added.

'I'll see you later then?' Ellen asked.

'You can count on it.'

They both hesitated for just the merest fraction of a heartbeat, and then Ellen turned to walk back to her house. She heard Jack walking in the other direction towards his ute. Her heart was still racing – and this time it was definitely with fear. But she wasn't going to listen to it. She *was not*! To silence it, she began to think about dinner. She had to prepare something for the young couple in the hospital. That would be easy. She didn't imagine they would be very hungry. Or very fussy. She would cook up some beef and vegetables in a stew, with mashed potatoes. That would be fine for them. She would pick up some fruit juice when she went to collect the kids. Put it on Adam's tab at the store.

But what would she cook for Jack?

He'd been coming to The Mineside every week for dinner – so she couldn't cook one of her standard recipes. Steak was out too. But she wanted it to be special. The store had plenty of meat – lamb and steak mainly. She wondered if maybe they had some frozen salmon. There was a pasta recipe she could try – with a creamy lemon sauce. With a salad and some garlic bread. Or was that too much? She didn't want him to think … or did she?

'This is just ridiculous,' she said out loud. 'He'll eat whatever I cook him. And I don't want to make too much fuss. What will he think?'

But as she walked towards the school, she started to wonder what she should wear.

It was going to be hard to say goodbye. The hardest thing she had ever done. Jessica looked down at the vast expanse of desert beneath her. That's how her life was going to be from now on. Empty. As empty as the co-pilot's seat beside her. As empty as the Adam shaped space in her life … as empty as her heart.

She automatically made another check of her instruments. He eyes and her hands and her brain were flying the aircraft, but her heart and her soul were so very conscious of the man sitting in the rear seat of the plane. He'd lost his patient. Sister Luke had given Jess the news as they prepared for take-off. It was the first time since she'd come to Coorah Creek that Adam had lost a patient. She had glimpsed the pain on his face as he'd boarded the plane. Her every instinct was to help him.

Once there might have been some small comfort she could give to ease his burden, but not any longer. All she could do now was make everything worse. Her only choice was to remain as distant from him as he was from her.

The radio crackled. Jack's voice was a welcome intrusion into her loneliness.

'Receiving you, Jack,' she replied. 'We are on our way home.' Her voice almost broke as she said the word. It wasn't going to be her home for much longer.

The long pause before Jack spoke again signified that he understood their mission had failed.

'Roger that.'

Even over the radio, Jack didn't sound his usual cheerful self. Was the whole world sad today?

'We'll be home for dinner,' Jess told her friend, not that she was going to be eating anything. She'd do what Adam wanted – pack her bags and go. If there wasn't a bus or a train, she'd hitch a ride with someone heading towards Mount Isa. Or Brisbane. Or Birdsville for that matter. Anywhere away from Coorah Creek. But first, she would talk to Jack and Ellen – and Sister Luke and Trish at the pub, too. Now that she was about to lose them, it was suddenly clear that she had made a lot of friends out here. People she cared for. People who cared for her and would be disappointed or angry or hurt when they heard.

'Roger,' Jack said again and signed off.

As she did the same, Jess felt something. She quickly checked her instruments. There was nothing wrong with the readings. Her eyes swiftly flew to the sky outside. But there was nothing there either. The sky was a pure and unbroken blue arc. Cloudless and calm. Still, some instinct deep inside her gut told her something wasn't right.

A minute passed. Another, with nothing untoward. She shook her head. She was imagining things. She just needed to keep her head together for a little longer, and then this would all be over.

It wasn't a thought that gave her any comfort.

Jack left the aircraft hangar unlocked. Jess and the doc would be back soon, he thought as he slipped behind the wheel of his ute. Damn! Much as he liked Adam and Jessica – that house where Ellen lived sometimes felt like some sort of meeting place – with half the town in and out every few minutes. Okay, that was overstating it just a bit. Having Jess and Ellen share the house was working out just fine for everyone – except perhaps for someone who wanted a little quiet time alone with Ellen and the kids. With Ellen.

There had been something different about her today. She'd invited him around for dinner before, but this time, something about the way she had smiled. The way she had looked at him. If he didn't know better, he would have said she was flirting with him.

And he did know better.

Ellen didn't flirt. God knew she had no reason to want to attract any man's attention after what had been done to her in the past. He knew she'd lied when she said Harry had protected his sister from a vicious dog. Jack knew exactly what Ellen wasn't saying about the life she and the kids had lived. He knew he was different. He could never hurt her. Or those two great kids. But she didn't know that, and he had no idea how he would ever convince her.

His mind stayed with Ellen as he drove back to his own small house. He lived in one of the mine cottages. It was small and neat and well kept. He'd never really thought about how lonely it was – not until Ellen and Harry and Bethany stepped down off that train and into his life. Now the cottage seemed very quiet and very empty. More than anything in the world, he wanted to change that.

He wanted to watch Harry grow up. He wanted to teach him how to drive and change a tyre. He wanted to teach him how to be a man. As for Bethany, he wanted to fold her under his arm and protect her from the whole world. He wanted to stand in the doorway scowling at some nervous young man who had come to take her on a date. He wanted to walk her down the aisle on her wedding day.

And Ellen? What did he want for Ellen?

He wanted to hear her laugh. He wanted her never to be afraid again. He wanted to come home at the end of a day and have her smile at him.

He wanted her to reach out and take his hand.

He wanted her as a man wants a woman.

He wanted to run his fingers through her hair and taste her lips. He wanted to stroke her soft skin, and have her understand that a man's touch should bring her pleasure. He wanted to press his lips into the hollow at the base of her throat and feel her pulse beating with his. He wanted to hear her cry out with joy as their bodies joined. And he wanted her to trust him enough to fall asleep in his arms, knowing she was safe and loved.

He wanted to wake up with her tomorrow – and every tomorrow for the rest of his life.

Maybe it was time to start working on that future.

Jack took the time to shower, washing away the sweat of his day's work. Then he picked up the new Uncle Scrooge comic he'd received in the mail two days ago. It was still in its plastic wrapper. Harry would enjoy opening it. It was a reprint of an old, old story called 'Back to the Klondike'. In it, Scrooge reacquaints himself with a long lost love by the name of Glittering Goldie. Jack smiled. Scrooge's romance did not have a happy ever after ending. Hopefully, he would do better. As he walked to the door, he glanced over at the place where his collection of Disney comics used to reside. That collection had taken years to assemble and included rare first issues that were valued at several hundred dollars each. The shelves were bare now. The comics were all in Harry's bedroom. He couldn't think of a better place for them to be.

It took just a few minutes for him to drive to Ellen's place. As he parked the car, she appeared on the front steps. She looked wonderful. She was wearing a simple summer dress that made her look like a young girl. Her hair shone where the setting sun touched it. And when she smiled at him, his heart wasn't the only part of him that reacted.

Perhaps it was actually a good thing that Jess and the doc were coming back. The way he was feeling right now, being alone with Ellen might not be such a good idea.

Chapter Twenty-Five

Never had time passed so slowly. Never had the journey seemed so very long or the outback so incredibly vast. Or so lonely. The blood red earth rolling beneath the plane seemed endless. She wished the journey was over. And she wished time would stand still. She wished that journalist had never come to Coorah Creek. And most of all she wished she had been honest with Adam from the very start.

It was no good wishing for things she could never have. And she would never have Adam's respect or friendship or ...

She tried not to even think the word. Even to think the word would be to define exactly what she had lost. The thing that she wanted more than anything else in the world. Adam's love. She wanted – needed – Adam as much as this plane she loved needed to fly. An aeroplane that didn't fly was a lost and broken thing – without purpose or beauty. Without Adam – what was she? Without Adam she might become what the newspapers had accused her of being – heartless and cold. Beautiful on the outside perhaps, but dead inside.

It was more than she could stand. Something deep inside her cried out in pain at the thought. Her breath caught in her throat ... and she felt the silent emptiness of the outback invade her soul. For the first time in her life, being a pilot and flying her plane meant nothing to her. She just wanted this flight to be over.

The port side engine missed a beat.

Instantly Jessica's every sense was focused on her aeroplane.

Her eyes checked her instruments. There was nothing wrong. She checked the skies about her. They were clear. Through the soles of her feet she could feel the rhythm of the propellers. The engine noise was a steady hum. Everything was as it should be, but her instinct told her there was something wrong.

For an eternity, everything seemed normal. Jessica listened to every beat of the engines. Every noise of the wind. Her fingers held her controls lightly, ready to sense the slightest change. She was beginning to think she must have been mistaken, when the port engine missed another beat. Then another.

Jess checked her fuel gauges. Both tanks were reading three quarters full.

The steady hum of the engines had resumed, but Jess knew now that something was very wrong.

A minute or two later, the port engine misfired loudly. This time her passengers noticed.

'Jess?' Sister Luke called from her seat in the cabin. 'Is everything all right?' She sounded a little frightened.

Jess was about to offer reassurance when the starboard engine also missed a beat. It was pointless trying to reassure her passengers. Sister Luke had every reason to be frightened.

'Jess?' Adam slipped into the co-pilot's seat, any tension between them forgotten in the face of a terrible new dread.

'Houston, we've got a problem,' Jess said.

'What is it?'

'I'm not sure. I refuelled back there. If the fuel was dirty or water had seeped into the drum ...'

'Is that why the engine is miss—'

His words were drowned out by another loud bang, and the starboard engine died completely.

'Damn it!' Jess exclaimed. 'We're in trouble now.'

She reached for the controls, her training taking over from conscious thought. She feathered the prop and it slowly stopped spinning.

'Sister Luke,' she called without turning her head. 'Make sure you are well strapped in. This is going to get rough. You too,' she added to Adam.

The metallic click of his seat belt locking closed was drowned out by the explosive sound of the port engine as it flamed out.

An eerie silence settled around them, broken only by the sound of rushing air.

'I'm going to try to restart the engines,' Jess said loudly to both her passengers. 'Brace yourselves.'

She didn't have time to panic. Or even wonder if the restart would work. Her training took over as she worked her way down the checklist. This was not the routine that had always given her such reassurance when she flew. This was a different checklist altogether – and there was very small comfort in it.

Power lever – on idle.

Fuel firewall valve – open.

Ignition … she glanced at the glowing red light. On.

Generator – on.

Engine auto-ignition – armed.

'Jess …' Adam's voice betrayed no sign of the fear he must be feeling.

He should be afraid. She was.

She turned the radio to the emergency frequency. 'Get on the radio,' she told Adam. 'We need to send a mayday.'

Jess hit the starter. Both engines responded, and for one brief moment she thought they were all right, but the engines spluttered a couple of times then fell silent.

She glanced at her altitude indicator. They were at twelve thousand feet. Her airspeed was just one hundred and thirty knots. If she wanted to try an air start, she had to make that decision now.

'Mayday. Mayday.' Adam spoke beside her. She glanced at him. His face was worried, but calm. There was no panic in his eyes. He was a good man to have beside you in an emergency. 'This is Goongalla Air Ambulance. We're ...' He stopped and turned to Jess. 'What do I tell them?'

'Say Beechcraft King Air has lost both engines. Passing through twelve thousand feet. We are five hundred kilometres south-west of Mount Isa. Three POB. That's people on board,' she added quickly in response to his frown. 'Pause for a few seconds after that and hope someone responds. If they don't, do it again. Just keep doing it.'

She mentally called up another of the checklists she had memorised so carefully during her training.

Propellers – full forward.

Fuel valve – open.

She didn't think this was going to work, but she had to try it. She knew that behind her, in the cabin, Sister Luke would have her hands clasped on the wooden cross she wore and would be praying. Jess hoped someone was listening.

'Mayday. Goongalla Air Ambulance. We have lost ...' beside her Adam's voice droned on. Controlled and clear.

These two lives were in her hands now. Her own too.

She dropped the nose of the plane, losing valuable height in an effort to pick up airspeed. The propellers were turning now, she waited ... waited ... and hit the starter.

Nothing.

She carefully raised the nose of the plane. She needed every foot of height she could get.

'Adam,' she said, 'add that we are going to make an emergency landing.'

She felt him tense beside her.

'Where?'

'Anywhere I can find that's flat and clear. I don't suppose you know of any properties around here with airstrips?'

'Not unless we go back to Clifton Downs.'

Jess shook her head. 'We'd never make it. And I'd rather not turn – we'd lose a lot of height.'

'Then what are you going to do?'

'We are going to start looking for some clear flat land.'

She turned to look at him. Without the drone of the engines, it was eerily quiet in the cockpit. His eyes met hers and all that had passed since the morning seemed to just disappear in the face of their danger. There was so much Jess wanted to say. Right now, all the secrets between them and all the reasons for keeping those secrets seemed so foolish. If only she could turn back time ...

But that wasn't going to happen. In a few minutes, she was going to have to put this aircraft down. Without engines. Without an airstrip. With nothing but her skill. The last thing she needed was to let her feelings for Adam stop her from doing her job.

'Look around us,' she said, dragging her eyes away from him towards her own window. 'We need some flat land. A bit of an uphill slope won't hurt. No trees. No big rocks either. And keep sending that mayday,' she said.

'What if no one hears us?'

'Just keep sending it.' Jess turned away from the

window and glanced towards the back of the plane. Sister Luke was sitting, her eyes shut and her lips moving in prayer. 'Sister Luke.'

The nun's eyes snapped open. Her face was pale, but she was in control of her fear. 'Jess?'

'We are going to have to make an emergency landing. I need you to make sure there is nothing loose in the cabin. Fasten all the seat belts. Make sure everything is stowed in the lockers. I don't want anything flying around the plane.'

'Very well.'

'Then get yourself strapped in nice and tight … and Sister Luke?'

'Yes?'

'If you can keep praying while you do all that, I'd be very grateful.'

Sister Luke almost smiled. 'You don't have to worry about that. I'm way ahead of you.'

Jess glanced at her instrument panel. She had to set for best glide. Her landing gear was already up. She adjusted the wing flaps and feathered both propellers. They slowed and stopped … useless now.

She allowed herself one quick glance at Adam. He was still making the mayday call, but his eyes were fixed on the window beside him, searching the ground for some safe place to land. She needed to do the same. She dragged her eyes away and looked out of the window.

The land below them was parched and dry. Jess decided that was a blessing because there were very few real trees, just low scrubby bush. But the wind, torrential rains and flash floods of the outback had carved deep gouges in the earth, limiting the amount of really flat land. And what flat land there was would be well littered with rock and stone. For a few seconds she thought of turning west. The desert sand would make a softer landing. There might even be a salt pan between the dunes. But that route would take them further from their expected flight path. The rescue planes might not look there. It was a tough call and the plane was losing height fast.

'Jess ... what about that?' Adam indicated a patch of ground to their right. Jess strained to look.

'It looks clear – maybe even sandy,' Adam said.

He was right. Some freak of wind had deposited a long wide drift of wind-blown desert sand along the base of a steep ridge. There wasn't a lot of it – but there might be enough. The sand would help slow the plane once they touched down. With only a handbrake and flaps, she was going to need a lot of room to stop. Or some help.

The problem was, to reach that landing site, she'd have to turn. Turning the plane meant losing height; and she didn't have any height to spare. If she turned and then found the site wasn't suitable, she wouldn't have any options left.

She didn't have a lot of options now.

'Adam. Get down to the back of the plane. Strap yourself in.'

'No. I'll stay here with you.' His voice was firm.

She didn't have time to think why he wanted to stay with her. 'It's safer in the back. Go.'

Adam shook his head and once more repeated the mayday call. Jess reached out and took the handset away from him.

'You've done everything you can. We are going down. Get back there and make sure everything is locked down tight. Make sure Sister Luke is strapped in. Once we stop moving, I want you to get Sister Luke out of the plane. The tanks are still full of fuel. The electrics are off – so the chance of an explosion is small. But after we're down, if the tanks have ruptured, just one spark ...'

She saw it then – the first flash of fear in his eyes. Fire! The thought of flames did to him what the idea of a crash landing could not. She could almost feel his flesh tighten in anticipation of the pain. She wished now she had said something about the scars on his body. Maybe she could have said or done something that would take that look from his eyes. Make it easier for him to face what might lie ahead. But it was too late now.

'I need to know you are both prepared for this,' she said quietly. 'And I need to know you will look after Sister Luke.'

Jess could feel the turmoil inside Adam and for a few seconds her feelings for him blotted out her pilot's instincts. She reached out one hand and gently touched his arm. This time he didn't push her away. Their eyes locked for a moment, then Adam nodded abruptly and climbed out of the co-pilot's seat.

Sister Luke's eyes were shut. Her normally serene face was too pale as her lips moved in prayer. The fine-boned hands clutching her wooden cross were white. Adam's heart clenched with concern for her. He dropped into a crouch beside her seat.

'Sister Luke?'

When she opened her eyes, she frowned. 'Adam? What are you doing? You should be strapped in.'

As if to accentuate her words, the plane began to bank quite sharply. As it did, it also started to drop. Adam grabbed the arm of the seat opposite Sister Luke and dragged himself in. He pulled the seat belt tight.

'Jess says that as soon as the plane has come to a stop,

we have to get out. There's a lot of fuel in the tanks ... and ...' his voice trailed off as the familiar fear tightened his throat. Not fear of dying. Fear of feeling the flames licking his skin. Fear of the terrible pain. Fear that he would want to die.

'Adam.' Sister Luke's voice was soft. 'I confess that I am terribly afraid. Would you hold my hand?'

No one knew better than Sister Luke how he hated to be touched. She was the one who changed his bandages all those years ago. She knew the pain the gentlest touch had caused him then. She knew how hard it was for him to accept such a touch now. She held out her hand towards him. It was shaking. Adam reached out and enclosed her hand in his larger, stronger one. He was appalled at how frail she suddenly seemed.

'Jess will take care of us,' he said. 'Trust her.'

'I do.'

Adam looked towards the front of the plane. Jessica's body was taut with concentration, her head held high. He suddenly had an overwhelming feeling that he had left something important unsaid. And now, maybe he'd never get the chance to say it.

'Brace yourselves,' Jess called, without turning her head.

Adam looked out of the window. The rocky red earth was racing up to meet them. They were going too fast! And where was the sand? If the plane dropped among those rocks it would be torn apart. And them with it.

He felt Sister Luke's fingers tighten around his. There was a flash of yellow sand beneath them and then the plane met the earth with a jarring thud. He heard Sister Luke cry out in pain. Then his whole world became a nightmare of noise and pain, the sound of tearing metal and the smell of hot fuel.

Chapter Twenty-Six

'That was a really good meal,' Jack said, as he picked up the first dripping dish and began to wipe it.

'Well, thank you. I'm glad you liked it.' Ellen smiled sideways at him. There were times she still found it hard to believe that this man seemed happy standing in her kitchen, wiping dishes. Or sitting on her big second-hand couch, with one of her kids pestering him for a story or yet another look at his cartoon tattoo. Yet he did. He acted as if every moment he spent with her and her kids was a privilege to be treasured. As if she was something to be treasured.

Ellen ducked her head back to her dishes. Oh – but she was terrible at this. She had set out to … not seduce Jack. That was too big a step for her to take. But to at least make him see her differently. Realise that maybe she could be more than a friend. But he didn't seem to be getting the message and she wasn't sure how to go about making it clearer.

Maybe it was because she was a couple of years older than him. Maybe it was because she was a mother. Maybe the way her husband had used – abused – her had left some mark that Jack could see. That made her unworthy of a man like him.

She cast another sideways glance at Jack – and saw in his face the same thing that she had seen in her own face in the mirror an hour ago. As she had combed her hair, and debated whether it was going too far to put on a touch of make-up, she had seen nervousness. And uncertainty. And longing in her eyes. Now she saw it in his. She bent over her task again, draining the sink and picking up the glasses to put them away. She was very aware of Jack standing next to her. So big and strong. But not threatening. Never that. He was always gentle. Even with the drunks at The Mineside. He never bullied them. Not even when one of them tried to pick a fight. He just took them safely home. He cared about people and took care of them if they needed it. She loved that about him.

She loved …

The last glass slipped from her fingers and shattered in the sink.

'Ellen – did you cut yourself?' Jack reached out to take her hands.

'No … I'm fine …' she stammered as he carefully examined her hands, turning them over to be certain she hadn't cut herself on the glass. Then slowly, ever so slowly he raised her hand, and pressed his lips into the soft palm.

Ellen almost cried out with the joy of it.

'Jack …' she whispered.

He looked at her and Ellen's whole world contracted to just the two of them and the hands that now cradled hers with so much care. With so much …

Jack slowly released her hand. 'I think maybe you should let me clean up the glass.'

'I can …'

'It's all right,' he interrupted her. 'Let me. My hands have seen much tougher work than that.'

Those hands of his. Those tough, strong, gentle hands that had held her children on so many occasions. That had breathed life back into a tired old home. That helped so many people. Ellen wanted to reach out and touch those hands, but he had already turned away to deal with the broken glass. Ellen felt almost bereft.

'Thank you,' she said, her voice not quite as steady as it should have been. She needed another minute or two to compose herself. 'I should go over to the hospital and check on Andrea and Lachlan. They'll probably be asleep, but ...'

'Of course you should. I'll stay with the kids.'

'Thanks. I won't be long. And when I get back, we can have coffee.'

'That would be nice.'

Ellen almost fled the room. Her heart was pounding as she walked over to the hospital. She raised her hand to look at the place where Jack's lips had touched her. Her skin still tingled with the kiss. How long was it since a man's touch had brought her anything but pain? She raised her hand to press the palm against her cheek, as if by doing so she would feel his lips there. She felt like a schoolgirl again. A giddy, excited schoolgirl in the throes of first love.

Jack had given that back to her.

Her feet were barely touching the floor as she entered the hospital. She walked quietly to the room where her charges were spending the night. It was the room that held the big double bed Adam had purloined from the house where she now lived. The door to the room was open, and she could see Andrea and Lachlan. They were both sound asleep. Andrea's head was cradled on Lachlan's shoulder, her injured arm carefully settled on a soft pillow. They looked so young and peaceful. How nice it would be, she thought, to sleep like that. Safe in the arms of someone who loved you. Maybe ... Just maybe ...

Not tonight of course. It was far too soon for that. And besides, Jess and Adam would be back shortly. But perhaps one day ... in the not too distant future ...

She turned off the light in the room, but left the hallway light on in case they woke in the middle of the night. Then she turned back towards her own home. Where Jack was waiting for her. She almost wanted to run. For one of the few times in her life, she wished her kids were not around. She'd get them off to bed nice and early. The sound of the telephone ringing cut clearly through the late evening air. The sudden hope flared that it was Jess calling to say she wasn't coming home tonight after all.

Jack reached for the phone, expecting to hear Jess or Adam at the other end of the line. They were due back about now. Jess would be tired after two long flights, and would be looking forward to getting home. Jack wasn't certain if that was a good or a bad thing. Those few moments in the kitchen with Ellen ... Maybe tonight, after the kids were in bed, he could begin to tell her how he felt. But the taste of her skin on his lips ... the sparkle in her eyes. It was going to be difficult to keep himself under control. To keep it light. The last thing Ellen needed now was to feel the depth of his desire for her. He didn't want to scare her away.

But maybe, he smiled to himself, he could ask Jess to stay away just a little bit longer.

'Hello!'

'Jack. It's Sergeant Delaney here.'

Sergeant. Not Max – that meant official business. 'Yes, Sergeant.'

'I was actually looking for Ellen ... or anyone for that matter. I was wondering if you have heard anything from Jess or Adam.'

A cold hard lump began to form in Jack's gut. He glanced out of the window. The summer sun was very low in the sky now. Jess and Adam and Sister Luke should have been back a while ago.

'No. I haven't. And neither has Ellen. What's wrong?'

'I had a call from Air Traffic Control. Another pilot heard a mayday. They think it might be them.'

Jack froze. 'When?'

'About half an hour ago. ATC has been calling them, but there's no answer. Jess filed a flight plan before they left Clifton Downs. They're overdue.'

'Did the mayday say where they were?'

'They didn't get an exact location – the signal wasn't good.'

'I'll head for the strip and try to raise them on our radio.'

'Good. I'll call Clifton Downs. I'll see if they can raise them. An officer from Birdsville was already on the way there because of the shooting. If Clifton can get their plane in the air, they can start a search.'

'I'll stay in touch.' Jack put the receiver down. He turned to see Ellen standing in the open door – her face frozen.

'What is it?' she asked. The fear in her voice matched his own.

'That was Max Delaney. ATC has picked up a mayday. They think it might be Jess and Adam.'

'Oh, no.' Ellen's hand flew to her mouth. 'Do you think they're ...?'

'No. I don't,' he said with a determination he didn't feel. 'I'm going to the strip now. If I hear anything, I'll call you.'

'Go.'

'Mum? Jack? What's wrong?' Harry stood in the doorway, looking at them with wide, sleepy eyes.

'Nothing at all,' Jack said forcing a smile. 'I just have to go to the airstrip for a while. You'll probably be in bed by the time I am done, so why don't I leave that comic with you, and we can read it together tomorrow night.'

'All right,' Harry said.

'Good man.' Jack ruffled the boy's hair, looking across at Ellen. He sent her a silent nod of support before turning to leave.

He forced himself to walk to his car. He didn't want to alarm Ellen or Harry, but his mind was racing. He pulled away from the house slowly, but as soon as he was out of sight, he pushed the accelerator to the floor, hoping against hope that it was all some terrible mistake. That he would find the Beechcraft in the hangar. Then he would laugh about the fuss with Jess and Adam and Sister Luke.

He raced down the dirt road to the strip and the car slid to a stop outside the hangar.

It was empty.

Jack got out of the car and raced towards the radio. He flicked the on switch.

'Goongalla Base calling Goongalla Air ambulance. This is base calling the Goongalla Air ambulance. Jess, are you there?'

Nothing but static. He switched the set to the emergency frequency and tried again. Still nothing. With a sinking feeling in his gut, he rang the police station.

'All right,' said the Sergeant. 'You stay there and keep trying. I'll alert ATC. They'll put up a search plane, but there isn't a lot of light left. Clifton can't help. Their plane flew back east last week for some maintenance work.'

'The search planes might pick up the emergency transponder,' Jack offered hopefully.

'Maybe we'll be lucky. If not, there'll be a bigger search

at first light. We know what time they left Clifton Downs – and we know roughly the track they were on.'

Knowing roughly the track they were on wasn't really good enough, Jack thought as he hung up the phone. The outback was a big place. A kilometre or two off the line, and no one would see them. If the transponder wasn't working. But it was. He knew it was. It was his plane. His responsibility.

He tried the radio again, not really expecting any response. There was none.

A few moments later, he heard a car pull up outside and Ellen walked into the hangar.

'Any news?' she asked.

'No. What are you doing here? Where are the kids?'

'I dropped them over to the pub. Trish will take care of them. I told her what was happening. In case anyone calls there.'

Jack nodded, accepting the wisdom of it. The pub was very much the centre of their small community. If someone was looking to contact almost anyone, they would call there.

'I figured you'd be staying here all night,' Ellen said. 'So I brought you some coffee and stuff.'

'Thanks. Just put it anywhere.'

She carried in a thermos and a bag of supplies for the night. Then she pulled up the only other chair in the place, and sat down next to him. For a long time neither of them spoke.

'If there was some mechanical problem with the plane …' Jack at last found a voice for his worst fears.

'No. Jack. Don't do that. No one could do a better job of taking care of that plane than you do. It's perfectly safe. It must be something else.'

He wanted to believe her. If only he could.

'Ellen, you should go home. I'll call you if I hear anything. There's nothing you can do here.'

'Yes there is,' Ellen said, her beautiful blue eyes firmly fixed on his face. Then she reached out and laid her hand over his.

Chapter Twenty-Seven

He could smell the leaking fuel. It made his skin crawl. As did the creaking of hot and damaged metal. It was no use telling himself that he was safely out of the plane. That they all were. He knew only too well that all it would take was a single spark …

'Adam?'

He jumped as if burned.

Jessica took a step back. 'Are you all right, Adam?'

'Yes. I'm fine,' he said quickly.

He and Jess were standing on the side of a low ridge, looking down at the aircraft they had evacuated just a few moments ago. Sister Luke was sitting on a rock, her breath coming in shallow gasps after their dash from the plane. It was nothing short of a miracle that all three of them had staggered away from the wreck without any serious injuries. They were a bit battered and bruised and Jessica's face had several small cuts caused by the shattered cockpit windscreen, but they were going to be fine. The Beechcraft, however, was a different matter. The underside of the aircraft was a mess of twisted metal. One wing had been torn almost off. There were gouges and dents all along the body of the plane and most terrifying of all, at least in Adam's eyes, was the steady leak of aviation gas from a torn fuel tank on one wing.

'Do you think they heard the mayday?' Sister Luke's voice was so soft he barely heard it.

'I don't know,' Jess answered. 'Someone should have. And I did file a flight plan. If we don't report in within an hour or so, they'll send out search and rescue.'

'But it will be dark by then.' There was a very definite tremor in Sister Luke's voice.

Adam moved to her side and dropped down on to the rock beside her. 'Let's not underestimate Jack,' he said forcing a confidence he didn't feel into his voice. 'He's got our backs. He always does.'

Sister Luke looked at him and tried hard to smile. Adam studied her with some concern. He didn't like the pallor of her face. Or the way her hands trembled as she clutched the wooden cross around her neck. He'd never seen her look like this. She looked old and tired – and ill. Now he thought about it, she hadn't been her usual self for a couple of weeks. Not since that trip back east ...

He was an idiot!

He got to his feet and caught Jessica's eye. The two of them moved slightly away from Sister Luke.

'I'm worried about her,' Adam said quietly. 'Realistically, when can we expect help?'

'Realistically – not till tomorrow,' Jessica said. 'Even if the radio is working, which I doubt, it doesn't have enough range. I want to save the battery power anyway. It's all we have. And it'll be dark soon. I'll set the transponder off in the morning – when it's most likely to do some good.'

Adam nodded, his mind racing. He wasn't at all pleased by the idea of spending the night here. Not for himself or Jess. A bit of discomfort wouldn't hurt them. Sister Luke was a different matter. He was afraid for her. But it appeared they had no choice.

'We'd better get some supplies from the plane,' he said.

'Yes. I'll get them. You stay well clear,' Jessica said.

'No,' Adam said in an urgent whisper. 'I am concerned about Sister Luke. I need some medical supplies. I'll go.'

'Adam. The leaking fuel. Planes don't explode that easily. But that leaking fuel could start a fire. Just one spark—'

'Do you think I don't know that?' His voice rose, anger growing out of the deep dread that gripped the very core of his being. Before Jess could say any more, he strode off down the slope in the direction of the crippled aircraft.

He thought she might follow, but she didn't. After a few strides he slowed down. His breath was coming in sharp jagged gasps, and he forced himself to calm down. The closer he got to the Beechcraft, the stronger the smell of fuel became. It curled inside his nostrils, into the back of his throat and into his gut.

He stopped just a few steps from the plane. The door was lying at an angle where they had forced it open to get out. He glanced back over his shoulder. Jess had moved to join Sister Luke, and they were both watching him. Even from this distance, he could see that Sister Luke's hands were clutching her cross. Jess had her hand resting on the elderly woman's shoulder, offering what comfort she could. Adam was conscious of two things ... that stepping inside the crippled plane was the last thing on earth he wanted to do. And those two women were the only people on earth for whom he would do it.

When he entered the damaged fuselage, he was surprised by how minor the damage seemed. A few of the windows were broken, and one of the lockers had sprung open, the contents spilling out into the aisle. The most obvious sign of the speed and shocking impact of the crash was the smell of leaking fuel. In his mind, he could hear it dripping into an ever-growing explosive pool beneath him. He pushed that to the back of his mind and looked at the open locker. Blankets. They would need those. It could get very cold overnight. He bundled up the blankets and carried them to the door. He stepped out into the open air and walked a few metres from the plane. He hesitated just long enough to deposit his load, then taking a deep breath of relatively clean air, he turned back again.

Medical supplies were his next priority. He retrieved his bag and opened it. From the overhead cabinets he took a selection of medication. He had no idea what was ailing Sister Luke – so he took anything that might conceivably be useful. The bag was almost overflowing when he carried it outside and deposited it beside the blankets.

The Beechcraft carried an emergency pack in a locker at the very rear of the cabin. It was stocked with food and water. Torches and ... matches. Adam's hand was shaking as he reached out to open the locker. The click of the latch made him jump. He felt as if the space around him was contracting. The smell of the petrol was overwhelming. The light changed. Flames! He could smell the smoke now! Feel the heat blistering his skin. The smell ... that sickening smell that was his own flesh burning. He raised his eyes. There, through the window, his father's face ... The awful sound of his own screams ...

His hand clutched the strap of the emergency pack and he turned and dragged himself down the length of the plane. He stumbled through the hatchway into the soft evening light, his breath coming in ragged gasps. Slowly the image faded.

It was the fumes, he told himself. Oxygen deprivation due to the fumes. Nothing more. He waved at Jess and Sister Luke, as he took several deep breaths. His head cleared and he looked at the gear gathered around him. Almost done. One or two more trips into the plane and he would have everything that they could use.

He took another breath, willed his hand to stop shaking, and turned back into the interior of the plane.

'I am going to go and help him,' Jess said. 'I can't just stand here. My plane. My responsibility. I feel so useless just standing here.'

'You can't help him. He has to do this,' Sister Luke said. She hesitated and Jess knew what she couldn't say.

'It's because of the past, isn't it? The fire.' She knew as she said it that it was true.

'You know about that?' Sister Luke's eyes became sharp. 'He's never told anyone before.'

'He still hasn't. I saw the scars.'

'Ah.' Sister Luke sounded deflated. 'I had hoped …'

So had Jess, but she wasn't going to admit it to anyone. 'Tell me about it,' she said, taking a seat on the rock next to Sister Luke.

Sister Luke shook her head slowly. 'He was an only child. The father was a dreadful man. God forgive me for saying that, but he truly was evil. Adam's mother had a restraining order out against him. But that didn't work. He kept coming to the house. One day, when he thought there was no one there, he set a fire. I suppose he wanted to destroy everything that Adam and his mother had. He couldn't have known that Adam had come home early from school. His mother was still at work. The fire brigade found him at the back of the house, hiding. He was so badly burned … for a long time the doctors thought he would die.'

'You were his nurse.'

'Yes. He was such a brave boy. He fought so hard to survive. It was a terrible thing to see a child suffer so. First there were the burns to heal. Then the plastic surgery.

Skin grafts. It was a miracle his face wasn't scarred – but the rest of him ...'

'Is that why he doesn't like to be touched?'

'You noticed that?' Sister Luke shook her head. 'That's partly because of all the pain. For many, many months, whenever someone touched him, all he felt was pain.'

Jess could feel tears pricking at her eyes. Her heart just ached. 'What happened to the father?'

'Jail. I found out years later that he had been released, but as far as I know, Adam never saw him again.'

'And his mother?'

'She tried. But she wasn't equipped to deal with such a broken boy. I imagine she blamed herself, in part. I could see it in her face. After a while, she found it hard to even look at him. They drifted apart. He's been alone a very long time.'

'Except for you.'

'Except for me. And now you.'

Jess shook her head. 'No. Not me. I ... I'm leaving when we get back.'

'I knew something was wrong. Tell me.'

She did. In just a few sentences she laid her guilt at Sister Luke's feet then sat, staring at the hands clasped in her lap. Waiting for Sister Luke to condemn her for what she had done.

'Jess, look at me.'

Jess forced herself to turn her head. Sister Luke's soft grey eyes held nothing but empathy.

'Jessica, you are not to blame for that boy's death. There were others who could have helped him. Should have helped him. You did nothing wrong. In many ways, you are a victim too.'

'But I flew the drugs into the country.'

'No. You flew a plane. The responsibility belongs with the person who put the drugs on that plane. Not with you.'

'I was blinded by Brian. His looks. His charisma. The money and the lifestyle. I thought he loved me. How could I have been so stupid?'

'You were simply being human,' Sister Luke said.

'Adam will never forgive me.' Jess's voice broke as she watched him carry another load out of the plane. 'He values human life so highly. He fights to save every one of his patients. How could he ever feel anything for someone like me – someone with blood on their hands?'

Sister Luke's small, wrinkled hand covered Jess's clasped fists. 'Forgive yourself, Jess. Adam will too.'

'I don't know if I can.'

'You must. Guilt is such a destructive thing. Love can never flourish if there's guilt like that. And the guilt you carry is not yours.'

'We are both such a mess.' Jess dashed the suggestion of a tear from her eyes. 'Each of us carrying a different burden. What a pair we are.'

Sister Luke's voice was firm. 'You've no reason for self-pity, Jess. And whatever you do, don't pity him. That's the one thing he doesn't need.'

'I pity the boy he was,' Jess said, her voice catching in her throat. 'The man he is now I admire and respect. And ...'

'Love him, Jess. That's what he needs from you.'

And what she needed from him. The unspoken words hung in the air.

'I'd better go help him with that load,' Jess said, rising to her feet. 'We'll set up camp just over the ridge. Away from the plane in case ... well ... just in case.'

By the time she reached Adam, she had composed her face, but her emotions were still raw. One look at his face told her he was equally vulnerable at that moment. She gathered an armload of blankets.

'I think we should set up just over the ridge. Away from the plane.'

He offered no comment, but simply followed her. It took them three trips to carry everything to a small hollow about a hundred metres away. A few scraggy trees offered a little shelter.

Jess dropped to her knees and started scooping out earth to make a fireplace. Adam, meanwhile, was sorting through their emergency kit. He set out torches and water.

'We've got enough supplies for a couple of days,' he said.

'It shouldn't take that long for them to find us.'

'But just in case, we're going to have to be a bit careful with the water.'

Jess nodded. 'Where's Sister Luke? I thought she would be right behind us.'

'I'll go get her.' Adam climbed back to the top of the ridge. Jess watched him go, her mind in turmoil. As he topped the rise and looked down, his body suddenly froze.

'Sister Luke?'

She heard the shock and anguish in his voice as he flung himself down the ridge and out of sight. Jess leaped to her feet, but before she could take a single step, Adam appeared again silhouetted on the skyline. He carried Sister Luke's limp form in his arms.

Chapter Twenty-Eight

'Get some blankets down!'

Jess was moving to do it even before the words were out of Adam's mouth. Holding Sister Luke gently in his arms, he slid down the rough slope, sending stones flying. When he reached Jess, he lay Sister Luke on the makeshift bed. Her eyes were shut, and her lips were slightly blue. He reached for her wrist, suddenly aware of how thin and fragile her bones were. The pulse beneath his fingers was thin and thready. She needed oxygen. There were canisters on the plane. How could he have forgotten them? He started to rise.

'What do you need?' Jess asked.

'Oxygen. On the plane.'

'I'll get it.' Without a moment's hesitation, Jess turned in the direction of her crippled aircraft.

The plane. The danger of fire! Adam felt a surge of fear – but not for himself.

'Jess!' he called. He tore his eyes away from Sister Luke to look at Jess. Her face told him she knew exactly what he was thinking. But her desire to help Sister Luke was stronger than her fear. 'Be careful,' he said.

She nodded and was gone.

Adam looked down at Sister Luke's face. Her breathing was so soft and shallow, he could barely hear it. For a few moments he was a terrified child again, hearing her gentle voice through a sea of pain. It was like cool water on his burning skin. Adam reached for his medical bag. Sister Luke had never failed him when he needed her. He would not fail her now. He pushed his emotions aside, and let the doctor take over. He had administered the necessary medication, and was listening to Sister Luke's heart when a noise behind him signalled Jess's return. Silently thanking whatever gods were responsible for Jess's safety, he turned to take the oxygen canister and a mask from her hands. Hands that were visibly shaking.

'How is she?'

'Not good.' Adam set the oxygen mask in place. 'It's her heart. I think she's known for a while that it's weak. When she went back to the mother house … Why didn't she tell me? I would never have let her come …'

'That's why she didn't tell you,' Jess said softly.

Adam kept Sister Luke's hand in his. As he looked down at the pale face, obscured by the plastic oxygen mask, he wanted to scream in frustration. All those years of training. All those books he had studied. All the hours he had spent trying to understand how the human body worked. How to help people. And there was very little he could do to help the person who meant most to him in this world. If only they were back at Coorah Creek. In the hospital with proper equipment … But even as the thought formed he knew he was wrong. Sister Luke was just … fading. And all his skill was not going to save her.

It was almost too much for him to bear.

'I'm going back to the plane,' Jess said softly. 'I am going to try the radio. Maybe I can raise someone. If there's a helicopter nearby. Mustering cattle … or something … anything …'

Adam nodded. He couldn't speak. He couldn't tell her that even a helicopter wouldn't help now. He let Jess go. Let her try to help. It might give her the comfort that was denied him.

'I've heard you telling people about me,' he said softly

to Sister Luke. 'Telling them that I talk my patients better. Well, if that's true. I want you to listen to me now. I want you to fight. They'll find us tomorrow and I can take you back to the Creek. You know what will happen then, don't you? Jack and Ellen. Trish … The whole town will want to help look after you. Because they love you. I'll have to chase them away or the hospital will be a madhouse.'

Her breathing seemed a little easier. The drugs and the oxygen were having some effect. He held her hand even more tightly, hoping against hope that his diagnosis was wrong.

'You can't leave the town. Those people need you. I need …' His voice broke.

He looked down at the hand he held. Sister Luke was stronger than any person he had ever known, but now she seemed so fragile. She was the only family he had. The only person in the world who knew his past … and loved him anyway. He rubbed the base of his neck, feeling the scarred flesh beneath his shirt. The pain he had suffered as a child had seemed beyond bearing. But it was nothing to the pain he felt now as he watched Sister Luke slipping away.

He leaned forward to kiss the harsh dry skin of her cheek. As he did, her eyes fluttered open.

'Hey,' he said. 'It's going to be all right. Just lie still.'

Sister Luke shook her head slowly. She moved her arm, trying to pull the oxygen mask away from her face. Frowning, Adam assisted her.

'No talking,' he told her. 'Or I'll put it back.'

Sister Luke nodded, and her lips twitched in what might almost have been a smile. Her free hand moved again, and Adam realised she was looking for her wooden cross. He placed it in her hand and her shaking fingers closed around it. Her lips started moving silently, and Adam knew she was praying.

She knew, as he did, that she was dying. And she wasn't afraid. How he envied her that. In all the years he had known her, her faith had never wavered. Not for one second. As a nurse she had faced the most appalling things. The scars on his body were proof of that. Yet still she believed in the essential goodness of people. As he sat holding her hand, he wanted so much to believe that she was right.

Was that what she had been trying to tell him all these years? Was that to be her gift to him?

He looked down at her beloved face, as she took one long slow breath. Then another. Then ... she was gone. The silence around him was complete. He felt utterly alone.

As he gently placed her hands on her chest, a tear fell onto the wooden cross. Then another and he realised the tears were his. He took a blanket and covered her, then lifted his face. The sky above was turning a deep purple. The first stars just winking into view.

'If you really are up there,' he said to Sister Luke's God, 'you look after her ... or you'll answer to me.'

He sat beside Sister Luke for a few minutes, reluctant to leave her. Then he rose and walked slowly back up to the top of the ridge. On the other side, he saw Jess just walking away from the wrecked plane. She looked up and saw him, and her steps faltered. He waited for her on the top of the ridge.

As she approached his eyes found hers. No words were needed. He saw the first tears form in Jess's eyes.

Far to the west, the last rays of the sunset vanished from the sky. All around them, the stars glowed. Adam reached out and found Jessica's hand. His fingers entwined with hers as if they had always belonged together.

Chapter Twenty-Nine

This had been the longest night of Ellen's life. She stood in the open doorway of the aircraft hangar and watched as the stars slowly began to lose their brightness. She was still amazed by the number of stars she saw every single night. They seemed to be endless. They seemed to offer so much hope and tonight, of all nights, she needed that hope.

Throughout the night, various people had dropped by the airstrip as news spread that the air ambulance was missing … that Adam, Jess and Sister Luke were missing.

Sergeant Delaney had also stopped by. He had no news of the missing plane, but he did offer Jack some words of consolation.

'I spoke to Clifton Downs,' the Sergeant said. 'They checked the fuel drum Jess used. It was contaminated with water. That would be enough to cause her engine problems.'

Ellen had felt Jack's relief at those words. Whatever had happened, he was not to blame.

'It's possible she just landed somewhere,' the Sergeant added. But he hadn't tried to explain why there was still no radio contact.

After the man left, Ellen and Jack had sat side by side through the long hours of the night, sometimes talking. Sometimes not. Once Jack had urged her to go home and get some sleep. But only once. She had never even considered leaving him and she knew that deep inside Jack was glad to have her there.

She glanced at her watch for what must have been the thousandth time. Dawn was not all that far away.

'It will be light soon,' she said.

'They have search planes standing by to go as soon as they can,' Jack said, as he came up behind her. 'My guess is that Jess is waiting until sunrise to turn on the transponder. Saving her battery until it can do her the most good.'

'Do you think …?' Ellen's voice faltered. She couldn't put the terrible thought into words.

'I think they had to land somewhere. I think Jess is a really good pilot and more than capable of making a safe emergency landing out there. They will find them,' Jack said firmly.

His arms came around her. For a heart-stopping moment, she couldn't breathe, and then she felt his strength and comfort. Without thinking about it, she leaned back into his solid warmth. It was like coming home. She felt so much of the past just wash away leaving her feeling … clean.

For several long, silent minutes they stood like that. Then Ellen took a deep breath. There was something she should have told Jack a long time ago. This seemed a strange time to do it but, after their long fearful night, she felt closer to Jack than she ever had to anyone.

'The policeman …' Ellen said slowly. 'When he was here earlier, I thought I saw something in the way he looked at me. As if he knew something about me.' She felt Jack tense and knew she was right.

'He's had a bulletin from the east,' Jack said calmly. 'You've been reported missing. The kids, too. And there are claims you stole money when you left.'

Ellen closed her eyes. The fear she thought she had left behind washed over her again. 'I didn't,' she whispered.

'I know that,' Jack said with such certainty that she felt

tears spring to her eyes. 'I told the Sarge that too. He said he would hold off for a few weeks. But Ellen, you have to go back some time and face it.'

'I know.'

'And there must be somebody you left behind who is worried about you. Who needs to know where you are. Who needs to know you and the kids are all right.'

There was. 'The kids would like to see their grandmother. I couldn't tell her where I was going ... in case ...'

Jack's arms tightened around her. 'There's a custody issue too.'

A small cry escaped Ellen. She felt her legs give way. If not for Jack, she would have collapsed to the ground. 'No. No,' she whispered.

'It's all right,' his voice was in her ear. 'They won't take the kids away from you. I saw what he did to you. When you arrived. I saw the bruises. No court would give him custody of the kids. I won't let him hurt you ever again.'

Ellen forced her way out of Jack's embrace, but she didn't turn to face him. He knew what she was. What her husband had done to her. Her humiliation was complete. Now he could never ...

'Ellen.' Gentle hands on her shoulders turned her to face him. 'Ellen, look at me.'

Slowly she raised her eyes.

'I will protect you. I'll come with you. I'll help you set everything right. Then, if it's what you want, I'll bring you home again. And, when you're ready, if you'll have me ...' His voice trailed off.

'You would want someone ... who has ... someone like me?'

A fierce light glowed in Jack's eyes. 'Ellen, you were a

284

victim in this. You did nothing wrong. You are just perfect – and how any man could ever hurt you …'

Ellen thought she saw the glint of a tear in his eye as he pulled her to him and wrapped his arms around her.

Ellen rested her head against Jack's chest. She breathed in the essence of him. Finally she lifted her face to him. His kiss was soft and gentle and she welcomed it.

After a few moments, he drew back and looked down at her.

'I won't break,' she said, and this time when he kissed her, it was with longing and desire and Ellen felt her own passion rising in response. There was a joy and a pleasure in Jack's touch that she had never felt before.

The sharp peal of the telephone finally broke then apart. Jack hurried to answer it. He listened for a few moments then slowly set it back in its cradle.

'The search planes are taking off,' he said.

The faintest glimmer of colour in the eastern sky heralded the coming of dawn. Sitting near the crest of the ridge, Adam took a deep breath of the crisp air. The leaking fuel had long since soaked into the dry earth, not even the fumes remained to mar the clear fresh smell of morning. As the fuel had dissipated, so too had some darkness deep inside him.

Jess was by his side, her hand still in his. At one point during the night, as the temperature had dropped, she had collected a couple of blankets from the plane and draped them over their shoulders. On the other side of the ridge, Sister Luke was also covered with a blanket. But she would never see this dawn. Despite his grief at losing the woman who had been more of a mother to him than the woman who gave him life, Adam felt almost at peace.

It was something he had not felt for as long as he could remember.

The first golden rays of the sun peeped over the horizon. Almost immediately, the air began to warm. Adam shrugged off the blankets.

'It wasn't like he said,' Jess said softly beside him. 'I didn't know the drugs were on the plane. I wasn't a part of it.'

'I know.' As he said the words, he realised they were true. 'You would never do something like that, Jess.'

'No.' She paused. 'But people's lives were destroyed by drugs I flew into the country. There must have been some hint of what was going on. Something I missed. Maybe if I had noticed something sooner …'

'Don't. You can't take on another person's guilt.' Was he talking to her … or to himself?

'After they raided the plane,' Jess continued, 'I was arrested along with Brian. I spent a few days in jail. My parents came to see me every day. I will never forget the courage they showed, walking into that jail, their heads held high. It almost broke my heart. I wanted Brian to pay for that more than for what he did to me.'

'You are very lucky to be part of a family like that.'

A few more minutes passed. The only sounds were the faint noises of the outback coming to life. The distant call of a crow. The soft rustle of a breeze in the scrubby undergrowth.

'I was ten years old,' Adam said. He was surprised to find his voice wasn't shaking. 'My parents were getting a divorce. My father didn't want me. Or my mother for that matter. But he didn't want to let us go either.'

He waited for the familiar pain to begin. It was there, deep inside him, but this morning it seemed less sharp.

'I sneaked away from school early. I hated school. Mostly because all the other kids seemed to have so much – and I had so little. I don't just mean the money. They all seemed to have happy families. Brothers and sisters. Mothers and fathers. And kids can be very cruel to someone who is different.'

He felt Jess squeeze his hand.

'I was in the kitchen. I was thirsty. There wasn't any milk or juice or anything. Even then, my mother wasn't very good at ... well, at being a mother. I was getting some water from the tap, when I heard him. He wasn't even trying to get into the house. He didn't want to steal anything ... he just wanted to destroy. I ducked under the table, because I didn't want him to see me. I heard sounds on the front veranda ... and then I smelt it. The petrol.'

Adam closed his eyes as the memories and the pain claimed him.

'I watched a lot of TV as a kid. My mother didn't care what I watched. I probably shouldn't have watched a lot of those crime shows so young. But maybe it helped. I understood immediately what was happening. I came out from under the table and ran to the front door, but the handle was already too hot to touch. I burned my hand trying to open it, but I couldn't.'

Adam raised his hand and studied it. Those scars were gone, but too many others remained.

'The house started to fill with smoke. Those old wooden houses burn so fast. I ran through the kitchen to the back door, but it was locked. I only had a key to the front door. I couldn't get out. I tried to get through to my bedroom. I knew I could climb out of the window, but the flames and the heat were too much. I crawled back into the kitchen. I climbed up on the sink ... smashed the window to get some air ... It wasn't a very nice neighbourhood where we lived and there were bars on the window... I was trapped.'

Adam stared out at the first glow of the sun on the horizon, but the glow he saw flickered and moved as the flames ate their way towards him. He shivered, despite the fact that the temperature was already rising.

'It gets a bit hazy after that. I think I dislocated my shoulder trying to force my way through the bars. The flames ... my clothes were on fire when the fire brigade arrived. They saw me and broke down the door to get me out. They took me to hospital and handed me over to Sister Luke. For a while the doctors didn't think I would live ... and God knows there were times when I wanted to die. The pain ... no one should have to live through pain like that. And certainly not a child. Sister Luke was my lifeline through all that. Without her ...'

He closed his eyes, blinking back tears as grief overwhelmed him. Grief for Sister Luke. Grief for the child he had been. When he opened his eyes again and looked at Jess, tears were streaming down her face too.

'There's one thing I never told her. I've never told anyone.' He took a long slow breath and reached deep inside himself for the scar that only he felt. 'He saw me. My father looked in the window. He was holding a lighter in his hand ...'

Beside him, he heard Jess gasp in horror. 'He knew—'

'Yes. He knew I was there when he set that fire. He looked right in my eyes, and then he dropped that lighter.' Adam's voice broke. For a few moments he struggled to control his emotion. 'All my life I have lived with the knowledge that my father wanted to kill me.'

'And you never told anyone?'

'No. I didn't have to give evidence at his trial. They said I was too young and too ill. There were other witnesses to what he'd done. So I never had to tell anyone that my father tried to kill me.'

'Maybe he wasn't trying to …' Jess's voice trailed off as he shook his head.

'He knew I was there. He wasn't a stupid man. He knew what he was doing. For a long time, as a child, I wondered what was so wrong with me that my father wanted to kill me. My mother wasn't exactly affectionate before the fire … afterwards, well, she just couldn't cope. With my nightmares. With the scars. And the hospital bills. I grew up thinking I was unlovable.'

'Sister Luke loved you, Adam.'

'And I loved her. She looked after me. Through my initial recovery, and the skin grafts. And the therapy. But she couldn't stop all the hurts. I eventually went back to school. If I thought the kids were cruel before it was nothing to how they were when they saw the scars. I still find it hard to believe the best in people. And years later – the women – they were either repulsed by me or wanted to sleep with me because I was some sort of freak show. I stopped believing … hoping that …'

His voice trailed off and at last he turned to face Jess. The early morning light had painted a rosy glow on her face. He waited for her to speak. To tell him that he was wrong. That he could find love. With her.

She didn't say those words that he so wanted to hear. Tears rolled down her face as she slowly reached out to touch his chest. She began unfastening the buttons of his shirt. For a few seconds, a terrible fear gripped his heart. He grabbed her hand. She gently shook her head. Slowly he released her hand to continue its task. When his shirt was loose, Jess gently slipped it from his shoulders. In the bright early morning light, the scars on his upper arm and shoulder seemed angry and red, as they hadn't for many years. Adam searched Jessica's face, and saw no shock. No revulsion. No pity.

He saw love.

The barriers around his heart broke as Jess leaned forward and gently pressed her lips to his scarred flesh.

Chapter Thirty

'They've spotted the plane,' the policeman said abruptly, the moment Jack answered the phone.

Jack felt relief surge through him. 'Where?'

'They were on the way back,' Max Delaney explained. 'They came down on some flat land on the south-east corner of Eight Mile Plains.'

Jack glanced across at the large-scale map of the area that was fixed to the wall of the hangar. His eyes found the property the Sergeant had named. He tried to visualise what sort of a landing place Jess might have found there.

'Have they made radio contact?' he asked.

'Briefly. Jess didn't have much battery ...' When the sergeant paused, Jack knew the news wasn't good.

'And?'

'Jess and the doc are fine. Sister Luke ... she wasn't hurt in the crash, but she had a heart attack. Adam couldn't save her.'

Jack nodded slowly, as he tried to take in the meaning of the words. Sister Luke was gone? She had been such an important part of their little community. So many people would miss her. The Aboriginal families she helped so much. All the patients at the hospital where she and Adam worked. Adam, he knew, would be inconsolable and no doubt would blame himself for failing her. Then there was Ellen.

Jack was alone in the hangar. Ellen had gone to pick up Harry and Bethany from Trish at the pub. She had promised to return after she'd given the kids their breakfast and left them once again with Trish. He had suggested she try to get some sleep, but Ellen was having none of it. She had declared her intention to grab a shower and a change of clothes, and then return with coffee and breakfast for him. She wouldn't let him continue the vigil alone.

But the vigil was over now.

'How are they getting back?' Jack asked, his voice as heavy as his heart.

'There's a ground team going in from Eight Mile homestead. They don't have a helicopter. It'll take them at least a couple of hours to reach the plane. Then they'll bring them back to Eight Mile where there is a good strip. The RFDS will meet them there and bring them home to the Creek.'

The Royal Flying Doctor Service wasn't technically needed if there was no one injured. But Jack understood that the RFDS would want to bring one of their own home.

'As soon as we have an ETA, I'll arrange for Mick Davis to meet the plane.'

Mick ran Coorah Creek's only funeral service.

'Thanks,' Jack said.

'Go home. Get some sleep,' the sergeant said. 'We'll need you back there when the plane arrives, but that won't be for a good four or five hours yet.'

Jack hung up the phone. He was deathly tired, but it wasn't sleep he needed.

He drove to the wooden house behind the hospital. The little blue car that Ellen and Jess shared was parked near the front gate. He pulled his ute in next to it and climbed the stairs as slowly as a man twice his age. The front door opened before he had even raised his hand to knock. Ellen stood there, looking fresh from the shower, her damp hair dripping water onto a clean cotton shirt.

'Jack? There's news?'

'They found the plane.'

The joy on her face faded quickly when he didn't go on.

'Please tell me they are all right ...' she said, her voice quaking with fear.

'Jess and Adam are all right. But Sister Luke ...' his voice faltered as Ellen gave a little cry.

'No. Not Sister Luke!'

Jack stepped forward and caught Ellen in his arms as she started to sob. He lifted her gently and carried her back into the house. Without a moment's thought, he carried her through to her bedroom and laid her gently on the bed. Then he lay beside her and gathered her into his arms as she cried. She cried for a long time, and when the crying subsided, they talked about Sister Luke. Ellen hadn't known her for long, but she still had stories of how Sister Luke had helped. Giving books to her children then bullying Jack into building a bookshelf. Jack listened as she told him little things that no one really noticed. Little things that meant so much to a single mum and her kids. Jack talked about Sister Luke, too. Of the times before Ellen came. Of working with Sister Luke and Adam. Of the times she had talked Adam into doing things he didn't want to do. Of the many times Jack had helped her. Of the affection and respect he'd held for the tiny woman with such faith and energy.

Jack's voice grew faint and after a time Ellen slipped into an exhausted sleep.

Jack lay on the bed; Ellen cradled in his arms, and watched her. She'd been awake all night, and now she slept deeply. Her face was so beautiful and so vulnerable. He could just look at her for hours. Jack also hadn't slept the night before, but he vowed not to close his eyes for one moment. He would lie here and watch over Ellen. This day and every other day for just as long as she needed or wanted him. It was his last thought before sleep took him.

Looking out of the window, Jess finally found what she had been searching for. A place where two roads met to form a giant Y. A place with a long thin ribbon of green to mark the creek. There was the now familiar pattern of houses and that rectangle of incongruous blue that was the pool in the school grounds. The open scar of the mine pit didn't seem as ugly as the first time she had seen it. That mine was the lifeblood of the town. Of her town. Of her home. The first time she had seen this town, she'd been seated in the pilot's seat and running away from her past as far and as fast as she could go. Now she was looking down at the town from the passenger seat in the RFDS plane, aching with grief but feeling an unaccustomed sense of homecoming.

She glanced to her right. Adam was seated across the aisle from her, also staring out of the window at the town below. Behind him, a stretcher carried Sister Luke's blanket-shrouded form. The search team had found them mid-morning. It had taken almost three hours to drive back to the homestead, where the plane was waiting for them. Greg Anderson, the pilot Jess had met at the Birdsville races, had come to take them home.

The plane banked as it came in to land. Looking down, Jess saw a small group of people waiting at the airstrip. There was also a long black vehicle. Tears pricked her eyes again, as the grief she felt for Sister Luke washed over her again. She felt, rather than saw, the movement beside her. Adam reached out for her. Their hands joined as the plane swept in to a gentle touchdown.

Jess was the first to leave the aircraft. Ellen and Jack were waiting and Ellen caught Jess in a hug the moment her feet touched the ground.

'I am very sorry about Sister Luke,' Ellen whispered. 'But I am so glad you and Adam are all right.'

Jess nodded, fighting to hold back the tears. Jack also hugged her briefly, before climbing into the aircraft. A few moments later, Adam and Jack carefully carried the stretcher from the plane. A tall sombre man opened the back of the hearse, and with great reverence they slid the stretcher inside.

'I'll come with her,' Adam said, but the man shook his head.

'No, Doc. You need to leave her with me now. I'll take good care of her.'

Adam opened his mouth as if to protest, but then his shoulders sagged and he nodded.

'Come by tomorrow morning, and we'll make all the arrangements.'

The small knot of people watched in silence as the big black car pulled away. As it drove through the gate out of the airfield, Jess noticed a man standing there. Taking photographs. Despite her grief and exhaustion, she felt a sudden wash of white-hot anger.

'What's he doing here?'

'The search made the news,' Sergeant Delaney said. 'I stopped him coming onto the airfield, but I can't stop him taking photos from out there.'

Adam made as if to approach the man, but the policeman stopped him. 'Leave him, Adam. There's nothing you can do about him. I need you and Jess to come and give me statements. It can wait until after you've had some rest. But I do need it today.'

All the energy seemed to leave Adam's body. He looked like a man totally defeated. Jess's heart almost broke as she looked at him.

'Let's do it now,' Adam said slowly. 'Get it over with.'

'Are you sure?' the policeman asked with a frown. 'It can wait.'

'I'm sure.'

Adam turned to Jess. 'What do you want to do?'

Jess wanted to go with him. To be by his side as he recounted the story of their terrible night. 'You go ahead,' she said. 'I'll be right behind you.'

Jess hated the look of disappointment on Adam's face. But there was something she had to do. And she had to do it right now.

Without another word, Adam turned and walked to the police car. A few seconds later, it was driving through the gate, under the lens of a camera.

'I'll only be a minute,' Jess told her companions and started walking towards the gate. She heard Ellen say something, but her attention was on the man in front of her.

'Jess, what happened out there?' John Hewitt asked, as soon as she drew near. The camera flashed one more time then he lowered it and reached for his tape recorder.

'Is that thing on?' Jess asked. 'Good. Because I want to make sure you remember every word I say. I don't care what you write about me. I really don't. The people I care about will know what is truth and what is a lie. But you be very, very careful when you write this story. Our community has lost someone very dear to them. A kind and caring person, who only ever wanted to help people.

You say one bad word about her, and I swear you will regret it. I am not running away from the likes of you ever again.'

She didn't give him a chance to answer. She turned on her heel and walked back to where Jack and Ellen waited.

'I'm ready now – let's go.'

Chapter Thirty-One

It was early evening when Jess woke. She lay on the bed for a few minutes trying to gather her thoughts. She was still fully dressed. She vaguely remembered deciding to have a shower and change her clothes. That had been after her return from the police station. After she and Adam had given statements. Jess closed her eyes briefly allowing a fresh wave of grief to wash over her. The pain was like a raw wound. It would heal in time, she knew. Sister Luke had lived a full life and had been content to meet her God at the end of it. Jess smiled, imagining Sister Luke bossing God around in much the same way she had Adam. Jess would miss her, as would the whole community, though none as badly as Adam.

They'd all come back here afterwards. Ellen was making a very late lunch when Jessica returned to her room to shower and get a change of clothes. She must have sat down on the bed and just fallen asleep. She had certainly been exhausted – both physically and emotionally. She wasn't sure how long she had slept, but she felt better for it. She stripped off her clothes and walked into the shower, enjoying the feel of the clean cold water as it washed away the sweat and dust of her night in the open. She felt almost human again when she walked through to the living room.

Bethany was watching television. Harry, as usual, had his nose buried in one of Jack's Uncle Scrooge comics. She smiled at them and headed towards the tantalising smell of coffee coming from the kitchen.

And found Jack and Ellen not drinking coffee.

'Oops … sorry!'

Surprisingly, it was Jack who blushed as the two leaped apart. Ellen simply glowed.

'Jess. How do you feel?'

'Better for some sleep. Coffee would help too.'

Jack set about pouring some, while Jess and Ellen sat at the table.

'Where's Adam?' Jess asked, knowing already what the answer would be.

'He went back to the hospital. He wanted to check on Andrea, the girl with the broken arm. Hopefully he got some sleep as well. You both needed it.'

It wasn't all that she needed. Jack placed three mugs of coffee on the table, then took a seat. Jess couldn't help noticing how close he sat to Ellen. She was pleased for them both.

'Do you want to talk about what happened?' Ellen asked gently. 'If you don't, that's fine. I just want you to know that we are here for you.'

That 'we' would have made Sister Luke very happy. It made the pain in Jessica's heart fade, just a little.

She looked at Jack and realised that he must be feeling terrible. The plane that crashed was under his care. But it hadn't been his fault. Sergeant Delaney had told her about the contaminated fuel. It fitted exactly with her own theory about the crash. There would be an official accident investigation, of course. But she knew what the results would show. She couldn't allow Jack to feel guilty for something that wasn't his fault. She knew only too well what that could do to a person. She wanted to talk to him about the crash. To reassure him. And it was also time she told her friends about her own past.

'There's a lot to talk about,' she said. 'And last night is

just a part of it.' She took a long draught of her coffee and started talking.

It was dark when Jess set off to walk to the hospital. Jack and Ellen had believed her, understood her and supported her. Jess knew that in them she had two friends she could count on in good times and bad. Now she needed to know what she had in Adam.

They had shared their deepest thoughts. Secret parts of their lives that no one else had ever seen. Knowing more of Adam's past had changed her feelings for him, but only to make them stronger. To make her more sure that Adam was the most honourable man she had ever met. The best man she had ever met. And the last man she would ever truly fall in love with.

But had their long night sitting vigil over Sister Luke changed how Adam felt about her?

Adam had been unusually silent, even for him, since they had spotted the rescue aircraft that morning. He had reached for her hand from time to time, as if seeking comfort, as they brought Sister Luke home. She was glad to offer him whatever support she could. And in her turn, Jess had taken comfort from him as they grieved for their friend. But that wasn't enough. She wanted more from Adam. Seeing Ellen and Jack together had made things even clearer in her mind. She hadn't known if Adam felt the same way she did, or if she was just a friend he'd looked to in a time of need. She wanted to be more to him than that. Needed him to be more than that to her.

And she had to know if he felt the same way.

Two windows glowed with light as she approached the hospital. One was the room where Adam's patients were spending the night. The other was not Adam's office. It was a light in the residence where he lived. That surprised her. On every other occasion she had been here late, she had found Adam working. It was what he did. It was who he was.

But not tonight.

Jess entered the hospital through the open back door, and turned immediately down the short hallway that led to the resident's quarters. There was a single door at the end of the corridor. Jess had never been in Adam's home before. She took a deep breath to calm herself, and then knocked.

'Come in.'

She opened the door into a large room. It was furnished as a studio apartment, with a large bed on one side, and a living area on the other. There was a small kitchen and a door leading to what was presumably a bathroom. Jess had expected to find this room uncluttered and functional. Perhaps a little spartan. Like Adam himself. Instead she was surprised to see shelves covered with books. A couple of lovely Aboriginal paintings hung on the walls. There was an expensive looking stereo playing blues music. She saw no television. No computer either. Those, it seemed, were part of his hospital existence. This was Adam's sanctuary. This was where he could be himself. Adam was sitting on the sofa, a book lying on the coffee table in front of him. He had obviously slept and showered. His hair was just a little damp. He looked tired, but peaceful. How many people, she wondered, ever saw him here? Like this. Saw Adam, rather than the doctor. She felt a low ache deep inside as she looked at him, and realised how close she had come to losing him.

'Let me turn B.B. King down,' he said, getting to his feet.

As the sound of the blues guitar sank, the silence seemed to grow. Now that she was here, Jessica wasn't certain exactly what to say. Or to do.

'Did you get some sleep?' she asked.

'A little.'

'Me too.'

'I know. You were sound asleep when I left the house.'

So he had looked in on her, and seen her sleeping. The intimacy of that small thing seemed to fill the room. Jess was uncertain how to continue. She moved slowly around, looking at the book titles. She examined one of the paintings. At length. She was so very afraid to reach out to Adam. Afraid that he would once again shy away from her touch. The first time that happened, she had been shocked and a little hurt. If it happened again now, after all they had shared, she would be heartbroken.

'Jess.'

She turned around slowly. Adam walked to her. Without saying a word, he raised his hand to run the backs of his fingers down her cheek. It was the softest touch. A gentle caress. Yet Jess could feel the tremor in Adam's hand. It matched the fluttering of her own heart.

His eyes were dark with emotion as he searched her face. Whatever he was looking for, he found it there. He pulled her to him and kissed her. It began as a slow, gentle kiss filled with longing. Adam's lips were like the finest suede, soft but firm. He tasted of long nights listening to rain on a tin roof, of slow sensual music and the fire in the sky at sunset.

Jess answered the kiss with every part of her being. With her loneliness and her fear and her need. She sank into his arms with a need that matched his. Her fingers twined through his damp hair and their kisses became deeper. More passionate. Both of them quivering with hunger.

Jess's hands moved to the waistband of his jeans, tugging at his shirt. And Adam was suddenly still.

He stepped back, just out of her reach.

'Adam ...' she wanted to tell him not to turn out the lights. That he didn't need to hide his scars from her.

He shook his head. Slowly he began unfastening the buttons of his shirt. His eyes never left hers as he slipped the garment from his shoulders and half-turned, exposing his scars for her to see.

She dropped her eyes to that tortured skin. For long moments she let her eyes rove his body. She felt no revulsion. No pity, just a surge of love.

Finally she looked back into his face.

'I'm not an easy man to live with,' Adam said, his voice hoarse with emotion. 'There are scars you can't see. There are times I wake in the middle of the night, shaking with fear at the memories.'

'We all have our memories,' Jess said. 'We all have our fears. When you wake in the night, I'll be there for you. As you will be for me. As for these,' he shivered as she ran her fingers gently over the scarred flesh, 'they helped make you who you are. I wouldn't have them, or you, any different.'

Jess never knew who was the first to reach for the other. All she felt was his touch on her skin. The strength of his body against hers. The taste of him. And the sound of him calling her name.

Chapter Thirty-Two

Sister Luke was laid to rest in the small graveyard behind the Coorah Creek Catholic Church. The small wooden church was built on a slight rise, and the graveyard looked out across the town towards the line of trees that marked the creek and the great red bluffs beyond. It was a peaceful spot, shaded by tall gum trees.

Almost the entire population of the Creek attended the service in the church. Adam and Jess sat in the front pew, with Ellen and Jack. Harry and Bethany came too, their small faces serious and sad. The rest of the pews held faces Jess had come to know. Even to love. Trish and Syd Warren from the pub. The police Sergeant Max Delaney wore his best uniform. There were uniforms also on display where the pilots and staff of the RFDS sat. Towards the rear of the church were the Aboriginal families. Some of the stockmen Jess knew. Others were strangers, but all came to pay tribute to a small woman with a big heart.

Two nuns from the mother house had made the journey by train to bid farewell to their Sister. The service was carried out by the priest from Mount Isa. He was a young man with a young man's passion for his calling. His eyes were suspiciously wet as he read from his well-worn prayer book.

There were flowers in the small church, plucked from gardens all around the town. The white roses lying on the casket had come from the garden of Nikki and Steve – the young couple whose baby Jess had helped to deliver. They were sitting at the side of the church, the baby plump and healthy in her mother's arms. Jess recognised other former patients. Dan Mitchell, the ranger from the national park put in a rare public appearance, alongside Mayor Coburn who was for once totally sober. So many people's lives had been touched by Sister Luke, and every one of them came to say farewell. Their presence and love helped lighten the sadness of the day.

After the ceremony, Adam and Jack led the pallbearers who carried Sister Luke's plain coffin out of the church and into the graveyard. The congregation followed them across the patchy grass. Tears streamed down Jessica's face as the coffin was lowered into the earth. Adam took her hand and squeezed it tight.

When the last prayer was said, people began drifting away. Most stopped to speak to Adam. He stood as Sister Luke's family. Jess noticed that he didn't pull back when Trish Warren hugged him. Nor when Mayor Coburn laid a broad hand around Adam's shoulders. And all the while, Jess stood by his side. Whenever he reached for her hand, she was there.

At last there were just the four of them left. Trish had taken Harry and Bethany home for milk and cookies. The priest and the Sisters had retired to the church. There was only Jess and Adam and Ellen and Jack standing in the shade of a tall gum tree. A light breeze rustled the leaves above them.

'You are leaving in the morning?' Adam asked Jack.

'Yes. I've found a lawyer who will represent Ellen in the divorce. He thinks the other accusations will come to nothing.'

'And the kids will get to see their grandmother,' Ellen added. 'I've spoken to her on the phone. She wants to meet Jack too.' Ellen blushed a little as she glanced sideways at the man holding her hand. 'We'll be back next week.'

'Sister Luke would be happy to hear that,' Adam said quietly.

'She'd be even happier to see the two of you together,' Ellen said. 'It would seem she was a pretty good matchmaker.'

Jess started to laugh. 'She wasn't very subtle about it, was she?'

'She might have been ... with you two,' Jack said. 'But she didn't ... I mean ... Not with me and Ellen.'

'No, of course not,' Ellen said smiling gently. 'She never asked you to stop by the house and help me with anything?'

'Well, perhaps once or twice, but I really didn't need much encouragement.' He lifted Ellen's hand, and kissed it.

'She was quite something,' Adam said. 'I am going to miss her so much.'

'We all are,' Jess said. 'Let's go back to the house. We can swap Sister Luke stories while Ellen and I start thinking about dinner.'

'You're going to help cook?' Ellen asked, astonished.

'No. I said I'd help think,' Jess said. The four of them smiled, and some of the sadness lifted from their hearts.

They turned and began walking back towards the gate. Adam held Jessica's hand. Jack's arm was around Ellen's shoulders. A gentle stillness settled over the graveyard, broken only by the distant laugh of a kookaburra.

About the Author

Janet lives in Surrey with her English husband but grew
up in the Australian outback surrounded by books. She
solved mysteries with Sherlock Holmes, explored jungles
with Edgar Rice Burroughs and shot to the stars with Isaac
Asimov and Ray Bradbury. After studying journalism at
Queensland University she became a television journalist,
first in Australia, then in Asia and Europe. During her
career Janet saw and did a lot of unusual things. She
met one Pope, at least three Prime Ministers, a few
movie stars and a dolphin. Janet now works in television
production and travels extensively with her job.

Janet's first short story, *The Last Dragon*, was published
in 2002. Since then she has published numerous short
stories, one of which won the Elizabeth Goudge Award
from the Romantic Novelists' Association. She has
previously published three novels with Little Black Dress.
Janet has also published an e-novella called *Bring Me
Sunshine* with Choc Lit, which is available online. *Flight
to Coorah Creek* is her full-length debut with Choc Lit.

https://twitter.com/janet_gover
https://www.facebook.com/janetgoverbooks
http://janetgover.com/

More from Choc Lit

If you enjoyed Janet's story, you'll enjoy the
rest of our selection. Here's a sample:

A Stitch in Time
Amanda James

**A stitch in time saves
nine ... or does it?**

Sarah Yates is a thirty-
something history teacher,
divorced, disillusioned and
desperate to have more
excitement in her life. Making
all her dreams come true seems
about as likely as climbing
Everest in stilettos.

Then one evening the doorbell rings and the handsome and
mysterious John Needler brings more excitement than Sarah
could ever have imagined. John wants Sarah to go back in
time ...

Sarah is whisked from the Sheffield Blitz to the suffragette
movement in London to the Old American West, trying
to make sure people find their happy endings. The only
question is, will she ever be able to find hers?

Visit www.choc-lit.com for more details
including the first two chapters and
reviews, or simply scan barcode using
your mobile phone QR reader.

Please don't stop the music

Jane Lovering

Winner of the 2012 Best Romantic Comedy Novel of the Year

Winner of the 2012 Romantic Novel of the Year

How much can you hide?

Jemima Hutton is determined to build a successful new life and keep her past a dark secret. Trouble is, her jewellery business looks set to fail – until enigmatic Ben Davies offers to stock her handmade belt buckles in his guitar shop and things start looking up, on all fronts.

But Ben has secrets too. When Jemima finds out he used to be the front man of hugely successful Indie rock band Willow Down, she wants to know more. Why did he desert the band on their US tour? Why is he now a semi-recluse?

And the curiosity is mutual – which means that her own secret is no longer safe …

Visit www.choc-lit.com for more details including the first two chapters and reviews, or simply scan barcode using your mobile phone QR reader.

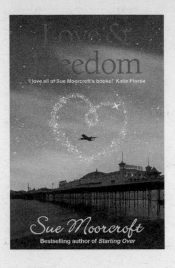

Love & Freedom
Sue Moorcroft

*Winner of the Festival of Romance
Best Romantic Read Award 2011*

New start, new love.

That's what Honor Sontag needs after her life falls apart, leaving her reputation in tatters and her head all over the place. So she flees her native America and heads for Brighton, England.

Honor's hoping for a much-deserved break and the chance to find the mother who abandoned her as a baby. What she gets is an entanglement with a mysterious male whose family seems to have a finger in every pot in town.

Martyn Mayfair has sworn off women with strings attached, but is irresistibly drawn to Honor, the American who keeps popping up in his life. All he wants is an uncomplicated relationship built on honesty, but Honor's past threatens to undermine everything. Then secrets about her mother start to spill out …

Honor has to make an agonising choice. Will she live up to her dutiful name and please others? Or will she choose freedom?

Visit www.choc-lit.com for more details including the first two chapters and reviews, or simply scan barcode using your mobile phone QR reader.

CLAIM YOUR FREE EBOOK

of

Flight to COORAH CREEK

You may wish to have a choice of how you read *Flight to Coorah Creek*. Perhaps you'd like a digital version for when you're out and about, so that you can read it on your ereader, iPad or even a Smartphone. For a limited period, we're including a **FREE** ebook version along with this paperback.

To claim, simply visit www.ebooks.choc-lit.com or scan the QR Code.

You'll need to enter the following code:

Q161312

Introducing *Choc Lit*

We're an independent publisher creating
a delicious selection of fiction.
Where heroes are like chocolate – irresistible!
Quality stories with a romance at the heart.

Choc Lit novels are selected by genuine readers like yourself.
We only publish stories our Choc Lit Tasting Panel want to
see in print. Our reviews and awards speak for themselves.

We'd love to hear how you enjoyed *Flight to Coorah
Creek*. Just visit www.choc-lit.com and give your feedback.
Describe Adam or Jack in terms of chocolate
and you could win a Choc Lit novel in our
Flavour of the Month competition.

Available in paperback and as ebooks from most stores.

Visit: www.choc-lit.com for more details.

Keep in touch:
Sign up for our monthly newsletter Choc Lit Spread for
all the latest news and offers: www.spread.choc-lit.com.
Follow us on Twitter: @ChocLituk and Facebook: Choc Lit.

Or simply scan barcode using your mobile phone QR reader:

Choc Lit
Spread

Twitter

Facebook